THE DISC

Widney Joseph

First Edition

NEWMAN SPRINGS PUBLISHING
320 Broad Street
Red Bank, NJ 07701

First originally published by Newman Springs Publishing 2021

ISBN 978-1-63692-864-7 (Paperback)
ISBN 978-1-63692-865-4 (Digital)

Printed in the United States of America

ACKNOWLEDGMENTS

First and foremost, I'd like to thank God for keeping me through this entire process. I'm so grateful that I have a brother that pushes me when I want to give up. I really appreciated all the encouraging words, Princelin. Without God and you, I don't know if I would've ever completed this project. No matter how hard it gets, or how difficult things may look or be, the process only makes you stronger. I'm thankful for the entire process because it made me better.

Life always has its struggle. Walls built to block the path. Roadblocks will be informed, and hurdles will be in the way. Life, as we know it, will have adversities. All of us will face obstacles, will be tested. That's either spiritually, mentally, emotionally, or physically. We must always be conscious of the choices that we make in life. Our choices have a way of affecting those we love and care for, so in a sense, when we make decisions, we can alter a person's life for good and bad. True enough, each individual is held accountable for their own actions. Nonetheless, a person's actions can be disrupted or affected by what someone does.

When I was feeling down or bent out of shape, if I don't have the strength to press on self, I find the strength to at least do it for someone that loves me. I'm always mindful that my choices also shape the life of others. I'd like to thank all my brothers, sisters, Anntrice, my devoted friend Natasha, and everyone who believes in me.

PROLOGUE

Sincere quickly rushed inside the train with his backpack strapped tight on his back. It took him a little over forty minutes to get to the train station. He did so running and jogging. Depletion of strength and energy had him drained and winded. Tears formed in his eyes. Tears that wanted to come down hard like waterfalls. He couldn't allow them to fall just yet. Once he was safe and alone, they can come down however they want to. The humidity and lack of air circulation on the train only enhanced the heat that came burning through his body. The flames of scorching fire never left his vision. The echoes and screams of his father came through his eardrums loud and clear. The scream of him dying was infuriating. Sincere couldn't believe he watched his mother get shot at point-blank range. He didn't even make an attempt to do anything about it. He felt like a coward. Regardless of his father's instructions, instead of fighting for the only woman he ever loved, he ran. Although his father insisted on him doing so, it made little sense for him to live without his mother or his father. Nonetheless, his father's views of things were totally different.

"You must leave quietly through your bedroom window. I know this is hard. We need you to stay alive. It makes absolutely no sense for all of us to die. Remember, I prepared you for this. Get what I told you and go!" his father instructed.

Without drawing any attention or making any noise, Sincere quickly grabbed what was needed and fled his home reluctantly. He didn't immediately leave the area.

He hid behind some large bushes, about fifty yards away from his home, hoping for some miraculous escape by his father. While waiting, a quick sound of a gun blast made his body jump. Five minutes later, he heard his father scream as his home went up in flames.

Somehow his father was aware of his fate. Preparations of his getaway had to be made in advance. Maurice always was one to make plans early. One thing he said a lot was, "Why wait for the storm's arrival to prepare when you can be ready before the storm."

As Sincere sat in the train, thinking about the misfortunes of his parents, the shift and movement of the guy standing across from him made him alert and more aware of his surroundings. The unknown guy stared deep into Sincere's eyes, holding a mischievous grin on his face. The scar across his left cheekbone made the grin appear more deadly. The guy had something up his sleeve in the form of a plot, Sincere initially thought, or maybe paranoia started kicking in. Instantly his father's words flooded his mind.

"Never let pain cloud your judgment. There's two things that can make a man put his guard down or make stupid decisions."

"What's that, Daddy?" Sincere remembered asking his father when he was ten years old.

"Pain and love. In the midst of pain, you can lose sight of things that's meaningful. Agony, in however form it comes in, can make you careless. It can make you do things without thought. Pain can make you unaware of what's taking place around you. It can make you act out of anger. And you already know, anger cancels good judgment. Pain is a form of weakness. The more you feel it and allow it to hinder your thought process, the more you will give people access to take advantage or harm you. And love... moments of excitement and pleasure are always dangerous when a man has a target on his back. Whether love is bringing a person happiness or sadness, that person is only opening himself to unexpected tragedy. Only if he's living a life that's not by the book. Truth of the matter is... love weakens a man. It blinds him and also takes away from his better judgment."

"You do love Mommy, right?" Sincere asked.

"Of course I do. And I will sacrifice myself to keep you and her safe. If someone wanted to hurt me, the easiest way to do that is to hurt the ones I love. You understand?" Maurice pointed out, hoping that what he said didn't fly across his son's head.

Sincere embraced the reminder and got up from his seat with a lack of concern. "Stay calm," he kept telling himself. "Don't panic."

Outwardly he seemed cool, calm, and collected. Yet inwardly, he was a bit shaky and on edge. *The man wouldn't do anything foolish in front of all these people*, he thought momentarily.

Don't underestimate anyone. Don't ever assume you know what a person will do, he remembered his father saying. So that thought was quickly erased. Sincere knew he had to be careful with this guy. Something didn't sit well with him. He felt it in the pit of his stomach. The guy had to be up to something. And that something happened to be him.

"Excuse me, sir, do you mind if I scan through the sports page?" Sincere asked a pudgy white man wearing oversized reading glasses. The man looked at him with an expression of disgust. Nonetheless, he retrieved the paper.

"Keep it," was all he said.

Sincere took the paper and placed it under his armpit, and walked to where the heavy crowd was. Sincere had no need for the paper. He just felt uncomfortable sitting down while being watched. As Sincere moved away from the guy with the mischievous grin, the guy followed him at a slow pace. The decision to move where the crowd happened to be was one he regretted. Being in an open space gave him more room to maneuver if he had to move. A crowd-limited movement. When Sincere stopped and turned around, he could easily see the tip of a knife visible in the guy's left hand. The train came to a screeching halt, and Sincere burst through the open doors. Not once did he look back. He wasn't gonna allow fear to set in.

Anger boiled in Sincere for a brief moment. He thought of his father's words and somehow released the feeling. He didn't know if the guy was in hot pursuit. Around a corner in a dark alley, Sincere pulled out the .38 special that he held in his waistband. The gun just happened to be a gift his father gave him last year for his thirteenth birthday. A gift he was glad to have in his possession. Sincere waited behind a dumpster, expecting the worst. A part of him wished the guy wasn't stupid enough to follow him. Another part wished he was. The sight of his mother getting shot enraged him. Now he was hoping the guy came. He heard the footsteps before he saw them. Surprisingly, he smiled.

"I know you're back there, B. Let me get that backpack and what's in your pockets, son," the guy said out loud, not knowing the mistake he wasn't gonna have the chance to live to regret.

Sincere purposely knocked over some soda cans to draw attention toward him. As expected, the noise drew the guy closer. Like feeding bread to birds, simple and easy. He took the .38 off safety. The instant the guy came in his sight, two shots hit him in the chest and knocked him hard to the ground. Sincere stepped closer and pulled the trigger again, the third shot hitting the guy in his head.

"If you ever shoot someone, always make sure they're dead. Don't ever pull a gun out on someone and not use it. If you don't have the courage to kill, there's no point in you totting the steel," his father told him before. Sincere never had any doubt about his courage.

At thirteen years old, Sincere killed his first person. Little did he know, it will be far from his last. To him, anyone should consider what he did justified. Maybe not in the court of law, but according to the rules of the streets, he had every right to do what had to be done. Shockingly, feelings of regret, anxiety, or remorse didn't consume him. He felt a burst of fuel being pumped inside of him. The thought of his parents triggered that energy. If any person posed a threat to his life, he would never hesitate to protect himself.

Sincere casually walked out of the alley and went to where the bus terminal was located. In the morning, he was getting on a Greyhound that was heading south to Miami. Evidently everything was already settled for him there.

CHAPTER 1

MIAMI

Rodney, a.k.a. Hot Rod, fumed with boiling heat of anger as he paced his spacious office. He was highly upset that a couple of his workers burned down the house of Maurice and Kiana. He hated when people didn't follow his instructions. With failure always came punishment. Punishment happened to be the only way to get his point across. Benny and Smoke had to be punished severely. They were given orders to burn the place down but not with the couple in it. As much as Hot Rod wanted Maurice dead, he couldn't change Maurice passing information and evidence that can get him a boatload of time to someone else. Hot Rod still didn't know how Maurice obtained the information that he did. He just knew it was material that needed to disappear. Maurice always held what he had as leverage to extort and milk Hot Rod for cash. A reliable source informed Hot Rod that Maurice wasn't the snitching type. Him being exposed or ratted out was just a bluff. So Hot Rod decided to take a chance in burning his place down to send a message. Maurice being dead had its good in it. Yet he also understood the great possibility of the evidence against him not dying with Maurice.

"How could you two be so stupid!" Hot Rod snapped.

"We were misinformed," Benny said, looking worried.

"By who?" Hot Rod asked, on the verge of losing his patience.

"That doesn't matter, boss. They're dead." Smoke cut in nonchalantly, not allowing Benny to get another word in.

"What the hell makes you think those drivers are not out there floating somewhere? They can easily be in someone else's possession right this very minute. You're telling me that doesn't matter?"

"I can assure you—" Before another word came out of Smoke's mouth, he was struck with a bullet in the back of his head. While Benny and Hot Rod were reaching for their weapons, Snake emerged from the door with his .45 to his side.

"Interesting," Hot Rod said with a smile. Knowing Snake, Smoke was engaging in some foul play. "The cause for that?" Hot Rod curiously asked, slowly taking a seat.

"He's a liability. On top of everything I've accumulated, he's untruthful. Benny was misinformed by Smoke. Benny did what he thought you wanted done. For the past week, I had surveillance on Maurice's home. I had no visual inside. With my limited sources, I still was able to fix something up outside on the perimeter. I have one audible transmission of Smoke saying he was given the order to burn the place down with the couple in it. Here's where things took a bad turn. Before the fire erupted, my camera showed his son climbing out of a window with a backpack on. He ran west and disappeared." Snake came closer to Hot Rod to show him the recorded footage on a camcorder.

"I see," was all Hot Rod said at first. "Do you happen to have any ideas where this kid is now?"

"I'm in the process of tracking him down now. Surprisingly Maurice or Kiana had no relatives that I know of in the States. It's gonna be difficult to locate him. Not far from impossible, though," Snake said, taking a seat.

"I wonder how he left the house unnoticed. And why did he leave without his parents?" Hot Rod asked out loud, thinking he was questioning himself.

"Don't know. I like dealing with the facts. I do my best to stay away from theories and speculation while I'm conversing with others," Snake said.

"Here's one for you." Benny jumped in. "Smoke has a gun to Kiana's head. Out of fear of losing her, Maurice complies with what we have to say and agrees on giving us the drives. I tie his feet and arms up with some zip ties. Smoke tells me to stand guard outside and keep an eye on anything suspicious or unusual. Instead of inquiring more about the drives, Smoke leaves Maurice downstairs, takes Kiana upstairs and rapes her. Which is my theory. While he's doing that, unbeknownst to us, Maurice's son sneaks in or out of wherever he is hiding. Doesn't have enough time to cut his dad loose. Hears the gun fire that kills his mother, and bolts," Benny concluded. Everyone stayed silent for a moment.

"Separate the facts from your theory. We just need the facts," Snake demanded.

"Maurice entered his home and saw Smoke holding a gun to Kiana's head. Maurice didn't put up a fight and allowed me to unarm him and tie him up. Smoke told me to go outside and see if anything looked abnormal. I went outside. After five minutes, I heard a single shot fired. I rushed back inside. Maurice was still tied up, and Smoke was coming down the stairs. He headed straight to Maurice and hit him with the butt of the pistol, demanding for the drives. Maurice never spoke. After a couple minutes of physical abuse, he was still silent. Smoke then shot him in the kneecap. Went upstairs and dragged his dead wife down and placed her in front of him. He questioned him some more but still got no answer. So we set the place on fire and dispersed. That's all facts," Benny said.

"So evidently, you never saw the kid. With that information, let's assume the kid knew y'all was in his home. When Smoke disappears with his mother, he follows them and watches her get shot. I don't think he rapes her. But there's no telling with Smoke and the sickness of his mind. The kid runs to his pop. And his father tells him what to grab and leave," Hot Rod said, painting his own picture on what he thought took place. "What do you say, Snake?"

"Like I said earlier, I don't like to speculate. What we need to do is find out where the kid went. That should be the priority."

"I agree. Benny, get the cleanup guys. Glad I went with tile instead of carpet."

*****

Sincere got off the bus, unsure on where to go. He had never been to Miami before. His Uncle Montell, his father's brother, had a place down here. Montell happened to be the only person he knew to contact. This upcoming summer, his father had made plans for them to go on vacation to Miami. Apparently circumstances changed things drastically. It seemed as if everything was pretty much situated for him from the letter his father left in his backpack. After reading it, Sincere realized, if his parents would've never died, his trip to Miami was inevitable. No matter what, it was bound to happen.

> Son, I love you. Things are gonna get dangerous around here. You know I'm not one to sugarcoat or water things down. I can only give it to you raw and uncut. It's not safe for you to stay here in New York. Some people want me dead. And in life, people use those you love to harm you. So to keep my head above the waters, I gotta remove you. If I don't, it's a possibility that someone will try to hurt you to get to me. I tried to send your mother down there to Miami with you. But you know how stubborn she can be. When she has her mind set on something, there's no altering it. She doesn't wanna leave my side. And her decision makes it difficult for me to move how I want. I have to account for her, which places me at a disadvantage. Being responsible for someone else's safety in the middle of a storm is not an easy task. Your mother is a fighter, though. So we will find a way to get through this. My brother Mo got a place under his name for you. The other hideout, you'll find out about later, is for you and *only you* to know about. Keep what's important inside of the safe house. Only go there when you need to. Do your best to live your life. Don't get too comfortable. Just because you're not around the storm doesn't mean you're sheltered.

> Rain comes even when the sun is out. So always be on point. If things don't work out for me and K, be alert. Don't trust anyone. Not even Mo. People disappoint. Go to school. Don't draw unnecessary attention to yourself by doing foolish things. Don't deal with fast girls. Females are a lot of males' downfall. I can't tell you what to do with your feelings. But if you find yourself in danger, guard your heart. If it's open to someone else. You'll be stuck like me. Having to protect not only yourself but also the one you love. Your Uncle Mo is all right. But people can be bought. Understand that. Here's your address, 2150 Northeast 169th Street, 304. Catch a cab there. In six months, find another place. You're smart. Use your charms to get an older female to rent you a place. Once you move, don't tell your uncle where you're living. Talk to you later. I love you, Dad.

Sincere held back the tears. He read the letter three times while inside the cab. In the letter, there were just certain things he couldn't quite understand. If Uncle Mo couldn't fully be trusted, why let him get the apartment? Why not have someone else rent it? After contemplating about it for a few minutes, he realized he needed someone to enroll him in school. Sincere also understood why his mother was choosing to be with his father over him. He didn't blame or knock her for that choice. His father had explained to him how love has levels and how the feeling is different when dealing with different individuals. A father doesn't love his son the same way that he loves his brother. Nor would a woman love her husband the same way she will love her daughter. Sincere knew if he was an infant, his mother's decision wouldn't have been the same. He was thirteen now. He barely spent time with his parents. Why should his mother sacrifice joy for someone who wasn't gonna be around her? His mother and father did a lot together to bring each other happiness. Yes, his mother loved him. There was no doubt in that. He just knew as her son, he couldn't provide her with what she wanted or needed. Only her husband was able to accommodate her in those areas. Sincere was taking care of himself fine. As a child gets older, a mother can focus more on herself and what makes her happy. Sincere understood that.

When Sincere got to his place. He was surprised to see that his new apartment was already well furnished. How long did his father have this planned, he thought to himself. The closet was filled up with school clothes and ten brand-new pairs of his favorite shoes: the '94 Deion's, the '95 Penny's, a couple of Jordans and Kobes, a pair of Griffeys, Charles Barkley, Bo Jackson, and Barry Sanders. On the bed was a phone, car keys, and another letter.

> No one has your house keys. I used your uncle to get the place. I also made him get two more, just to throw him off. He doesn't know what you're down there for, keep it that way. Use him to enroll in school. Six months, leave that apartment. The sooner, the better. When you turn sixteen, get your license. That blue Dodge Charger out front is yours. I know you're gonna drive it. Never go over the speed limit. When you decide to drive it to school, do so when you're in high school. There's $5,000 inside of the Kobes. You have a Ruger inside the left side of the couch. Pay close attention to the seams. Bullets and a suppressor is inside of the mattress. Make other spots once you settle yourself in. Get to the safe house. All letters I write you, make them disappear. Letters can be used as evidence. No one can take what's in your head, unless you give it to them.

Forty-five minutes later, Sincere headed to the safe house. He was unfamiliar with the roads and the streets. So he took a cab. Compared to New York, Miami streets were a lot smaller. People weren't bunched up everywhere either. It was a lot easier to move around in a vehicle.

The safe house basically had nothing in it. One mattress sat in the only room. There was a couch and a TV in what appeared to be the living room. Upon searching the place. He found a safe inside of the walls in the closet that held $300,000. He only knew the amount due to a piece of paper that stated it. Sincere placed the backpack in the safe and grabbed the envelope with his name on it.

> We spoke so many times about the importance of managing your money properly. A lot of individuals allow their money to control them. And a lot of individuals are not disciplined. So their spending habits cause them to go or be without money. I'm trusting you to do the right thing. Stay away from jewelry and anything flashy. They attract the wrong type of attention. Pretend to be broke. It's easy to determine who truly cares for you when you're without. With money, people will be around that won't be if you didn't have anything. You have enough clothes and shoes. Find you a good job to pay your bills and feed yourself. Make money and add to what you already have. Don't subtract from it. At the end of the day, you're gonna do what you wanna do. But my sincere advice is for you to stay away from the street life. It may seem enticing. It may draw you in. Unknown factors that most don't even consider can cause you to lose your life or freedom. So please, son, don't sell drugs, steal, or rob. I will contact you when I need you.

Sincere wondered if there were any other letters around for him to read. He had a feeling this was the last one. He reread it and flushed it down the toilet, like he did the rest of them. Why were his parents in danger? What was hidden in the backpack? Where would he work? How could he possibly go on? As the questions came, the tears came. Like the child that he was, he cried himself to sleep on the mattress.

CHAPTER 2

The Inc.

Snake was Hot Rod's right-hand man. They had met back in junior high school. Both of them were the head of their respective rival gang. Both of them were born gorillas. Born leaders. Instead of clashing heads and going against each other, they agreed to work together. They automatically separated themselves from the foolishness of adolescent troublemaking. And they strategized to make money. From burglarizing, to scamming. From snatching books to robberies. A little bit of drug dealing and pimping was in the mix. Nothing separated them from each other ever since.

As they aged, Hot Rod placed more emphasis on building a legitimate establishment. On the business side, he had car washes, automechanic shops, clothing stores, sports bars, and restaurants. Snake wasn't one that cared too much for money. He wasn't defined by his bank statement. To him, the urge to have a lot of money was a weakness, even though money brought respect and power. It ran neck and neck with women when it came to the downfall of most men. Money and women were men's biggest weakness. Whenever a person needed to gain information on someone or try to get someone killed, money or women always happened to be the best weapon. It's what men chase the most. Seldom you'll see someone who's after knowledge and spiritual peace. Money and women were always the motive most of the time.

Snake was well known for his marksmanship in Jersey, Philly, the BMV area, and the five boroughs in New York. When it came to trigger play, he was extremely deadly. Like a poisonous snake, he was quick and lethal. His rapid attack was always fatal. His name didn't derive from any shyness, craftiness, slickness, or creepiness. He wasn't that type of snake. His name was given because of his killer instinct. He wasn't one to flex his muscle, run his mouth, or push his weight around. Clowns boast about things. Killers move in silence. When an assignment was presented to him, his commitment and performance was never a failure. If a price tag was on someone's head, a death certificate was being served. Snake killed for the thrill of it. The expenses and money were just material to make his work more efficient.

No one knew that Snake trained with former Deltas and Navy Seals. He wasn't your typical street killer. Erasing guys like drug dealers, pimps, robbers, and sexual predators was elementary work to him. Most people that believed they had street credentials really had nothing to think about. They never knew they were being watched or followed. They spoke recklessly over the phone and around people they didn't know. They had too many personal attachments that jeopardize their safety. They loved to be the center of attention. They spend too much money, buy too much jewelry, flaunted in expensive cars that legally they couldn't afford. They dealt with way too many women. They stayed too close to where they did dirt. They underpay their workers. They weren't loyal to those that deserved their loyalty. The list went on and on. Snake needed a challenge. He needed something to pump him up and get his blood flowing.

Killing people was second nature to Snake. Over the past two years, he accumulated at least twenty bodies. And those were the ones that were worth counting. The junkies, kids, and women he had to eliminate weren't even a part of his list. And yes, kids and women were not an exception to death. Young or old, it didn't matter to him. A child and a woman can easily be the cause of someone's death. So to Snake, they weren't exempt to death.

Snake was on his way to Baltimore when he received the call. He didn't expect the call to come soon. Money had a way of speeding up the process.

"MK is throwing a party in Miami. You down to go?" the caller asked.

"I'm good. Don't like the weather down there. When are you gonna pick up your stuff at my place?"

"I'll be there in two hours."

Snake hung up the phone and smiled. From the information he just collected, Maurice and Kiana's son was in Miami. Once the caller arrived with more info, he planned on making it hotter down at the bottom.

*****

Victorious Inc. was a prestigious company in Miami, Florida, that held unlimited information for almost every resident in the city. Information ranged from name, birthdate, Social Security numbers, health records, addressed, credit scores, school records, sexual inclination, criminal history, restrictions of any kind, cancellation of credit cards, phone and house bills. Whatever information that can be pulled up that was in the database was managed by the Inc.

A strong black woman in her midforties named Alexis Prince was the CEO and cofounder of the company. Alexis was born and raised in the Ocean State. The moment she graduated high school, she left Rhode Island and accepted her academic scholarship at the University of Miami. She attained her marketing degree, business management and business administration degree in twelve years. The choice to start and own her company was one of the best decisions she ever made.

Alexis's vision was to expand her business and find more working opportunities for the black race. She wasn't born in poverty. Seeing the destructive structure and lack of unity in black communities inspired her to at least try more for those who weren't giving a lot of chances. The system wasn't designed to be against black. If it was, she wouldn't be in her current position.

In her place of business, there were former dancers, ex-felons, ex-drug dealers, and people without diplomas. Every position wasn't required for individuals to have certain experiences or college degrees. Those specific spots were filled in by those who she believed deserved a second chance. The only exception she made was with people with sex cases. Sexual crimes in any form was something she just couldn't tolerate.

The decision to sympathize with those with shaky backgrounds came from seeing how hard their work ethic can be. True enough, it was a risk she was taking because things weren't guaranteed to work out. But that could be said about any individual she hired. So far, she's been fortunate. No complaints. No troubles. No problems from the nine employees she took a chance on.

Yolanda has been employed at Victorious Inc. for the past four years. She was currently Alexis's secretary. Five years ago, Yolanda was a dancer at a strip club. Having a child at a young age forced her into that lifestyle. The father was a pushover, and she had no support system elsewhere. Stripping was the fastest way for her to make some quick money. One night, while working her normal night shift, a very close friend of hers at the club got caught up in a rapid gunfire while giving someone a lap dance. The intended target was the guy she was dancing on, a guy who turned out to be a snitch. Her friend was just collateral damage. After that night, she knew she had to make another way to make a living.

Seven months after that incident, Yolanda was working at Walmart. The payment was enough to get her through the next month. Every cent had a name on it already. It wasn't the kind of life she could keep living. One day, while getting ready to withdraw some money at a bank, she parked her beat-up Altima next to an E350 Mercedes-Benz. The four-door sedan was what Yolanda considered her dream car.

While admiring the interior, she recognized that the key was still in the ignition. Like a good Samaritan, she waited for the driver to arrive, knowing whoever he/she was would be thankful for her good deed.

Fifteen minutes later, a stunning woman was walking directly toward her with purpose. The beautiful woman had to be the owner of the vehicle. Her walk and aura shouted power, confidence, and sophistication. It had to be her car. The Benz had a feminine touch to it. And it roared strength, confidence, and sophistication.

"Excuse me, is this your car?" Yolanda asked as the woman got closer.

"Yes, it is. Is there a problem?" Alexis wondered why someone she didn't know was standing by her car.

"There's no problem since you're here. You left your car keys inside, so I was playing security guard." Alexis immediately looked inside of her vehicle, then checked the door handle. To her relief, it opened.

"I hate being in a rush. We're not even halfway through the year, and this is the second time I did this," Alexis said to no one in particular. Yolanda watched her and was still amazed at how beautiful she was. For some odd reason, she felt like a little girl.

Compose yourself, she thought. "You gotta be more careful. Anyone could've gotten in your car. Someone could have stolen it. Thank God that wasn't the case. Just glad I stopped to admire your car." Yolanda started with a smile.

"Likewise. How can I repay you?" Alexis asked. The first thought that came to Yolanda's mind was asking her out on a date. She didn't know where the thought came from. Her slight hesitation was probably a good thing. "If you ever desire to have drive and be ambitious, you must be confident. You never know when an opportunity is in front of you. This is one you can't let slip away."

When Alexis made that statement, Yolanda knew she had nothing to lose. Chances had to be taken. This woman looked like she had something going for herself. And Yolanda wanted to be a part of that something.

"This may be far-fetched, but I need a job," Yolanda admitted.

"What's your name? Alexis asked.

"Yolanda."

"Well, Yolanda, nothing's far-fetched. Here's my card." Alexis reached in her bag and gave Yolanda a card as she entered her vehicle.

"What's your name?" Yolanda heard herself asking before the beautiful lady pulled off.

"It's on the card."

The rest is history. That's how they met. Their bond and friendship only grew with time. Yolanda first started as a receptionist. Now she's Alexis' secretary. Elevation in position constitutes elevation in pay.

*****

Gregory Black was the mail delivery guy at the Inc. He not only sorted all the incoming mails, he also had the responsibility to pass them out. The fact that he was one of the few individuals without a diploma or specific skill set didn't bother him. From his view, he was making easy money. He just got released from prison after doing ten years for a murder charge. Landing a sweet job weeks later, when all he had to do was walk around passing things, didn't bother him one bit. A female friend of his that was supporting him through his incarceration helped him get the job. She put in a good word. And on her pretty face, he was a working man for the very first time.

Gregory, also known as Shadow, stood at 6'1". He weighed a solid 210 pounds. His skin tone was jet black. He sported waves on his head. He had no golds or tattoos. He was against putting things on his body that can do more harm than good. Tattoos and golds were markings of identification. It made no sense to get them. Being jet black often worked against him. So adding things to his description wasn't smart.

Almost eleven years ago, Shadow was confronted by a couple of gang members about a drug turf he was accused of distributing in. One of the guys that approached him made the mistake of poking his finger in Shadow's face, which resulted in two people being dead. The only thing that linked Shadow to the crime was his skin complexion. Nothing else. Several witnesses stated they saw a real dark-skinned man fleeing the area. It was all circumstantial evidence. Nothing concrete. But in real life, in the courtroom, lack of evidence in a case doesn't mean anything. It's all about who performs the best in trial. And performance on both sides, prosecution and defense, is choreographed with lies. Shadow was found guilty and given two life sentences running concurrent. He eventually got overturned due to the erroneous jury instructions. It was crazy that a convicted person had better chances to win his/her case off procedural errors by the courts as opposed to going to trial.

Gregory was glad he was free. He planned on keeping it that way. There was no need to go back into the drug world. There was no future in that life. As he was making goals and strategizing on his next move, his phone rang.

"This Black, speak."

"How do you like your job?" the caller asked.

"Couldn't be any sweeter."

"Anything new popped up on the surface?"

"Not really. But tell your cousin he should definitely visit Miami. The water here is amazing. And the girls are even better." Shadow laughed.

"Say less. I'll be sure to deliver the message. Stay out of trouble." The caller ended that call and made another one.

CHAPTER 3

SCHOOLHOUSE

Montell wasn't sure how long Maurice intended to keep his nephew down in Miami. As an uncle, he didn't do much for Sincere. That was the perfect time to change that. Although Sincere was a teenager, and at that stage in life where he probably was gonna try to figure out everything on his own, there were still a lot of things and areas he could be helpful in.

"You know, whenever you are in need for something, anything, I'm only one phone call away. Don't be a stranger to my number. True enough, we were really close. But you're family, and I wanna look out for you in the best way that I can."

"We are good. Always have been. Thanks for getting me registered," Sincere said, hoping he didn't inquire about his father and why he was down here.

"No prob. You want me to pick you up after school?"

"I'm not in grade school, Unc. I can walk home. Thanks, though. If I ever need you, I'll call."

"All right, be easy. Was gonna pick you up in my candy-apple vert," Montell said, smiling. Sincere thought of what his father said about flashy things.

"I'm still good."

"Cool." Montell reached into his pockets and gave Sincere $500. "Money for you to spend. Each week, look forward to that."

"Thanks again." Montell made his way out of the school and went about his business.

The first day of school didn't go so well. He really didn't expect it to. Making a school change in early spring was rare. Cliques, groups, partners, friends were already formed. Not that he intended to fit in or be friendly with anyone. He just knew from observation how tough people can make it on newcomers.

Minutes after the teacher made him introduce himself, he sat in his assigned seat, and immediately, he was being tested.

"He got some nice shoes, Chris." Sid started, looking to start trouble.

"I know. They look like they're my size," Chris responded.

"I bet you them shoes are not even his," Sid continued, baiting and amping Chris up.

"I don't even care. He better know how to fight. Because when school is out, they will be mine."

On and on they went. First it was his shoes they were gonna take, then his clothes. Sincere just ignored them. He noticed a couple of girls looking sadly his way as Sid and Chris continued to make jokes. A couple of guys in the class were laughing, trying to fit in to make him feel bad. Apparently Sid and Chris were the class clowns or school bullies. Sincere didn't like either one of them. He calmly kept his cool. As long as they didn't put their hands on him, they can talk all they want. Every individual had control over the choices they made. Yet a lot of people failed to realize they had no control of their consequences. The choice Sid and Chris made wasn't gonna go unpunished.

Later on that night, Sincere left his apartment and went to the corner store to grab something to snack on. Surprisingly he saw Chris coming out of the store. The sight of him lit his eyes with rage. Sincere quickly rushed toward him and mopped him to the floor with an avalanche of blows to Chris's face. After kicking his head into the pavement, he walked away, only to see one of the girls that was feeling sorry for him earlier in class looking astonished.

Sincere knew his father told him to stay out of trouble. But as a young kid, some problems just had to be dealt with. If certain issues are not addressed or get nipped in the bud, they will only grow or get worse. And having dudes chump him around wasn't something he was ever gonna allow.

The next day in class, everyone got silent when he entered the room. All it took was one set of eyes to make word travel. Witnesses weren't always good.

Reports they confirm or inform could be damaging. In this case, the information that was being spread was damaging for Chris. Chris didn't show up in class. Word of mouth said he was recovering at the hospital from a broken jaw and fractured skull. Sid or any of the other boys didn't look or glance sincerely. All the girls' eyes were fixed on him, though; the girl that witnessed the whole thing was shaking her head in disapproval. Sincere didn't get or understand girls sometimes. One minute the girl felt sorry for him. And the next minute, she acted like he was some kind of monster. Well, needless to say, he could care less how anyone felt. An example had been set. And for the rest of the school year, no one picked on him again. That's what mattered.

*****

Two years ago, while in the sixth grade, Sincere was on the court playing basketball with nine other kids in his physical education (PE) class. Sports wasn't something Sincere was into. They were short one player, so he decided to even things up. The game ended up being real close. The next point for either team was gonna win the game. A tall kid on Sincere's team stole the ball and threw an outlet pass to Sincere for the game-winning layup. A kid named Max came out of nowhere and pushed Sincere in the back, which made him hit the floor hard. Max stepped over Sincere without apologizing. His father told him, when he was in the first grade, to never let anyone push him around. He didn't care how old or how big they were. The moment someone disrespected him, he better man up and try to hurt him.

"There's no suckers in this household. If someone hit you, you better try to break his jaw. If someone catches an attitude with you, check them and make sure they come correct in the future. Everyone got their own lane. Don't let no one cross yours. Don't ever hesitate to put a dude in his place. If you ever come home, and I hear anything about you letting some kid try you, you're gonna regret not doing anything."

"What about if a girl gets out of line?" Sincere asked, hoping the same didn't apply to them.

"You carry yourself right and respect them. You don't have to worry about them getting out of pocket. Never hit a female. If one attacks you, restrain her. But never hit her."

Sincere got up off the floor and dusted himself off. He walked past Max, as if the push was nothing.

"You all right?" Laz asked, a teammate of his.

"I'm good. Check ball."

On the ensuing possession, Sincere purposely turned the ball over. While Max was focused on the game-winning point, Sincere blindsided him with a right hook to his jaw that knocked him to the ground. Instantly he dropped haymakers on him. Then all of a sudden it was a five-on-five fight. It lasted until security guards got control of things. They rounded everyone that was involved and took them to the principal office. Six students got three days' suspension. Three received five days. And Sincere got the maximum of ten days. When Sincere went home, his parents were already aware of the incident.

"Why are you beating people up in school?" his mother asked with concern in her voice.

"Some kid was trying to hurt me. So I put him in his place," Sincere replied. Kiana shook her head and looked at her husband with a lot of sadness in her eyes.

"I don't want him growing up to be just like you. He shouldn't be fighting," she said, shaking her head in disapproval.

"What's wrong with him growing up just like me?" Maurice joked.

"I'm serious," Kiana said firmly.

"Boys fight. There's no way around that. And sometimes, he's gonna have to send very strong messages." Maurice shot back seriously.

"No he doesn't. He can walk away—" Maurice cut his wife off.

"Our boy is not gonna walk away. If he does that, it's gonna only make things worse on him. You know that there, KK. Remember how it was for Tony in the third grade. All that came from him not waiting to fight back. From walking away like you want our son to do. They humiliated Tony throughout middle and high school. Our son will not go through that."

Kiana started to protest. But Maurice cut her off. "Son, you should never look for trouble. But you have the right to defend yourself. Avoid problems as much as you can. Some problems shouldn't be avoided. Like I said before to you, if a dude gets out of line with you, try to break his jaw." Kiana mumbled something under her breath and went to her room.

The memories of the past were all Sincere had of his parents. So he intended to keep them as a reminder when he was going through things.

*****

Before heading to Miami, Snake had to cover up some loose ends. He was currently at a strip club in Virginia called Passion, keeping tabs on an upcoming big-timer named Li'l Gangsta, who ran off with $100,000 on a dope deal from one of his contacts in Maryland. Snake didn't like strip clubs. It was a death trap and a waste of money. Seeing a bunch of loose and beautiful women shaking their ass didn't excite or move him. Women that flaunt their bodies turned him off. The same chick that was capable of bringing excitement could be the same chick to get a person killed. Females were nothing but trouble. They were the biggest destruction of mankind. The right amount of money will make any one of the strippers cough up information. Strippers couldn't be trusted. Needless to say, that statement can be made for a lot of people.

The females at the strip club stripped, sucked dick, played with their pussy, and bust it open for the cash flow. A dude was just another come up to them. So easily they manipulated men with their scent, voice, and bodies. Their seductive nature and mannerisms were just webs being thrown out. Evidently men got trapped in them. Almost every woman knew her potential. Those that recognized their capabilities use it to empower and elevate their status. Even an impoverished woman used her sexuality to improve her situation. Snake refused to be tricked by any female.

To play his part, Snake had $2,000 in singles, one while pretending to be a bit intoxicated by the alcohol he never sipped. He made it rain on a couple of dancers. From his position, he had a great view on L. G. After cashing out, he headed to the bar. One thing he learned a long time ago, great killers were patient. Great killers didn't do sloppy work. They didn't get discouraged by how long they had to wait on someone. Delays or changes happen. Opportunities always pop up.

L. G. was having a blast. He had no intentions of leaving early. One of the prettiest women Snake ever saw mounted on top of L. G. Another reason not to trust a woman: looks were always a form of deception. A man was weakened by what he saw. Snake could never see himself slipping like that. L. G. swiftly inserted his dick in the pretty face. She pretended to give him a lap dance, while two other strippers shielded them. L. G. was entranced in the pleasure of lust, unaware of eyes watching his every move, unaware of his future fate. While bopping his head, pretending to be interested in the music, a stripper with an amazing body blocked his view.

With hands on hips, she shot. "What's up, big spender? Are you taking me home tonight?"

It amazed Snake how bold women were. Twenty years ago, females weren't this aggressive and forward. They had no modesty or shame in what they did now. That was more reason not to trust them. There was nothing but trouble.

"I would love to, but I'm somewhat here with my lady," Snake lied, hoping the woman with the great body would go about her business.

"You two can share me. I'm like Dej Loaf, I go both ways." She smiled, then purposely changed her stance to give Snake a side view of her body. Women had to work on their poses, facial expression, and walk when they were alone. It had to be something they trained himself to do. It didn't come naturally. Another reason not to trust them. They prepared themselves to find ways to get a man's attention without verbally saying anything.

"How about I come scoop you up tomorrow? Got a place I want you to sit on."

"You don't like to share, I see," she said, grinning.

"Why would someone want to share a beauty like you? I'd rather have you all to myself.'

"If I didn't know better, I'll think you and I will be more than just a one night."

CHAPTER 4

Snake

At exactly 8:17 a.m., L. G. was heading to his car without the two females. In so many ways, that made things a lot better. The woman wasn't the target. Collateral damage can bring unnecessary heat. Multiple bodies turning up dead drew way more attention than a single one. Snake wasn't gonna slip up or do anything reckless. That's not how he operated. Getting to L. G. efficiently was better now since he was alone. The extra body count wouldn't have done him any favors. Females were always blinded to the danger they were in.

Snake followed L. G. through the main road. The traffic was real light this Saturday morning. Like every other typical drug dealer and street guy, L. G. had no clue that he was being followed. Not that Snake was making it look obvious. Not knowing where he was heading didn't bother him. The unknown had the tendency to show fear, bring out problems and complications. Those were the moments Snake excelled in. People are normally afraid of what they didn't know or what they couldn't understand. People had a habit of fearing doors they never entered. Not knowing that, that same door they are afraid to walk through could be the best entrance they ever have.

Fear wasn't a feeling Snake was acquainted to. There was no such thing as pressure on him. Pressure was the air you pumped into tires. Air is an element that can be deflated. Snake wasn't made of air. His heart was hard as steel and cold as ice. He wasn't one to be pumped up or deflated by fear. He knew death was coming to everyone. That's a door no one can avoid. Death was guaranteed to the living. When those doors open up to him, it's something he will welcome.

L. G. pulled his car into a small breakfast place called The Egg Ums. The restaurant happened to be in a secluded area. Snake wasn't the type to believe in luck. Opportunities were either there, or they had to be created. A person never get lucky. Everything was based on the laws of nature. Individuals reap what they sow. On this occasion, the opportunity just happened to be there. At least for the moment, that's how it appeared to look. The restaurant was away from traffic. It also wasn't surrounded by apartments or other businesses, where unseen eyes could be a problem. The Egg Ums was in the cuts. And Snake liked that.

L. G. parked his car next to a Cadillac truck. After grabbing something out of his trunk, he entered the restaurant. The thought of parking his car next to L. G.'s vehicle crossed his mind. But he wisely stayed put in the alley across the street. Staying stationery in one spot for so long sometimes is not always safe. Especially if that spot is a parking lot. Hiding in a closet or under a bed is far more different than laying low in an open area. The thought of someone looking out of the restaurant's windows kept Snake at his current position.

For over an hour, he watched cars slowly enter and exit the restaurant. Something wasn't quite right. A person doesn't eat for over an hour. Questions circulated through Snake's chain of thoughts. Was L. G. on to him? Was he meeting someone? Was this his place of business? When will he step out?

The Source didn't give him enough information. There were a lot of holes in what was given. Nonetheless, he opted to not abort his mission. Patiently he waited again, feeling highly confident that an opportunity will eventually present itself.

Two hours later, L. G. and the alleged person he was accused of stealing from walked out of The Egg Ums, kicking it like real close friends. Now the question was, why was The Source misleading him and being manipulative? Evidently L. G. didn't run off with the Ghost's package. One plus one never came up to three. No matter how you switch the numbers around, it was mathematically impossible. This picture didn't add up. Snake didn't like what he saw. He was also kind of glad he didn't have the opportunity to kill L. G. He wanted to see how things were gonna unfold.

One hundred thousand dollars was already given to Snake to seal the deal. Normally The Source gave him half up front. This was the very first time he received the full payment. He didn't know what kind of games The Source was playing. Business wasn't always just business. Lies tend to be a part of the game. Snake didn't like being lied to. When people deceive you or try to do so, there was no room for them to be trusted. One lie always led to another. Too many lies can lead to death. Snake had no intentions of being the recipient of death because of trickery.

For the moment, he spared L. G.'s life. There was a reason he was wanted dead. Nonetheless, the fabrication of Ghost stolen product was where unrevealed information was hidden. Snake overlooked the Tahoe truck L. G. pulled off in. He decided to follow the Cadillac instead. Questions had to be asked. Answers was something Ghost had. He either had involvement in the cahoots of the missing product, or Snake was being played; one way or the other, Snake was gonna find out.

Snake disliked how things were developing. He replayed his conversation with The Source repeatedly in his head. He knew now some foul play had been orchestrated, that he happened to be in the middle of. Ghost and L. G. were said to be alleged enemies; it didn't appear that way. Although looks can be deceiving, there was no denying that they were all right. At least on the surface, it seemed that way.

Snake didn't know much about Ghost. That somewhat excited him. Normally Snake conducted things a certain way and went by certain codes. But he was gonna violate how things were usually done. He felt as if he needed the challenge. Snake never made a plan without knowing as much as he could about his enemy. He never was afraid to change his plans when new information was received. Snake never assumed he knew everything. And he knew it was received. Snake never assumed he knew everything. And he knew it was wise to not want to know everything. In this sequence, Snake was gonna improvise. Ghost wasn't the initial target. Yet there was something up his sleeve that Snake just had to see.

*****

For most of the school year, Sincere stayed to himself. Being the new kid on the scenery had its good in it. The girls constantly flirted with him. They all seemed to really like his New York accent and style. Off the top, Sincere realized the slight difference of the girls from Miami. Their attitude and grammar were unlike what he was used to with the girls from New York. Outside of that, they were all the same. Some were sneaky and secretive. And some were just loose and wide open. The entire female sex was amazing to him. Conversations or discussions with them were way more appealing than the ones he can form with his make counterpart. His father's advice of not dealing with fast girls was on his mind. But with so many girls being forward, it was nearly impossible to restrain or discipline himself by rejecting all the girls' advances.

One day after school, while walking home, Sincere heard some females giggling behind him and hissing at him. He couldn't believe it. Girls were doing things boys did. Turning around, he noticed three girls that were in his English class: Monica, Sandra, and Lisa. He never had a conversation with any one of them. The fact that they were trying to get his attention surprised him. All three of them thought they were royal or some privileged group. Especially Monica. She always walked around with her nose in the air, as if she was God's gift to men. The normal thing to do was to see what they wanted. But he wasn't gonna give them that satisfaction. Without breaking his stride, he kept walking.

"Sincere! I know you hear us calling you," one of the girls said in a commanding voice. Sincere stopped and fully turned around as the girls approached.

"I didn't hear my name until now. What's up?" Sincere smoothly said, looking at each girl.

"You know who we are. I'm Monica. That's Lisa and that's Sandra," Monica stated, firmly indicating with a finger who was who. It seemed as if all three girls were looking down at him, even though they all were shorter. How did they do that?

"I know you got ears, and you hear the talk about who you're gonna take to the dance," Monica said.

"And we know you got eyes. So seeing us doesn't make you blind." Sandra chipped in.

"Right now, believe it or not, it's in your best interest to choose one of us," Lisa added with hands on hips.

Sincere couldn't believe these girls. The way they spoke was like they planned this conversation. In class they never acknowledged him or appeared to be interested. Now all of sudden, they were. In a strange way, these three girls fascinated him with their aura and demeanor. They were all respected and very popular. It's a trip about how they tried to make a claim in an area they have no control over. They seriously thought what they said was law. Sincere had a trick for them.

"So it's in my best interest to choose one of y'all, you say. In that case, I want the best. You all are beautiful. And I'm not gonna make my decision just off what I see."

"So how are you gonna decide?" Monica asked, looking intrigued.

"Since the dance is only a month away, each one of you has a week to show me why you deserve to be that girl."

"They're my friends, I'm not competing against them," Lisa quickly said

"Then that means you've already eliminated yourself from being chosen." Sincere pointed out.

"I don't mean it that way," Lisa replied, letting it be known, in her own subtle way, that she wanted to compete. Sincere didn't miss the look Monica gave her.

"Listen, I don't know anyone of y'all. This is my very first time speaking to you all. A chance to get to know who I want to go with shouldn't be a problem."

"Hold up. What makes you think you have the right to dictate how things are gonna be? My friends and I need a moment to speak on this," Monica said.

It was clear that Monica was the leader or the spokesperson of the group. She always took charge and always wanted to be in charge. There were no royal chairs in a palace or a crown that was gonna be pulled. She was the kind of girl a male couldn't give an inch. Her confidence was cool. But her nose being up in the air all the time didn't sit right with Sincere. The girls were huddled up and kept glancing back at him, shaking their heads with the affirmative nod.

"All right, let's get this clear. We choose the order and everything starts tomorrow. Lisa will be first. Then Sandra. And I'm last," Monica said with authority, as if what was said was finalized.

"You are also not allowed to flirt or spend time with another girl." Sandra put in.

"Do you agree to those terms?" Lisa asked.

"Those rules are easy enough to follow. There's one exception. We start today. So Lisa, may I have your number?" The request surprised everyone. Lisa and Sandra looked at Monica momentarily. Apparently they were expecting her to lead. She just stared Sincere down with an expression that was lost to him. Was she really upset that he made a small tweak to the way she wanted things?

That probably was the case. She was used to things being her way.

"I guess that will be okay since we'll be getting to know one another this week," Lisa finally responded after the awkward silence. After giving Sincere the number, the girls did an about-face and walked off without saying goodbye. Those girls were something else, he thought as he headed home.

*****

Ghost pulled up and parked his truck in front of a nice-looking town house. Snake blinked twice when he saw the woman who greeted Ghost at the door with a passionate kiss. It was the same woman he exchanged numbers with at the club. The same woman L. G. took to the hotel. Snake knew that women had their ways of getting around. And most times, their movements go undetected. This particular woman was nothing but trouble. Snake couldn't knock her conniving and slick ways. At the end of the day, a woman gotta eat too. Everybody's craft and hustle is different. If dudes are foolish enough to be tricked by women, that's totally on them.

The mysterious woman was on her way out the door. Indeed, she was a woman on a mission who got little rest. Snake had plenty of money at his disposal, but he didn't wanna use her. For one, she couldn't be trusted. And he had no idea what her relationship was with Ghost or L. G. So she couldn't be a tool.

Snake knew that he couldn't prolong getting the job done. A lot of things were subject to change once certain people knew L. G. was still living. A thought quickly shaped up in his head while watching a locksmith walk down the streets. Snake slowly got out of his vehicle. As soon as the locksmith made a turn on the next corner, he quickened his step.

"Excuse me sir! Excuse me!" Snake said as if he was out of breath. The locksmith turned around and stopped.

"Do I know you?" he asked, looking perplexed.

"No. No. This is weird, but my girlfriend wants to role-play, and she wants me to be a handyman. How much are you willing to sell me your shirt, hat, and toolbox?"

"Are you crazy? Get out of here! This is for the company. I can't sell you this," the locksmith said, wondering if the guy in front of him was joking or doing some prank.

"You can always get another set. Make an offer."

"Why don't you go to Home Depot or a tool store," the locksmith said, getting ready to walk off.

"I'll give you a thousand for what I asked for." As Snake was pulling out his money, the locksmith's eyes widened.

"I guess it can be replaced."

The man quickly took the ten hundred-dollar bills. He handed the toolbox over and quickly took off his hat and shirt and went running down the streets. He probably made a $500–$700 profit. Money meant nothing to Snake. He used it to make his job easier. Snake got dressed on the spot and circled the block before heading back to his car. Everything was being done on the fly. Winging it wasn't pretty much bad after all.

CHAPTER 5

Five years ago, during their very first encounter, Alexis sparked something within Yolanda that she never thought existed. Yolanda knew every woman was and is beautiful in their own way. But she never believed she would feel for a woman the same way she felt for a man. Gradually over the years, that spark ignited into a burning desire of passion, heat, lust, and love. Yolanda never wanted a person as much as she wanted Alexis. Everything between them was either cordial, platonic, business related, or friendly. It was never the way she yearned for it to be—sensual, emotional, sexual.

Yolanda never revealed her emotions or suggested anything in reference to her feelings toward Alexis. She kept her feelings bottled up inside. It was her fantasy to have an exclusive relationship with Alexis. But she wouldn't dare take that risk. She was afraid of not only losing her job but her friendship as well. And the fear of being rejected kept her from approaching.

In her office, Alexis was preparing a draft on a mutual agreement her company had with their sister company to enhance their telecommunications network services for the betterment of their marketing sales and revenues. Her special adviser was on vacation. So she and her secretary, Yolanda, had to cover up all the details. Alexis was looking forward to expanding her business and merging with other companies that were owned by blacks. Seldom will you see people of color working together. It was a movement Alexis hoped that can inspire other black owners.

Lately Alexis noticed that Yolanda was a bit withdrawn and distracted when it came to getting the job done. Yolanda was grade A. Always on time.

And she consistently did what was required of her and more. Though as a friend, she was slowly changing and becoming distant. It was a change she didn't like and one she was gonna address the next time Yolanda stepped in her office.

*****

Katherine, also known as Kat, was the only female computer technician in the building. In a field that was dominated by men, she held her own and stood out when it came to cracking codes and getting around viruses. Most of her work was legitimate. The side jobs she took, which consisted of her breaking into other companies' systems, her boss knew nothing about it. Gregory Black happened to be the other boss she was working for. Little did people know, Gregory was more than just an errand boy. Surprisingly he paid her more than the company. It was great to be under his payroll. Under his arms. Under his sheets. Among other things there was no need to mention. Katherine hurried down the steps, anticipating her lunch break with Gregory.

Shadow was on his lunch break, waiting for Kat's arrival. She was an ordinary Jane that was easy for him to seduce. Since his release from prison, Shadow only had eyes for snow bunnies. It derived from them really being the only group of women in the institution he was in. Now he was infatuated with them. They were the only females he had sex with. He wouldn't give a black woman the time and day.

After exploiting Kat's weakness and realizing how helpful she can be with providing information, Shadow got his palms on Sincere's location. That information alone really increased his bank account. Kat wasn't the kind of woman that thirsted for money. She was thirsty for something else. She was eager, more than ever, to do anything for him after their sexual marathon. Sex was all she wanted from him.

"Hey, beautiful."

"Hi, Gregory. Sorry I'm late. I lost track of time. I do that sometimes. Actually I do it a lot when I'm juggling different prospects in my head. I think I have the wrong concept of… Sorry, I'm rambling again," Katherine said as she took a seat.

"It's okay. I love hearing your voice and the way you speak," Shadow said, turning the charm on.

"Stop that," Kat said, blushing.

"What, you don't like when I make you feel good?"

"It's not that. I just get… Well, I'm unlike me when I'm around you." And she meant that. Gregory was the first black guy she slept with. It was always her fantasy to sleep with a black man. He intimidated her. Although the feeling was strange, it was very much welcomed.

"Do you like who you are when you're around me?"

"I love it. I'm filled up with so much energy just thinking about you," she admitted.

"I got another job for you that needs to be done in two days." Shadow buttered her enough. Now it was time to get to business.

"If it's in my power to do it, consider it done." Kat was ready to do anything for him. Was she already in love? What would her parents think? They didn't have to know everything about her personal life, she thought.

"Nothing is impossible for you to do. I'll give you the rundown tonight. Will you be available?"

"For you, of course I will."

*****

Snake kept the car running across the street as he walked up the steps of the town house. He knocked on the door a couple of times and waited. He paid very close attention to the movement in the house. It was going to be important to know how many people were in there. He only heard one set of feet. That didn't mean it was the only pair in there. Without asking who was at the door, And probably not even looking or checking to see, Ghost carelessly opened the door.

"Good morning, sir. I was called in reference to a leakage in the kitchen sink." Snake reached in his pockets and looked at the name that was written on the napkin with the phone number. Doing this was a risk if she gave him a false name. "By a Veronica."

"Yeah, that's my wife. The kitchen is to the left. You can't miss it," Ghost replied and turned to walk away.

Snake didn't know what was more astonishing—that Veronica was his actual wife, or that he was so stupid to let him inside of the house so easily. Wasting no time, Snake pulled out his Sig Sauer P226, with the silencer in place, out of the toolbox. He crept and hit Ghost with the butt of the pistol. Ghost stumbled to the ground.

"Take off your shirt slowly and sit down over there," Snake said in a low voice. After seeing Ghost wasn't armed, he stated, "Who's in the house with you?"

"I'm alone."

"If anyone comes down them steps or out of any room, they are gonna die. Do you understand?" Ghost just nodded yes. "I'm not gonna drag this out. I need answers without delay. Someone contacted a person I know to put Li'l Gangsta in the past. Word is that he stole a package from you. Yet earlier today, you two were together. What's going on?" Snake asked, wondering if Ghost knew who he was.

Ghost decided not to speak. Which was a grievous mistake. Snake aimed the pistol at Ghost's kneecap and fired. The silencer drew out the blasting sound of a gun without one. But Ghost's scream carried through the walls. Snake stuffed a dirty rag with oil out the toolbox, in Ghost's mouth. Snake learned a long time ago, most times, it was best to make a person feel pain so they can know the seriousness of the situation. If pain is not inflicted, people often think the danger is not real.

"Like I said, I'm not gonna drag this out. I need answers and you're delaying. The next shot will kill you. What's going on?" Snake asked again, taking the rag out of Ghost's mouth.

"My cousin paid someone, that I think is you, to kill L. G. After L. G. died, someone was to kill you," Ghost informed.

"Who is your cousin?"

"Big Sam. But his contacts know him as The Source."

Snake didn't feel no type of way that The Source was plotting on his death. It wasn't an act of betrayal. The Source wasn't a friend. Snake was someone that The Source couldn't control. So that alone made him a threat.

"Did your product come up missing?" Snake asked.

"What product?" Ghost asked back, looking confused. "Your coke?"

"Coke! I don't deal with drugs."

"One last question. Do you have any idea who is supposed to kill the person that kills L. G.?"

"Somebody named 2Shooter." When the name left Ghost's mouth, Snake released a shot that hit him in the middle of his head.

*****

Lisa just got off the phone with Sincere. She was shocked that they had an amazing conversation. It was definitely unlike anyone she had with previous boys. She and Sincere had so much in common. From her favorite R & B singer, ice cream, time of the year, movie, perspective on injustice, and, most important thing, in a relationship. That one conversation with him shot a wave of joy through her that flooded her insides with happiness. The feeling he brought her was electrifying. She wanted more of him. Monica was a damn fool to not just ask him out. She fronted as if she wanted them to tease him. But Lisa saw through it all.

Lisa had made her mind up. She was in the competition to win it. Every day Monica, Sandra, and she were supposed to discuss their time with Sincere. There's things Lisa would never speak of to her friends. She was anxious to see what tomorrow would bring once they were alone and face-to-face.

*****

Monica was stunned that she didn't put her feet down. Who did Sincere think he was? He had no right to change things. On top of everything, he needed to learn some manners.

"We shouldn't be going along with this with you or for you. It makes no sense to involve Lisa and me in this farce," Sandra said, staring down Monica.

"I don't think there was another or better way," Monica replied, ignoring the way Sandra was looking at her.

"Are you kidding me! You could've just flat out asked him to the dance. That was the easiest way to handle this. You know that. What if he picks me or Lisa and not you?" Sandra asked, hoping that Monica would look at the situation from all angles. Ignoring the question and avoiding making eye contact, Monica grabbed a dress.

"What do you think about these shoes in this dress?"

"Oh, Monica, Monica, Monica," Sandra stated playfully, knowing exactly what was going on.

"What!" Monica asked, becoming agitated with Sandra. Well, that really wasn't the case. She was frustrated with herself.

"You've finally met someone that got you off balance. I saw how you froze up when he changed things up and asked Lisa for her number. Who would've thought Monica, of all people, would be tongue-tied in the presence of a boy. Don't think I missed that," Sandra said, smiling.

"You're delirious." Monica shot back.

"Am I? You know what, I'm not even gonna go there with you. It boils down to this, girl. Fact remains, you should've just asked him out. Now that you put the ball in his court, you relinquish whatever power you have. Because where you stand now, you have no control over who he decides to pick. And you know that." Sandra said.

"You two will make him not choose y'all from me." Monica shot back, raising her voice with a touch of anger in it. "I see you don't understand boys, sweetie. They like us girls sometimes in ways we can't even comprehend. It's not always simple with them or just about sex all the time. Who knows how he likes a girl? Me or Lisa turning him down can just be something that turns him on."

Monica had nothing to say. She knew her friend was right. Oh, how she wished she was wrong. Monica had to get herself together. She was the most popular girl in the school. It was an hour for anyone, boy or female, to speak to her. She had to take control. One thing her friend was wrong about, had she given up her power? She had an ace in the hole. When it was time for her to be with Sincere for the week, she won't dare look up or freeze up.

*****

Snake had to postpone his trip to Miami for the time being. His life was more important than what Hot Rod had going on. He suggested to Hot Rod that it would be wise to send someone down there to pay Sincere's uncle a visit to see what kind of information they can make him cough up. Hot Rod wanted Snake to be hands on with everything. Once loose ends were straightened out on his end, He was gonna take that trip down to the bottom.

CHAPTER 6

TEMPTATIONS

A little after one, Alexis got on her phone. It was time to get to the bottom of why Yolanda was acting the way she was.

"Yolanda, report to my office immediately." As soon as the words came out, she wanted to take them back. Summoning her to the office wasn't the approach she wanted to take. Yolanda was a friend and needed to be treated as such. There was always time for professionalism. This wasn't it. Alexis was nervous. She didn't know what was going on with Yolanda. She just knew that she didn't wanna lose a friend.

Yolanda didn't like Alexis's tone and the way she told her to come to the office. It was way too professional. Something was up. Yolanda put her coffee down and rushed to Alexis's office.

"Is there something wrong?" Yolanda asked as soon as she burst through the door.

"As a matter of fact, there is. Take a seat." Alexis didn't like how she was using her authority. Reluctantly Yolanda sat down, wondering what was going on. "The air needs to be cleared out. Lately you've been acting real funny. You do an incredible job in this building. But you've been pulling away from me as a friend and being real shady. What's up with that?"

Yolanda didn't know what to say. So she remained silent. She didn't have the courage to express her thoughts and feelings.

"Have I done anything wrong toward you? I've never undermined your position. I treat you as my equal and give you the utmost respect as a person. Why the change?" Alexis asked, placing a hand over Yolanda's.

The touch of Alexis hand shot currents of electricity through Yolanda's body. Yolanda flinched and unconsciously pulled her hand away. She knew she couldn't stay silent. Alexis deserved an explanation to her awkward behavior. Yolanda didn't know where to start.

"I need some time off," Yolanda said out of nowhere.

"How much time do you need?" Alexis asked, wondering how time off would rectify the problem at hand.

"Just a couple of days. I need to get some things sorted out. Once I do, I promise to be a better friend."

"Whatever you're going through, you don't have to go through it alone. Just know that I'm here for you."

Alexis watched Yolanda walk out of her office. There was something odd about the way she was acting. Yolanda's reaction to a simple touch may have confirmed one of the thoughts she had. Yolanda snatched her hand away as if she was being burned by fire. Alexis remembered doing that in high school with her childhood crush. James was the first guy she had sex with. Before he even knew she was head over hills over him, he had touched her, and Alexis pulled away, just the way Yolanda did. Maybe her outlook to the situation was far-fetched. Yet she really doubted that it was.

At the moment, Yolanda could no longer be in the presence of Alexis. She gathered her belongings and rushed out of the building. She jumped in her car and drove off without a destination in mind. She had two choices: either quit or let Alexis knew how she felt about her. She could still feel the softness of Alexis's hand over hers. At a red light, she was so deep and lost in her thoughts that she was unaware of her hands pressing firmly on the prime between her thighs. Cars honking behind her got her attention. She was really tripping, she thought.

Instead of going home, she checked herself in a hotel. With Alexis in mind, she called a long-time friend she used to hook up with sexually.

"Hey, this is Yolanda. Are you busy?"

"It depends."

"I'm at a hotel, and I need some company."

"Say no more. Text me your address, and I'll be on my way."

Yolanda really needed someone to talk to. Corey was a friend that kept an open mind every time they connected. Not only was he a great listener, he always had the right advice. Sex never complicated what they had. When her tank was empty, Corey did what he could to fill it up. A friend like that was always handy. Right now, she was in need of his words.

An hour later, Corey was at the door knocking. Before Yolanda had a chance to say hello, he was all over her, showering her with kisses and trying to pull her clothes off. Yolanda tried to fend him off. But he was too strong and too drunk. Her pushing him back only pulled him forward. She didn't call him over for this.

"Stop it, Corey! We need to talk," Yolanda said, hoping to slow him down. He ignored her and ripped her shirt off. Yolanda slapped him, and in return, he punched her. "Please, Corey, don't do this!" Yolanda pleaded.

"Shut up and stay still." Corey barked.

"Please, I'm begging you." Corey punched her again and held a hand over her mouth as he had his way with her. Yolanda lay there and just cried with her eyes closed. She didn't know how long he was on top of her or when he left the room. When she had the strength to get up, she called the first person that came to mind.

"Alexis, I need you to come pick me up. I just got raped."

*****

The following day in school, Sincere had a surprise for Lisa. He really enjoyed speaking to her over the phone last night. It was the very first time he spent damn near the entire night on the phone with a girl. One long conversation doesn't make a relationship. There's too many spaces and holes that have to be filled up. Too many things that had to be covered and discovered. The ones that he explored made speaking to Lisa and wanting to be around her something to look forward to.

Early that morning, Lisa was waiting behind a particular portable that they agreed to meet at. Away from all other eyes. Away from her closet friends.

"How long have you been waiting here?" Sincere asked.

"About five minutes," Lisa replied nervously with her eyes cast to the ground. It was a sight to see. Around her friends, she was sure of herself and possessed a boatload of confidence. This was a totally different girl.

"I don't wanna keep you waiting. I know every morning you gotta meet up with your friends—" Sincere stated and was cut off.

"I can always catch up with them later. They know the arrangements." She shot back firmly. She was right, Sincere thought. Lisa had seven days. And he liked the fact that she wanted to be around him.

"Well, I got this for you." Sincere reached in his back pocket and took out a small crystal sculpture twin dove. "My mother gave me this and told me to give it to the first girl that really makes me happy."

"That's so sweet of you," Lisa said, finally looking up.

"It's a symbol of friendship. Whatever happens, let's always be friends."

"I really like that." Lisa came closer, softly took Sincere hands into hers, and pulled him in for a kiss. "I'm sorry," Lisa blurted out quickly, obviously shaken up by a kiss she initiated.

"There's nothing to apologize for," Sincere assured her, wondering why she was acting like she did something wrong.

"I think I should go see how my friends are doing."

"Cool."

The rest of the week, Lisa was avoiding Sincere. She screened all his phone calls. When he saw her in school, she was usually always being shielded by her friends. Sandra and Monica kept eyeing him down as if he was the most horrible person they saw. He didn't know what Lisa told them about him. It was all confusing. The first girl he really liked and slightly opened up to didn't wanna have anything to do with him. Whenever he saw her alone, she quickly went the opposite way or went hiding around a corner. This was the same girl who made the move to kiss him. One thing he was beginning to learn and see that girls were strange and full of complications.

*****

Snake heard of the young killer named 2Shooter. He was the leader of a small local gang in Connecticut called The Death Squad. They consisted of six guys that were well known for terrorizing the streets. M1 was twenty-seven years old. He was already acquitted of three separate capital homicide cases. So the name Murder One stuck. You also had S. K., Tech Nine, and Forty. They all were known for using those specific weapons. And last was Pistol P. He was actually second-in-command.

The group brought a lot of fear to those in the community. Snake knew he had to kill them all. He wouldn't put it past The Source or 2Shooter to not say anything else about the hit on his head. Everybody had to go. There were no cutting corners or sparing anyone. Fortunately for L. G., he was gonna live a little longer.

After going to Maryland to change his choice of transportation, Snake was on his way to Connecticut.

*****

Seeing Yolanda in her state flooded Alexis with all kinds of emotions. Sympathy, care, worry, love, but most of all, anger. Why would someone abuse her this way? She felt a bit guilty for not praying more about what was troubling her. If she never had approved the two-day break, there's a strong possibility that this wouldn't have happened. Alexis knew she had to focus. She couldn't bury her thoughts in self-pity. She needed to be there for Yolanda the best way that she can.

Moping about things that couldn't be changed wasn't gonna get her anywhere. She immediately grabbed the phone with the intention of contacting the police.

"No don't," Yolanda stated, placing a hand over her arm tightly. "No police. Please… Just take me somewhere."

"Okay. Let's go to my place so we can clean you up."

Yolanda was sitting on a couch in Alexis's spacious living room. She couldn't believe Corey, her childhood friend, of all people, raped her. Him being drunk didn't justify his actions. He had no right to take advantage of her like that. What he did to her wasn't gonna go unpunished. She didn't wanna involve the law enforcement in the middle of her problems. Too many times she saw how they mishandled things. She knew the perfect guy to deal with Corey. He needed a personal touch. Vengeance was required in this situation.

Alexis didn't like the expression on Yolanda's face. Her eyes were dark, full of fury. She never flinched or twitched as she applied the items in her medical kit over her bruises. She was in a zombielike state.

"You're safe now. I will protect you," Alexis said, trying to soothe her with words. "I'm gonna be here for you as long as you want me to be." Alexis felt Yolanda soften underneath her. The tension was gone and replaced with tears.

"He raped me." She cried.

"It's okay. I'm here now," Alexis whispered softly, brushing her fingers through Yolanda's hair.

"All I wanted to do was talk. And he raped me." She continued to sob into her chest.

"I know it hurts. But we will find a way to make the pain go away. We will do it together," Alexis assured her.

Alexis felt Yolanda's head rising and inching toward her neck. Yolanda softly kissed her neck. Before she knew it, they both were engaged in a passionate kiss. Alexis knew that Yolanda needed to be cared for. So she gave her what she needed. She gave Yolanda comfort. She gave her a pillow and a blanket to rest on. She gave her something to take her mind off the horror and tragedy of the night.

Yolanda accepted Alexis opening up to her. Her mind was clear of the anger and hate she held for Corey. It was now a place with desire and hunger. They both melted under each other's touch. Releasing emotions within that seemed to be hidden for centuries. There on the couch, they abandoned reason, fear, and questions. There on the couch, they explored each other's bodies.

*****

Sincere received a phone call from Lisa on the last night he was supposed to have with her. Officially after school tomorrow, their seven days were gonna be over with, and it was on to Sandra. Hearing her voice took him back. She did her best to avoid and stay away from him. And out of the blue, she just called. This girl had to be crazy, he thought.

"Hey," was all she said.

"Hey to you too." Sincere wasn't gonna be the one to start the conversation.

"I'm sorry about how I've been acting. You scared me." Sincere didn't know what this girl was talking about. How did he scare her? This had to be some kind of games she and her friends were playing with him. He remained silent.

"I'm really thankful for the gift. Tomorrow is our last day together," she said with sadness in her voice that confused Sincere even more.

"I know. After you kissed me, you hid from me."

"I'm so sorry. Come to my house tomorrow morning. My mother will be at work," Lisa said. Sincere didn't read anything into the invitation.

"I have to be in school, so do you."

"Please… I wanna make up for last time. And missing the entire day of school is the only way to do that." Lisa was dead serious. Spending the day with her sounded good.

"How about we do this. We go to our homeroom class so we can get credit for the day on attendance. Then we go to your place."

"That's a great idea. You must've done this before."

"It's the logical thing to do," Sincere said.

"So we're gonna have to sneak out and walk to my place," Lisa said, but not in the form of a question.

"Sneaking out isn't hard. I'll see you tomorrow then."

"Okay. Thank you for not being mad at me."

"You good." Sincere ended the call, wondering why he would be mad at her. He didn't think he would ever understand females.

*****

Hot Rod gave Snake the needed information he requested to locate the group that resided in Connecticut. He truly hoped the situation was resolved as soon as possible. He understood his friend's predicament. As much as he needed his aid, he was aware that his friend's life was in danger. In a way more drastic and fatal way than his. He sent a couple of his lieutenants down to Miami to put some pressure on Montel. If he didn't accept payment, his other option was death. There weren't too many methods to go by. The kid had what he needed. By any means, he would have it.

As Hot Rod was preparing to go to one of his establishments, he received a dreadful phone call. His half-sister just recently got raped. Yolanda was someone he hadn't spoken to in almost thirty years. How did she get his number? And why would she run and tell something like that? As kids, they were always close. But her mother didn't want her daughter around him. So they relocated down South without a single word. Hot Rod always had a soft spot for her.

The unexpected news enraged him. But as he learned from Snake a long time ago, it's never wise to let anger control your decisions. It was a Chinese proverb that made sense. He wouldn't dare risk going down there. But he would inform his lieutenants to give his sister a hand.

*****

After a long session of incredible sex, Katherine laid her head on Gregory's chest. She felt so alive when they were together. He gave her life purpose and meaning. She knew it was silly to depend on a man for strength and substance. It was straight elementary and a quick way to be disappointed. Yet the feeling Gregory brought her was addictive. The risk she had taken with her heart was well worth it. Life was dull and dry before he came into her life. Now it blossomed and bloomed. Whatever he wanted her to be, she would be. Whatever he needed from her, she would supply it. If she did as she was told, she could prove her loyalty to him. And he would never leave her.

Shadow knew that Kat was crazy for him. She was lost in a world that he created in control. The snow bunnies from his assessment were easy to manage. Far better to seduce and mislead. Black women wanted control or wanted to be on an equal footing. The snowflakes had no problem following. They yearned to submit. They looked forward to being dominated. Shadow knew that all women were different. He knew that the Beckys had the same character traits as the sisters. And the same vice versa. At the end of the day, they were under the same gender—female. But different encounters proved to him that it was easier to persuade a snow bunny.

"Thanks for the information you gave me last night. Tomorrow morning, I'm gonna wire the money in your account," Shadow said

"I told you that's not necessary. We're on the same team. I do what you want because that's required of me," Katherine replied.

"You know, Kat, I've been giving this some thought. Would you like to be my lady?"

Katherine was speechless. Tears formed in her eyes. She was excited, delighted, and overwhelmed with joy.

"I will cherish you as my man and do my best to never let you down."

"I know." Shadow smiled. Yes, indeed, she was trapped.

*****

The next day, after the first period, Lisa and Sincere met by the gymnasium. The teachers' parking lot was not too far.

"Hey," Lisa said shyly.

"Hey. You trust me?" Sincere asked.

"I guess I do," Lisa responded, not knowing where that question came from.

"Either you do or you don't." Looking into Sincere's eyes, she said she did. "Follow me."

Sincere led her to the teachers' parking lot and opened the doors to his Charger. He told Lisa to get in. Quickly she went to the passenger side.

"Whose car is this?" she asked with doubt in her voice.

"It's mine. My father brought it for me on my last birthday."

"How come you always walk home and to school?" Lisa asked.

"I'm supposed to drive it once I start high school."

"You are so cool." Lisa flipped through Sincere's music folder and put it on Kut Klose, "I Like." When that song went off, she put TLC's "Red Light Special" on. The mood in the car was peaceful. The drive to her place was real short. They arrived before the second song ended.

When they reached her place, Lisa was shocked to see her older sister home.

"What the hell! Why are you not in school?" Before Lisa had a chance to answer, her sister saw Sincere. "What is he doing here? You know what, this is none of my business. You girls are so fast nowadays. Make sure he puts on a condom." Lisa's sister was out the door after that statement.

Lisa's face flushed with embarrassment. Sincere felt stupid that he didn't read the signs. She probably invited him to hang out. But those two songs she played in the car screamed what she wanted. Sex was never something he actually thought about. Now that the picture was clear, why else would she bring him to her place? He didn't even have or own a condom.

"Are you hungry?" Lisa asked, trying to lighten the mood.

"I'm good. How old is your sister?"

"Seventeen."

"Shouldn't she be in school too?" Sincere asked.

"My point exactly," was all Lisa said. For almost ten minutes, they stayed quiet. Neither one of them knew what to say. They didn't know how to make the first move. Eventually they both knew it was gonna happen. They just didn't know how to get things started.

"I never had sex before," Sincere admitted, breaking the ice."

"Me too."

"I didn't even think you wanted to have sex. So I didn't bring a condom." Lisa pulled out a small package out of her pocket that Sincere recognized at the store. "You planned this?"

"I gave this a lot of thought. I want you to be my first. I don't know why. I just feel this connection with you."

Lisa made the first move. It all started with one kiss. Which led to the removal of their clothes, and then rounds of experimenting.

After two hours of exploration, they cuddled up together, watching two movies: *Think Like a Man* and *Waist Deep*. No words were exchanged. They enjoyed each other's company. When both movies were completed, Lisa was fast asleep. Sincere didn't disturb her. He wrote her a short note and left.

> Thank you for opening yourself up to me. Although the seven days have expired, hopefully our time together doesn't. I look forward to speaking to you again after all of this. Written with warm regards, Sincere.

Lisa read the note over and over again as tears came down her eyes. For the first time, she was in love, and as much as she loved the feeling, she was afraid, afraid that the feeling wouldn't be reciprocated.

CHAPTER 7

2Shooter and everybody in his crew were out on the front porch of S. K.'s baby's mother's house chilling. In an hour, they had plans to terminate some new guy from California who thought he had a right to make money in the neighborhood without paying a fee. He was gonna be hit with a news flash, the East Coast way. Staying around doesn't give you access to make some changes. Since this new kid named LA was playing around, he was gonna get it to. 2Shooter didn't know how they did things out West. But over here, the cake on the plate wasn't for everybody to eat. At least on this turf it wasn't. If you weren't part of the Death Squad, you had to pay your community tax. If not, you better get your cash flow in another area.

Minutes before bending the corner to give LA a message, 2Shooter received a phone call from The Source.

"That acquisition I proposed to you. The offer is double. Take care of it immediately."

Before 2Shooter could reply, a rain of bullets showered him and his crew. No one had the chance to fire back. The wound he now had in his throat was gonna turn out to be fatal. As he lay on the ground, pressing both hands on his neck to suppress the bleeding, a man—one man—jumped off his motorcycle and precisely put rounds in everybody that was on the ground. His whole crew was dead; 2Shooter accepted his fate. They caused mayhem and brought havoc to a lot of people. They had many enemies. They stepped on so many toes. It wasn't a group of dudes that made the attack. This guy was by himself. Instantly it hit him when he heard the voice on the phone, saying, "Hello." He should've never have dealt with The Source. As Snake approached, 2Shooter smiled.

It was time to go. He lived a good life. Outside of dealing with The Source, he had no regrets. Without saying a word, Snake pulled the trigger and left.

*****

The Source never trusted Snake. It wasn't because he was reckless. The Source admired his courage and tenacity. Snake's ability to get a task done was second to none. His skill set was impeccable. His ruthlessness, lack of emotions, and thirst for bloodshed was the reason why Snake couldn't be trusted. He was unpredictable. When it came to killing, he had no boundaries or set no limits. He was tied or committed to no one.

Ever since the assignment on L. G. was a compromise, everything went haywire. L. G. was supposed to be dead. But he was still roaming the streets. Somehow Ghost was the one that ended up dead. And after hearing those gunshots and no response from 2Shooter, things didn't appear to look too good for him. The Source picked up the phone and made the call.

"Yo, B. Come through. We got a problem," The Source said.

"Science or Mathematics?"

"Science."

"In the means of what?"

"Creation. Reptiles. Chemist."

"Say no more. I'm on my way."

*****

Snake was speeding off in his motorcycle, putting miles away from him and the bodies he left in a gruesome fashion. With all the killing the group did, they wouldn't be missed. He did the city a favor.

Finding 2Shooter and his crew wasn't difficult. Hot Rod had connections. Trish was S. K.'s baby's mother. Everyone in the city of Norwalk knew that her house was the hangout spot. The Death Squad didn't fear anyone. They walked every block as if they owned it. The older heads who made a name for themselves were forced out of the game. They all had families now and didn't wanna risk their lives. Almost five years ago, 2Shooter and his crew set the tone when they killed this big-timer named Poppy, his wife, and three young girls in broad daylight at a gas station. The rest was history from there.

Now that the Death Squad was out of the way, another upcoming group will try to establish themselves as bosses. That's how things always turned out. The cycle never stops. It may slow down or be put on hold momentarily, but the heat always goes on.

*****

After that night with Monica, Sandra was seriously considering not going through the seven-day ordeal with Sincere. What would she gain out of it? Sincere wasn't the type of guy she could see herself with. She liked them tough and with a lot of edge on the corner. He was too quiet. She liked a boy that made noise, and one that can also challenge her intellect in conversations. While daydreaming, Sincere came out of nowhere with flowers in his hands.

"Good morning. I wanted to make a good impression. I went with plastic because it will last longer," Sincere said.

Sandra didn't know how she let him sneak up on her like that. Flowers. No one ever gave her flowers before. This boy wasn't even her boyfriend or someone she knew. Nevertheless, on their very first official meeting, he wowed her. Someone sweet and considerate seems or feels so bad.

"I take you like the flowers. I'll catch up with you later. I look forward to getting to know you," Sincere said and was gone.

Sandra stood there, stunned. Where did her voice go? Why couldn't she move? How did he do that to her? When her body came back into form, she quickly hid the flowers in her locker. If Monica knew who it came from, she probably would throw a fit. One thing was for certain, she would definitely feel some type of way about that.

Sincere learned from his father, a couple years back, how to drop a girl's guard down. It first started with kindness. Getting them to like you after that was simple, his father said.

"The more you do to bring a female pleasure, the more they will want to make and keep you happy. Females love to feel good, important, and special. They want us guys to put them in a class of their own."

After having sex with Lisa, Sincere really didn't wanna continue the seven day project with Sandra and Monica. It was his idea, so he had to keep his word. As of now, he disliked the fact that he put his foot in his mouth.

*****

Hot Rod and Snake were in one of his offices at a sports bar in B-More, strategizing on the best way to deal with the operation down South. Hot Rod sent word to his sister that a cousin of his was gonna pay her a visit. He promised to visit in the future. It was unlikely that he was gonna keep that promise. One thing he would do was help take care of that scum that violated her.

Hot Rod watched Snake and couldn't fathom how he could be so calm. Killing people had no effect on him. Being hunted by killers didn't seem to bother him either. His facial expression was as still as a statue. How did he do it?

"It seems as if Ghost partially told you the truth. The Source is his cousin, but he gave you a fake name. Remember back in middle school, there was this kid who threw another boy over the third-floor rail."

"Yeah. Bernard Little." Snake pointed out.

"They tried to charge him as an adult. Yet the judge ended up giving him ten years for manslaughter. He was released in seven. No one knew that he was the hidden force behind The Enforcers. Everyone thought Big Luke was the muscle and power. And Lamar was the brains. But all along, Bernard was pulling the strings. According to what I just gathered, every member on The Enforcers didn't get jammed up during the raid by the feds. Bernard was under no radar because he didn't exist. Other faces were put in place for fame and credit."

"That was very smart of him. So Bernard is—" Snake started to say.

"The one and only."

"If Bernard didn't exist, where did you dig up this information? Is it even something that's not altered?" Snake questioned.

"I know you would have your doubts." Hot Rod made his way out of the office and came in with a bruised-up woman. Her beauty was still obvious through the damages on her.

Snake waited to see how this female played into anything. Women were very deceptive and always had ulterior motives. Not one could be trusted. Sooner or later, it was best to discard them. Sometimes they showed more loyalty and honor compared to men. Nonetheless, the truth remains. They were mainly liabilities.

"This is Bernard's fiancée. Everything was according to her," Hot Rod said and took a seat.

The woman with the bruised face was Stacy. She gave up every information she could of Bernard. Apparently he had been physically and mentally abusing her for years. She reached her breaking point and was finally tired of the constant mistreatment. A woman scorned had no boundaries to what they'll do. More reason for Snake to not trust them.

"How did you two meet?" Snake asked, wanting to fill up some holes.

"When I made the decision to leave, I felt the need to contact you. I discreetly inquired about you in the Bronx. Someone led me to seven different people before I was introduced to him," Stacy said, pointing to Hot Rod.

"Seven different people?"

"Yes. One in the Bronx, Queens, Brooklyn, Manhattan, Staten Island, Richmond, Newark, and now I'm here in Baltimore."

"That's a lot of traveling."

"I'm serious about what I want. You can help the both of us out," Stacy said with a desperate look in her eyes.

Snake really didn't have any option to weigh. He sucked up every piece of information he could about Bernard. When he was satisfied with what he had, he shot Stacy.

"What the hell!" Hot Rod yelled, looking at Snake in disappointment.

"You know I wasn't gonna let her live."

"I don't care about her. I gotta change my damn carpet now."

*****

While getting to know Sandra, Sincere quickly realized how different girls were. He still understood them. Almost every conversation he had with Sandra, she kept reminding him that she wasn't the one he should choose. It didn't make any sense. If she didn't wanna be chosen, why go through the seven days? One minute, it was, "I think Monica will be the one for you." And the next, "I wish I had a boyfriend like you." Sincere's mind was made up—all the girls were crazy. They may not think so. But he was convinced.

As confusing as Sandra was, she was by far the smartest girl that he ever spoke to. He was a bit intimidated by her knowledge at first. But it helped enhance his mindset and ways of thinking. She always surprised him with her topics. The truth of Thanksgiving and how the Americans slaughtered for a country they didn't own. How Christmas was set up for people to spend money. Modern-day slavery. Female modesty. Division in religion and humanity. Sandra read numerous amounts of books and did countless research on things they spoke about. Sincere didn't always share the same views as her. And those disagreements led to friendly debates.

On the fourth night of their time together, Sandra invited Sincere to her house to read a passage in the Bible and a book she had called *Knowledge of Self.*

"You see, it clearly states that people are also God. So there's more than one God. God is not just the Creator." Sandra threw out there to see what his response would be.

"It all depends on your definition of God. There's only one Creator. I think that's why the Muslims call him Allah, to differentiate the complex name God."

"So you don't think you're a God?" Sandra asked, raising an eyebrow in curiosity.

"No. But I do know anything or anyone can be a god. The name God is just a thing of worship. Money, jewelry, stones, statues, the sun, people, they all can be worshipped. But there's only one Creator."

"I'm gonna agree and disagree. Humans can create. Cars, plants, food, kids," Sandra said just to test Sincere.

"Before anything ever existed, someone had the structure—the ground, skies, stars, sun, moon, rainbows. The rivers, ocean, and lakes came from somewhere. Mammals and humans were created. How one sperm can reach an egg to produce is an extraordinary design that only a supreme being can come up with," Sincere said.

"What are your thoughts on the big bang theory?" Sandra asked, pleased with the answers she was hearing.

"It's just a theory."

"That it is. I know you once stated you don't claim any religion. But if you had to choose, which one will it be?"

"I think there's something you can take from each religion. I'm single. If I had to choose, I'll probably be a Buddhist."

"A person of love. I'll choose Islam. I love modesty in females and how disciplined they are."

Sincere and Sandra spoke for hours. They lost track of time. It was nearly one o'clock in the morning when they looked at the time.

"Since we don't have school tomorrow, and it's late, you might as well spend the night," Sandra said, releasing a fake yawn.

"Where's your mother?" Sincere asked.

"She should be asleep. Let me check." Sandra left the room. Sincere thought about sneaking out. But why pass up on an opportunity to sleep at a female's house? Minutes later, she came back to her room. "She's fast asleep. I didn't even hear her come in. She's a heavy sleeper, so we are good. I don't think she'll hear us."

Sincere immediately caught what Sandra indicated, even if it was a slip of the tongue. There was only a certain type of noise that would probably wake her mother out of her sleep.

"Where would I sleep?" Sincere asked, trying to change the air in the room.

"It's enough space on the bed for me and you," Sandra said, turning her back to him, pretending to get comfortable on the mattress.

Sincere went to the restroom to take a leak. Once again, he was nervous. He wondered if the other girls knew what was going on. This entire seven-day thing had to be something they spoke about. Girls had a tendency of sharing things. It wasn't much they kept from one another.

When Sincere reentered the room, the lights were off, and Sandra was acting as if she was asleep. She even put in a fake snore. Females were good actors, he thought. He took off his shoes and made his way to the end of the bed, as far away from her. When his body hit the mattress, she started stretching.

"When did you get in, baby?" she asked.

"What?" Sincere was lost again. This girl was really crazy.

"I've been waiting on you since eight. I didn't think you'll be working late tonight," Sandra said, moving closer to Sincere.

Sincere didn't know what she was talking about. She had to have bumped her head on something hard when he went to the bathroom. She really had problems.

"Do you know who I am?" Sincere asked with concern in his voice.

"Of course, silly. My husband, Sincere."

Sandra wrapped her arms around him. Sincere was surprised to feel her nakedness. He came prepared. Ever since that day with Lisa, he kept protection on him. That experience made him handle this situation better. He slowly undressed as they kissed with their bodies pressed together. If in her mind they were married for the moment, he would act out the scene with her. Quietly they pleased each other. Quietly they cuddled up, and it was all done.

CHAPTER 8

KEISHA AND BRENDA

A woman in a red dress was bent over, looking under the hood of her car. The back view that was on display was really a sight to behold. Normally Corey wasn't the captain-save-a-woman type. But one look at this woman's pure beauty made him lose all rational thought.

Keisha, the woman in the red dress, was burning up under the blazing sun. The wires on her batteries were actually loose. She already knew that she had to get her carburetor fixed. She also needed a tune-up and an oil change. The car she had was not one she owned. It was necessary for the time being. As she lifted her head up, a car slowly drove by and pulled over. She smiled and unbuttoned her shirt to show more cleavage.

"Good morning. Is there anything I can help you with?" the man asked, not once looking in her eyes. His eyes roamed all over her body, especially her breasts.

"A friend of mine should be on the way any minute."

"I'm a mechanic. Since I'm already here, I might as well see what I can do." The guy offered.

Keisha didn't reject his helping hand. She had a beach towel on the floor. The towel was purposely placed there. Everything was calculated to be just the way it was.

Corey tightened the wires on the batteries and made his way under the car. He was glad a towel was on the floor. Unbeknownst to him, another person stepped out of the vehicle. When he finally came up from under the car, his eyes widened, and all kinds of lustful thoughts rushed into his mind. He was now facing two beautiful women. Not once did he consider how the newcomer appeared. Her sight blinded him.

There was no other vehicle to announce her arrival.

The first female in the red dress did as he did and went under the car. All his attention was focused on her thighs and trying to get a better look at what was in between. He never saw or heard the movement of the other woman. He never saw the hypodermic needle in her hands. Corey felt a sharp sting on his neck. He turned around, trying to grab the woman that was slowly stepping away from him. His vision started to blur. He felt his body weaken, and it quickly went unresponsive as he passed out.

Keisha and Brenda quickly lifted Corey off of the ground and placed him in the back of his trunk. Keisha pulled out a knife and slit his throat wide open. As the trunk closed, they jumped in the beat-up Honda and drove off. Corey would no longer be able to put his hands on another woman again. That minor problem was solved. Now it was time to visit who they came down here for.

*****

The information Snake received from Stacy was accurate. It wasn't a hundred percent. Everything was subject to change. So the percentage of things staying the same could dip. Bernard, also known as The Source, could easily change his current location or his daily routine.

Stacy running out on Bernard and staying away for days, and sometimes weeks, was a regular thing. Stacy wanted financial comfort. She lacked independent security. So she degraded who she was and accepted things that brought her discomfort and pain. She was stupid. Every other woman that ran back to someone who beat them up was stupid too. And men who physically harm a woman they were with were even dumber. Any female could be replaced. Not dealing with them at all was the best option. It made absolutely no sense to risk going to jail or have certain things exposed. Every single woman was sneaky. All women tried to discover things their men kept hidden. They smoothly squeezed things out of them, like squeezing a sponge dry. The Source slipped up. He kept doors opened that were best kept closed.

Snake felt good and optimistic as he headed to Jersey City, where Bernard's mother stayed. Like clockwork, Stacy said he took his mother to church every Sunday. Sunday was family day. A day he took seriously. A day he kept his phone off and did nothing but spend time with his mother. For most people, Sunday was considered a day of worship. A day to praise the Lord, depending on a person's religion. Sundays were the best of days, according to Snake this week. It was the day Bernard got to see a new light.

*****

Yolanda just received confirmation that Corey was no longer a part of this world. A part of her was still saddened about what took place that night at the hotel. Corey's death didn't bring any healing to her. The memories of that awful night remained with her. Nightmares of it were a constant thing. Alexis supported her mentally and kept her satisfied in other areas. But the pain never went away. And she never thought it would.

Alexis did everything she believed she could do to relieve and suppress the stress and hurt Yolanda held within. The time they spent alone together was beyond remarkable. They weren't officially an item. Gradually they took steps to become one. Alexis always cared and had sentimental feelings for Yolanda. She never saw this coming. She couldn't explain how she placed herself in this position. Kissing another woman, loving another woman, all this just happened. Maybe it was always in her. Maybe being alone and lonely for so long pushed her to accept this way of life. She was unsure of many things. Maybe this will work.

If it didn't, she would hate to imagine how things would turn out.

*****

Shadow stood in an alleyway observing the cars that were passing by. His contacts from up north were sending a couple of people his way to collect some information that he had gotten from the company. He was instructed by a woman to wait in this specific alley at 7:30 p.m., and then go to the male's restroom at the McDonald's across the street at 7:50 p.m. Some of the people he was dealing with really thought they were on some Mafia-type stuff. No one had any reason to follow him or suspect him of anything. The same couldn't be said about the people he was dealing with. They probably had their reasons to move cautiously.

At 7:50 p.m., Shadow headed to the McDonald's and went straight to the male's restroom. A pretty woman caught him off guard when she followed him in.

"Let's make this quick. Hand over the package," the pretty face softly said.

"Who sent you?" Shadow asked, wanting to make sure he was dealing with the right person.

"The person that helped you get out of prison," she said with her face balled up now. This was why Shadow didn't like dealing with black women. He asked one question, and she took offense to it. Sisters always wanted things to go the way they wanted.

"I was told it was gonna be two of you," Shadow said, reaching in his pockets. The stone face of the pretty woman remained silent. She grabbed the envelope and looked over it and gave him an envelope as well.

Brenda was sitting at the back table by the restrooms, sipping on her milkshake. If Keisha didn't come out in sixty seconds, she was going in. As soon as she rose from her seat, Keisha was making her exit. Brenda collected the rest of her meal and started to follow the guy Keisha was just doing business with. Her assignment was to find out where he stayed. Doing that was elementary.

*****

On a late Saturday night, Snake was riding slowly down the block of Bernard's mother's house. He noticed a family of five that stayed directly across from the street of Bernard's mother's home. They were entering a family car with luggage and suitcases. From Snake's assessment, that indicated a road trip or flight somewhere. Minutes after their departure, he easily broke into their home. He scanned the place for other occupants. Once satisfied, he sat by the window, watching the house across the street.

The next morning, at 8:05 a.m., Snake watched Bernard from across the street entering his car with his mother. A big part of him was itching to unload bullets in him. But he dared not overlook the Chrysler and Dodge Ram truck that sat on opposite ends of the block. He saw both cars park seconds from each other. The fact that no one got outside of the vehicles raised his antennae. It had to be his security team, Snake thought. He was gonna be in desperate need of them. It was a good thing the two vehicles left as Bernard did. Fifteen minutes later, Snake also left.

Snake was inside Bernard's mother's house hours ago. He thoroughly searched every room to make sure they were all empty. The house was currently vacant. He didn't want any unexpected in Bernard's mother's room. The view was the best than any other room. The blinders were already shut. It was uncomfortable staring out the small opening. But soon, it will come with rewards.

At 11:37 a.m., a new vehicle pulled up inside of the driveway. Bernard's mother slowly stepped out. But her son was nowhere in sight. Snake didn't like the picture. Stacy told him after church, Bernard always—not sometimes *but always*—came back home with his mother. This wasn't happenstance or something to be taken as an oversight. It was never wise to think you have the upper hand on someone. No matter how detailed your preparation or how well equipped you are in a specific area. You never know exactly what the other person knows. Looks alone or paperwork or even precise information doesn't make things certain. Snake didn't wanna question his decision with how quickly he ended Stacy's life. A few more questions could've been asked. What's done is done.

The Infinity truck left as soon as it appeared Bernard's mother was safely inside. Snake could never determine how many people or who was in the truck. He only had Bernard's mother to deal with now. Snake waited in her bedroom, still looking outside by the window with the blinders slightly opened now. Twelve minutes later, his mother finally came in. When she saw him, she barely flinched. She didn't scream or try to run.

"I don't know who you are, but if you know better, you need to get the hell up out of my house," she said with a lot of ice in her voice.

Snake didn't understand how a woman who was unprotected could assure she has the power to speak in that tone with him. Money doesn't give a person total control. A weak person or someone who cherishes it are frightened by those who have it. Power or money that another possesses can easily be taken away.

"Take a seat on the bed," was all Snake said.

"I'm not gonna tell you no more. Get the—" Before the words could formulate in her mouth, Snake released a shot that hit her on the left shoulder blade.

"Sit like I told you to do."

Bernard's mother hurried to the bed. Fear was all over her face now. Softly she was weeping and praying. Following a direct order could've avoided this. Yet pain is the only understanding people know.

*****

The Source wasn't slipping by a long shot. Stacy's disappearance wasn't abnormal. Every time he had to teach her a lesson for her disobedience, she stayed away. There was no pressure in her doing so, with what she knew. Someone always had an eye on her. She couldn't blink without him knowing exactly where she was at. Unfortunately his surveillance team blinked. Now she was nowhere to be found. It's been three days since anyone had any visual or audio on her. What unsettled him the most was the fact that she didn't contact his mother. After every punishment, she sought consolation through his mother. She actually called his mother daily. The Source has been in the game long enough. It was evident to him that Snake had his hands in this.

The Source was at a warehouse looking over numerous footages of some cameras he had installed to overlook the main areas he frequently went to. The Scientist was beside him, flipping one of his knives from one hand to the other.

"So the reptile is Snake?" The Scientist asked.

"Yeah. And I'm positive that he grabbed Stacy somehow. He may have forced her to talk. So I expect him to be at my mother's house today or next week.

I'm gonna need you to watch the house Sundays."

"Let's assume he's there now, waiting on you. What you think would happen to your mother? You should've had surveillance at her place." The Scientist pointed out.

The Source never considered that. His mind was solely on keeping himself safe. His relationship with his mother wasn't the best. As a child, he was the least favorite. He harbored a lot of resentment because of that. His mother didn't love him the way she loved his older sister. That lack of emotions came from how he was conceived. His father killed his sister's father over a gambling debt and raped his mother. That's how he arrived here. He and his sister never got along. That same statement held true with his mother.

Since The Source left prison, he reserved Sundays for his mother. He tried to put some broken pieces together. But it was to no avail. Yet weekly he still searched for approval from his mother.

The Scientist was right. He should've kept a close watch at his mother's home. With a wild man like Snake on the loose, there's no telling what he'll do.

"Install some equipment at her house so we can keep it monitored," The Source said.

"I'm on it."

"When you see him, just kill him, even if he doesn't see you coming. Got it?"

"Understood." The Scientist hid his knife under his sleeves and exited the building.

*****

Snake had no intentions on staying long. He had no idea or clue what Bernard was up to. One thing he was certain of—this house had no extra eyes. It was why he took the risk to come here. Stacy told him about the warehouse and what places he kept eyes on. There was no flow of money or business being conducted at his mother's house. It could be the only reason Bernard had no purpose to supervise the place. It was just the opening Snake needed.

"Where's Bernard?"

"I don't know. He normally stays the entire day with me. But something urgent came up, he said."

"How often does he call you?"

"He never calls me. He just comes every Sunday," she said, sniffling.

It amazed Snake how the feeling of pain could drastically change one's behavior and attitude. He didn't think he would learn anything new from her. He pulled the trigger before she could protest or scream. It was fruitless to let her live. Bernard will know, one way or the other, that he was here. What better way to let him know than this.

*****

The Scientist arrived at Bernard's mother's home fairly quickly. She wasn't expecting him. She actually knew nothing about him. His job was to directly install the cameras in their proper positions. Moving along the side of the house by the flower bed. The Scientist saw a man, about sixty feet away from him, jumping over the fence on the side of the yard. Instantly one of his knives flew and hit the man on his right shoulder blade. Another knife flew, just as quick, over where the man's neck would have been. The guy rolled on the floor and hid behind some bushes. By the time The Scientist got there, the guy was gone. He collected the knife that didn't hit true and went inside Bernard's mother's home. It didn't surprise him to see her dead.

On his way out the door, he made the call to The Source. Snake was a step ahead of them.

"I'm coming over," was all The Scientist said before hanging up.

*****

Brenda kept a close eye on Shadow. The house he just entered wasn't his. It couldn't be his. Instead of opening the door with a key, he knocked. She barely got a view of the woman that allowed him in. The most distinguished thing that was noticeable was the woman's color.

Brenda was hoping for a short night of work. But it extended for hours. Six o'clock the following morning, Shadow and the white woman got inside a different vehicle. Brenda started her ignition and got back on his trail. She was positively sure the house they just left wasn't his. A person owns a key to his own home. She highly doubted that he lost his key.

They arrived at a company a little after six thirty. They both were dressed the part. Brenda called Keisha to relay how the past eleven hours went. Shadow wasn't due to get off of work until four o'clock. Keisha relieved her for three hours so she could rest. The rest was very much needed. Not resting properly could be detrimental to the body and how she worked. With the brief rest, she was alert and more energized.

Six minutes after 4:00 p.m., Brenda was back on the road following Shadow. The white woman was still with him. The route they took wasn't the same as the morning drive. They were heading to another location. They eventually pulled up in a three-story apartment building. Brenda got out of the car and followed them. Shadow and the white lady made their way to the elevator. She quickly caught up to them and went inside the compartment. This was the main reason Keisha and Shadow already had.

While in McDonald's, Brenda's back was to Shadow while he was coming in. Her gray wig covered half of her face on his way out. A wig was something she no longer had on. In the elevator, Shadow didn't take a single glance her way. The same couldn't be said about the white lady on the side of him.

*****

Snake pulled the knife out of his back shoulder. His instincts were the only reason he was still living. That second knife came real close in ending things for him. One minute, he was the hunter, and seconds later, he was being hunted again. The field he was in was like a flip of a coin. You never know what side you were gonna get. Sometimes you won, and sometimes you could lose it all. There were no draws. Snake knew he lost this flip. Bernard was still living, and he had people after him that Snake knew nothing about. As Snake tended to his wound, he smiled thinking of the challenge he was faced with.

*****

Katherine knew she had to seize this opportunity. Her life would be complete if she could pull this one off. Gregory already agreed to it during their many conversations after sex. Now the third party had to be willing to participate.

"Hey! Do you stay here?" Katherine asked, not sure how to approach the situation. "I'm sorry. I'm not really good at this. I'm wondering… I mean, I was thinking. If…" Katherine was locking up. Gregory immediately noticed what was going on. So he saved her from further embarrassment.

"Her intentions. My intentions are not to disrespect you in any way." The elevator opened to the third floor, and they all stepped out. Gregory continued speaking, "We know this is an odd request. But we would like to invite you to our room. We would like it even more if we can explore you in ways that will make you smile."

Katherine loved how Gregory spoke. He was a natural speaker with the gift of gab. He could talk as smoothly with the best of them. But this was her fantasy, not his. She cut him off and tried to take control.

"I always wanted to kiss a black woman. We know you are not part of an escort service, but we will pay to have you." Gregory looked at her in disappointment. She wondered if she said anything wrong. The black girl just laughed.

"I can't believe this is happening. This is my fantasy. Lead me to your place," Brenda said.

"It's actually my boyfriend's place," Katherine said. The female's smile broadened, and Katherine had a feeling she was gonna have the time of her life.

Brenda couldn't believe how events were turning out. She was given access to Shadow's apartment with his consent. Having sex was like wanting sweets. It was something that was craved but not needed. She could do without it. Her body could be used as a tool to get a job done. It was, in fact, a powerful weapon.

CHAPTER 9

GIRLS

Monica was anxious and ready for her turn with Sincere. She loved Sandra and Lisa as sisters. But they couldn't hold a candle to her. In a popularity contest, Monica had them both beat. She also had more money, better fashion, and her looks to supersede theirs. Not saying her friends were not pretty, because they were. But it was like comparing a pearl to a diamond. Both were beautiful. One just stood out more. Monica felt as if she was way ahead of the curve. From her conversation with Lisa and Sandra, Sincere was awaiting his time with her. They both stated that Sincere was kind and would be a cool friend. Monica wasn't looking for a friend. She had one too many of those. Friends tend to disappoint. It was why she kept her circle small.

While chilling at her usual spot after school, waiting for her friends, she noticed Sandra and Sincere walking together. She didn't think much of what she saw. Sandra's eyes grew in surprise when she saw Monica. It made Monica suspicious of what was being talked about. She felt a stab of jealousy. She tried to reject the feeling and regroup. She approached the two with a smile that wasn't genuine.

"Hey, girl," Monica said to Sandra

"Hey," Sandra replied.

"Our time starts now, Sincere," Monica said, giving him a hug. Lisa came toward them, and Monica didn't like the way she was staring at Sincere. Both of her friends were obviously hiding something. It didn't take a rocket scientist to know that Sincere was in the middle of it all. Did her friends really take a liking to him? Did they wanna be more than just friends? Were they really trying to get him to go to the dance with them? Monica didn't know if one or both of her friends were trying to backdoor her. This was a competition. If they wanted to compete, she'll have them both chewing on rocks at the end.

"I'm glad you showed up, Lisa. There's a change of plans today. Sincere is gonna walk me home."

"I thought since your parents are out of town, we were coming over to do your hair?" Sandra chipped in.

"I'm sorry," Monica said, looking as if she meant it.

"And when did you and him speak? It's been Sandra's turn. So speaking to him was off-limits," Lisa said with way too much attitude.

Monica didn't appreciate how she was being challenged. Her friends totally forgot that Sincere was supposed to be hers. It shouldn't matter if she did break the rules.

"We never spoke. I just decided that he's gonna take me home. There's something I wanna show him." Monica didn't catch what Sandra mumbled under her breath. She did catch Lisa rolling her eyes. So her friends really liked him. "It's so rude of me to even make the statement that I did," Monica said, turning her attention to Sincere. "There's several outfits I want your opinion on. Females don't share the same taste as males. Do you mind coming to my place? That is, if you don't have anything to do."

"I'm free. My time with you does start after school." Without saying bye to her friends, Monica took Sincere's hand and walked off. *Chew on that*, she thought.

Sincere couldn't believe these girls. They were supposed to be best friends. Yet they were acting like enemies. If eyes could tell a story, Lisa was throwing daggers at Monica. And no one could've missed Sandra softly calling Monica a girl dog. The tension among them was high. And he understood why. Sandra wanted him to come over her place tonight. She disregarded the fact that the next seven days were strictly for Monica.

Lisa was also upset that he was sticking to the rule and not speaking to any other female. He didn't get these girls. It was their rules, and they were mad at him for not breaking it.

Monica's mind was already made up. The day she gave him control was the same day she made the choice to have sex with him. Boys didn't like playing games or going around in circles. They didn't like girls that were stuck up, snobbish, and a girl who thought the treasure box had no keys. They liked straightforwardness. They liked to feel in control.

When they entered her home. Monica told Sincere to get comfortable as she went to freshen up. She came out of the bathroom in the nude.

"How do I look in these?" she asked, walking up to Sincere.

"You look incredible."

Monica wasted no time and was all over him. She wanted to be remembered. She wanted to stand out. She wanted Sincere to know that she was all his. She failed to realize that she no longer held any power. Precious jewels are better when they are withheld. It's not something that a female should just up and give away. Monica wanted to separate herself from the rest. She did just that. Every day after school, Sincere walked her home. And every day after school, she gave it up.

*****

The Scientist just left Rosedale, Maryland, where he was a part-time substitute middle school teacher. The job was just something to keep him off certain radars.

It also gave him something positive to do. His scale of bad deeds already was tipping over because it was filled. Maybe the little good deeds he did would one day count for something.

The Scientist was now going to White Oak, where he had a ranch there and a small farmhouse that he called the lab. Losing Snake and letting him get away may have come at a cost. He or The Source had no inside leaks to track him down. The only way to reel him in was to create and set up a bait that he couldn't resist to pass up. The bait had to be something worth attracting his attention. The Source happened to be the only person to fit that description. But he knew The Source didn't have the heart to put himself out there like that. So another plan had to be orchestrated.

In the lab, The Scientist had various artilleries at his disposal. He collected pistols, rifles, explosives, and semiautomatics, just for sport. Those were not his weapons of choice. Guns and bombs made way too much noise. Although using a can suppressor can silence the sound, nothing was better than knives. The Bowie knife was his favorite. Knives were so much easier to conceal. He could carry at least twenty of them with no problems. Guns and explosives get the job done too quickly. He liked to savor the moment in seeing a person in pain while he drained the life out of them slowly. A cut here, a cut there reveals how much pain a person can take. It also shows a person's true nature.

*****

Sincere was glad that his time with Monica was over with. That girl's batteries never ran on *E*. Every day she drained him sexually. The time they had and shared together was fun. But a boy needed time to recuperate. Monica was all go. No breaks, time-outs, or stop signs. Unlike Lisa and Sandra, when it came to sex, Monica was seasoned and well trained. It was far from her first sexual encounter. She did things he was pretty sure the other two wouldn't even consider doing at their age. She was a certified beast in bed. And he wasn't afraid to admit that he couldn't keep up with her. She was way too much for him.

During school, the first morning when things were supposedly back to normal, Monica, Sandra, and Lisa were laughing and kicking it as if they weren't trying to take each other's necks off last week. Why were girls so full of complexities, he thought. They could never be figured out. It was a headache and like wrestling with his brains trying to understand them.

Each female in her own mind had the right to believe that she should be the chosen one. Lisa was the female he had the most similarities with. Their chemistry was great together. Sandra was more challenging. And that was good. She always had him thinking of ways to make their conversations more intriguing. She actually challenged his intellect in the modes of conversations. Monica was the best-looking of the three. She was a straight nympho. They hardly talked. So he never got the chance to know who she was and what she was really like. If sex was what he wanted, one thing that was for sure, he could count on her to deliver the goods.

The choice on who he was taking to the dance was a one-night thing. It's not like any one of them were gonna be his girlfriend. What was so important about the dance, he thought. What he did during his week with each of them should easily supersede the dance. Why would friends wanna compete with something like that anyways? Friends supported and helped each other out. He couldn't say this enough. Females were just crazy.

Monica saw Sincere first and waved him over. When he was within arm's reach, she placed a wet kiss on his lips, looking at her friends in triumph. Not to be outdone, Sandra placed an even wetter kiss on his lips that had Monica fuming in anger. While Monica and Sandra were exchanging dirty looks, Lisa placed a soft kiss on his lips with a lot of tongue.

"You sneaky sluts," Monica said to them. "All this time, you two were trying to have him for y'all selves."

"Slut. You probably gave it up on the first night. That's what ratchet and scandalous girls do." Sandra snapped back.

"Ratchet. What kind of friends try to take a person's man? That's ratchet." Monica shot back.

"He wasn't, isn't, and will never be your man." Lisa jumped in. Before Monica could fully turn around to address Lisa, Sincere stepped in.

"Why was I being kissed by all of you this morning? We didn't agree on no kissing contest," Sincere said, throwing them off.

"I was just glad to see you," Monica said.

"I missed you," Lisa said.

"I wanted to show you who's a better kisser." Sandra shot back matter-of-factly.

Once again, Sincere was dazed and mentally bent out of shape. Every one of them had their own angles. One that had too many cracks in it.

"The time I had with each one of y'all was special. I never experienced joy, happiness, and pleasure the way I have the past three weeks. It's hard for me to single any one of you out. So I can't make the pick."

"You have to pick one of us," Lisa said sadly.

"That was part of the agreement," Sandra replied calmly.

"An agreement we agreed to that you made," Monica reminded him.

"This was your idea, so you can get to know us. You know enough of me to choose me," Sandra said, looking a bit angry.

"She's right. Not on her being chosen, of course. But this was your idea, so you can pick one of us. We all fulfilled our duties. It's only right that you do the same." Monica chipped in.

They all were standing by one another's side. Them bickering a few moments ago was long gone. They were besties again. They were also right in their argument. No matter who he chose, two females would feel left out.

"This is hard. I like you all equally. So I wanna take all three of y'all to the dance. I can't just pick one."

Lisa and Sandra didn't look too disappointed. But Monica walked off. She truly believed she was entitled to having whatever she wanted. Sincere knew she just needed time to cool off.

*****

Snake had nothing to go off of to catch Bernard with eyes closed. He couldn't send anyone as a decoy to entrap Bernard. His security was definitely gonna be tighter around him. His only place of vulnerability was when he was with his mother on Sundays. Now the attempt on Bernard's life was unsuccessful, and his mother ended up dead. It will be more difficult to get close to Bernard. Not impossible, just harder. No matter how tight a screw is or how hard something is welded, there's always ways to loosen or break it. It was imminent for Snake to find a way.

Snake knew whoever the guy was with the knives was gonna turn out to be a problem. He had to be dealt with. The knife wound he took was better than a bullet wound. The mysterious guy didn't like to use guns. Snake never saw him when he was leaving Bernard's mother's house. If the guy was using a gun, more than likely, Snake would be dead by now.

Snake didn't have an army or a group of men with him. It wasn't his style to work with other people. Having numbers had its advantages. It also could put a person behind the eight ball. It's harder to find someone that's working alone as opposed to watching several people that are in a group that can lead you to who you want. In a group, each person accounted for brings different sets of personalities and egos. Snake had no time for the headache it brought.

The warehouse Stacy told him about was probably the next best place to catch Bernard or this knife-throwing dude. Although it may take days or weeks to get results. He had nothing better to do. Hot Rod had to wait a little longer. Snake drove to a spot he ducked off at, in East Riverdale, Maryland. He knew that to kill whom he was after, he had to change his description.

For two whole weeks, he stayed isolated in East Riverdale. He let his beard and mustache grow out. He spread different layers of clay over his hands and face to darken it. He also added wrinkles to his face with the clay to add age to his look. Then he patched up his head with loose nappy hair. Next he put on his outfit. A long-sleeve polka-dot black-and-blue shirt that was oversized, dirty jeans with holes in them, and some beat-up boots.

Looking at his new identity, Snake was satisfied. The only resemblance to who he really was, was his eyes. If a person ever got the chance to see them, it'll be too late.

*****

Katherine couldn't believe how a woman had her paralyzed from the waist down. For about two minutes, she couldn't feel anything. It was like her body was in a coma. Her thoughts were filled with joy and sensation. Sexually no one ever made her body spasm or cum so much. She thought it would never get better than Gregory.

But what Crystal did with her tongue, lips, and hands couldn't fully be described in words. She wanted to—no, she needed to be alone with her. The things they could do one-on-one gave her a rush.

While Gregory was asleep, Katherine slipped Crystal her number. She couldn't wait for her to make that call. Her body was burning up and full of anticipation. That night, she had her first threesome and first woman to woman experience. She fell asleep with Gregory no longer being a dominant part of her thoughts. At the moment, there was only room for one person.

*****

The Scientist has been going to the warehouse twice a week. There was no sight or word on Snake's whereabouts. The Source was laying low at one of his homes in Brockton, Massachusetts. He intended to make one more stop at the warehouse before he completely went rogue for six months. There was no need for him to come around any of his businesses. The people he put in charge were well equipped and trustworthy. The Source just needed to fall all the way back. He wasn't built for getting in the trenches and killing people. Although he had a body under his belt, that didn't count. It was accidental. The Source wasn't a killer. There was no cutting corners on that.

The Scientist, on the other hand, loved to spill blood. When he was eight years of age, he stabbed his stepfather to death. At eleven, he snuck up on the woods and stabbed a kid in his neck for pushing the girl he had a crush on. He wasn't linked to any of the murders. When he saw how easy it was to kill and get away with it, he was hooked. He loved watching people grasping and struggling for air as he took their breath away.

The Scientist knew the Snake was out there lurking, waiting to slip inside of an open crack, he had a surprise for him when he popped up.

*****

Shadow didn't like what he saw when Kat gave that black woman a note. He specifically told her he preferred a white woman if they were gonna have a threesome. And she went after a black one. Black women lived to make things harder for him. It angered him to see Kat losing control under that hot pretty skeezer. He tried to break the black woman in two when he was behind her. She threw it back and took it like a champ. Even though he didn't like how Kat was moaning, the black woman was by far the best he ever had.

As Shadow lay on the bed, staring at the ceiling wall, he started to wonder what he was really mad about: Kat trying to hook back up with the skeezer on the low, or him not being able to give her his number. Shadow fell asleep thinking how good it felt, digging up inside the unknown woman that he had to meet again.

*****

Pretty Tony didn't like that he had to impersonate being The Source. He always wanted to be on the front line to prove that he wasn't just a pretty boy. He got tired of working behind a desk. He wanted to get into some action. Now that he was called to do a duty, a duty that could place him in the line of fire, it scared him. He realized it was best to not try to be more than what you were. He just hoped that realization wasn't too late.

CHAPTER 10

Keisha and Brenda were at their temporary apartment discussing the best way to address Montell. The assignment was to put him under payroll until they had what they needed from his nephew. They agreed not to seduce or manipulate him. Since he loved money, they were going to him with a business proposal he wasn't gonna be able to reject or refuse.

Brenda knew everything she needed to know about Shadow through Katherine. The flick of a tongue had power, just like what was beneath her spur tongue. Katherine couldn't get enough of it. She was begging for it every day. Even Shadow was chasing her like he was Pepe Le Pew. He never got another sip or taste, which had him thirsty and hungry. Brenda wasn't gonna keep him dehydrated and starving. Everything was about timing. Shadow was in the palm of her hand on a yo-yo string, being strung along. When he wasn't needed, which would be very soon, he would be discarded.

*****

Monica didn't like or appreciate the games her friends were playing. They actually had the guile and audacity to kiss Sincere right in front of her. To make matters worse, he stood there and kissed both of those backstabbers back. He never tried to push them away or brush them off. The kisses didn't even come as a surprise to him. There was no doubt now that the encounters Sandra and Lisa had with Sincere for their seven days were more than friendly.

Monica thought she did enough to become the last girl standing. It hurt her to be considered on an equal level as the other two.

Monica felt empty. Other than sex, she didn't know what else she could give him to keep his interest. Maybe giving him money would seal the deal. Boys did love sex and money.

Lisa really didn't like going to the dance with her other two friends. But going with them and him was better than not going with him at all. In a way, she felt wrong for not being honest and loyal toward Monica. From the jump, Monica expressed how she felt about Sincere. She was the one who initially wanted to be with him. Lisa knew she wasn't acting as a friend. She was being really selfish. She never expected to feel the way she did about Sincere. He kept her off balance in a good way. The trust she had with Monica was probably broken. After the dance, she promised to do her best to mend and fix the friendship she and Monica had. What Monica and Sandra were going through was irreparable.

*****

Sandra was sick and tired of playing second fiddle to Monica. How did she even become the alpha female of their group? Monica was cool in her own way. But she wasn't above everybody else. Especially not her. Sandra wanted to make sure Monica wasn't gonna have Sincere. Ever since they met in grade school, Sandra envied Monica. Before Lisa joined the group there, it was always them two. Monica garnered all the attention. Sandra was good-looking and smart. But people always flocked toward her friend, leaving her feeling bitter.

The competition with Sincere brought things to the surface that was covered up for years. Sincere may not be a street dude or a bad boy, but he knew how to sweep a girl off her feet. He knew how to hold his own in a conversation. And he was a great listener. Sandra was really starting to believe that he was connected in illegal activities. She had two brothers in prison for drug-related cases.

She knew how they were. Sincere stayed in the freshest clothes and kicks. And what eighth-grader had a car? He definitely had to be a bad boy. If that's the case, there's no way in hell that Monica was gonna have him.

*****

Snake was lying down on the ground of a filthy sidewalk that wasn't too far from the warehouse. His current position gave him an all right view of the place. It wasn't quite good enough, though. He saw a dumpster nearby that would take him closer to where he wanted to be. It came with more exposure. Doing things that people didn't expect was imperative to him. Being exposed for this mission was necessary. Every time a person tried to kill someone, there were always two lives on the line. The killer had to put his body out there. And sometimes the person that came in for the kill ended up being the victim of death.

In real life, things didn't play out like movies or action shows filled with drama. In real life, no one is untouchable. There was always someone out there who did things better, a person who worked harder, a person who was just a lot smarter. Snake also knew that everyone slips and makes mistakes. There was no exception. Someone was bound to take the wrong step. If it was Snake who made the wrong move, he could live with the results.

When the sun descended, Snake took his dirty blanket and his shopping cart, that was filled with soda cans, and slumped on the floor by the stinky dumpster. He wrapped himself up and kept his eyes locked on the garage doors and parking lot. At night, the dumpster would be his supposed sleeping spot. And during the day, he decided to roam the sidewalks and blocks asking for money and food.

On the fifth day of Snake staking out by the warehouse, he was eating an energy bar that he just purchased, with a beer. Not once did he go anywhere without some kind of visual of the warehouse. It didn't appear that the warehouse had any back or side doors. Everyone entered and made their exit through the front. While inside of the convenience store, Snake noticed a woman getting out of a Ford Focus and going into the warehouse.

For the past four days, Snake watched three of the same people changing shifts. He made note of the woman because it was outside the normal operation. Who was she? Snake appeared to drink his beer and rested back by the dumpster.

The warehouse had a three-man eight-hour shift: 2:00 p.m.–10:00 p.m.; 10:00 p.m.–6:00 a.m.; and 6:00 a.m.–2:00 p.m. When the mysterious lady arrived, it was 2:37 p.m. The guy that came in at two left forty-five minutes after checking in. At 10:00 p.m., no one showed up. Snake felt something happening. He was up for a 122 hours straight. And he was wide awake, scoping things out with eyes that weren't heavy or fatigued.

*****

Sincere was tempted to have his uncle drop him off at the school dance. He almost pushed his father's advice of keeping a low profile to the side. The more he thought of it, the more it made sense. Some cars draw the wrong kind of attention. It attracts the likes of robbers and people that try to play up under you. Sincere didn't need that. On top of everything, why have someone drop him off and come pick him up when he can go on his own on the low?

Sincere thought of wearing a suit his father placed in the closet for him. But it was kind of too hot for that. He opted to wear something simple yet still elegant and fly: a gray-and-blue dress shirt, blue dress pants, and a pair of gray Billy's. He thought of wearing a fedora hat, but he wasn't trying to look like no pimp. It was funny that concept came to mind. He was going to the dance with three girls. It wasn't pimping one on one, but a person can easily get the wrong perspective of what they saw.

The plan was for Sincere to pick up all three girls and take them to the school dance. Monica was highly against the idea. Her home was the furthest, and she wanted to be the one sitting in the passenger seat. That seat evidently was reserved to whom he picked up first. The girls actually had a big argument about who he should pick up first and who was gonna be taken home last. Monica said if she was picked up last, she should be dropped off last. Sandra countered that and said if she was picked up first, the order should continue from last to first. Lisa said it wasn't fair for her to be stuck in the middle both times. So she had every right to choose the final order. Nothing anyone of them said made sense.

"Listen. I'm not gonna show any favoritism. This is what we're gonna do. We're all just gonna meet each other at the school. Afterward I'd like to show you three something. That's cool?"

"It sounds fair," Lisa said.

"I have no one to take me to the dance." Sandra pointed out.

"You have feet. Walk," Monica said with a sly grin on her face.

"No you didn't." Before Sandra could snap, Lisa jumped in.

"Please stop these two. My sister will drop us. You want us to pick you up, Monica, even though you got a ride?"

"That's kind of you, Lisa. My mother already canceled her plans to drop me off."

"Since that's settled, tomorrow," Sincere said.

*****

The Scientist and The Source were inside of the warehouse observing the footage on every camera. The Scientist rewound all cameras a week back so he can pinpoint anything or anyone that was out of place. He knew that one misstep, one detail overlooked can be very damaging.

After careful reviews of the past week's activities, three things were new. In Tenafly, New Jersey, a block away from the cabinet shop The Source held some of his weapons, an unidentified man, whose name wasn't listed, moved in. The man never came out. Never had any company. Only a person hiding something stayed inside his home for three whole days. The second thing that caught his attention, there was overflow of traffic next-door to a beauty salon The Source owned in Staten Island, New York. Someone just rented the place two weeks ago. The last unusual thing he couldn't ignore was the homeless guy appearing out of nowhere. Homeless people were common around certain areas. The specific one just appeared out of the blue. It probably wasn't anything. In years of doing this, The

Scientist was aware that nothing can turn out to be something. The bum was the closet as of now. So a heavy eye was gonna stay on him.

The Scientist sent two separate teams to check on the individuals in Tenafly and Staten Island. The team that was going down to New Jersey was told to kick down the door if they received no response.

*****

Brenda was on top of Shadow mountain, giving him the ride of his life. Katherine made it clear to her that she no longer wanted to be with Shadow. And she was more than willing to do anything to please her. A woman like Katherine couldn't be trusted. Whoever pleased her the best sexually was the one she felt obligated to. That was always subject to change. Brenda had value. So Katherine wasn't one that needed to be disposed of; on the other hand, Shadow no longer had any relevance or purpose to live.

Brenda heard the knock at the door she was waiting for. She didn't bother to get dressed as she checked through the peephole. Brenda put on a robe, then went back to the door.

"Who is that?" Shadow asked not trying to cover his nakedness. Brenda opened the door, and Katherine made herself seen. She stared at a surprised-looking Shadow. Brenda stepped back, looking at Shadow as well.

"Do you know her?" Brenda asked him. Shadow looked at her in disbelief. What type of question was that? And how did Katherine know where he was at? He never saw Katherine fumbling through her purse when she drew out the small .22 caliber. It was too late for him. Five rounds hit him in his chest.

Brenda started to get all hysterical. She apologized and pleaded for her life. Katherine was stunned and confused at Brenda's reaction. Before Katherine could speak, Keisha exited out of the closet with a camcorder in her hand. She walked up to Katherine and showed her what she just recorded, and left.

"From here on out, I own you. You don't spit unless I tell you to. A witness recorded you committing murder. I'm also an eyewitness and victim. You are my property now. You understand?" Brenda asked. With tears in her eyes, looking at Shadow, who was barely breathing, she nodded her head in the affirmative. "I'm gonna train you on how to use your tongue. Get undressed and come please me."

*****

The Source really didn't wanna be at the warehouse. It wasn't that he was afraid. He just didn't think it was wise for him to take an unnecessary risk. With his financial funds exceeding a little over $77 million, he was gonna pull a rabbit out of his hat and go to his ace in the hole if this failed. When Pretty Tony entered the building. They immediately changed clothes. Pretty Tony departed in the vehicle The Source came in. Pretty Tony had the responsibility to go to every spot that they had surveillance on. He was thrown out there to the wolves to die in The Source's place—well, thrown out there to a snake.

*****

The dance was not something Sincere was feeling. The DJ was playing a lot of down South booty-shaking music. Right now, "I Wanna Rock" by Uncle Luke was on. Sincere wasn't a dancer. The girls didn't care about that. They all sandwiched him and threw their bodies at him. They took turns dancing with him one-on-one. The three of them pressed their breasts to his chest. And they pushed, bounced, and shook their butts repeatedly on his manhood, they didn't give him any air or break. Within an hour, he was ready to go. He expressed that to the girls, and they were all eager to leave as well.

"I have a great solution about the seating arrangements. We all can just sit in the back," Lisa said.

"That's a real great idea," Sandra agreed.

"In a way, it is."

"Say what you gotta say, it's always something with you, Monica." Sandra snapped, knowing Monica was hinting at something.

"There's still the issue of who's gonna be dropped home last," Monica said.

"Could we enjoy the rest of the night and worry about that when the time comes?" Lisa said.

"That couldn't be said any better," Sincere said.

*****

Snake watched The Source as he entered the warehouse. His instincts were hardly wrong. The woman played a big factor in what was happening since she was still inside. Another car pulled up, and another individual Snake never saw made his entrance. Minutes later, The Source came out. Snake was pretty sure he was being closely watched. The woman and another guy remained inside. Snake had no way of sneaking up on The Source without going unnoticed. So he waited. Being desperate can come with penalties. The more Snake watched The Source, the more he questioned what he saw. The guy he was looking at walked exactly like the guy that just recently walked in. A person doesn't just get up and change their walk. Certain feelings and moods added a little swag or took some bounce off a person's step. This person walked with no confidence. His shoulders were slouched, and his strides were too shaky. This couldn't be Bernard. Snake was no fool.

Snake remembered six years back when he was in Philadelphia, two men were following him on foot. He entered a restaurant and found someone in the bathroom with his same complexion and body size. He forced the guy out of his clothes with his pistol. They switched clothes. Snake purposely left $1,500 in the guy's new pants. Snake handed him his keys and wallet and told the guy he better be nowhere in sight when he leaves the restroom. The guy quickly left. When he checked his pockets, he moved quicker. Two men followed him out, unbeknownst to him. Snake followed the two. When they arrived in an area that didn't have too many bystanders, Snake open fired on them, checked their pockets and left. The two deceased were cousins of someone he took a contract from a year earlier. They didn't approve that he killed the target's nine-year-old son as well. Snake was firm in his stance. No one—absolutely no one—was exempt from death.

That incident with the misdirection was becoming a common thing. This guy who was supposed to be The Source was a walking duck with no wings. He probably was not even aware of the danger they had put him in. Following him was pointless. Minutes after his departure, the lady came out and lit up a cigarette, staring in his direction. A car came to a screeching halt in front of Snake. Three men stepped out, the three guys that normally were on shift at the warehouse. They approached Snake with guns drawn. Snake stayed on the floor, pretending to be drunk. When a person was afraid, they made mistakes. Snake wasn't afraid. He knew he did nothing to draw attention to him. So he didn't panic. Whoever this lady was, she was smart. He couldn't discredit facts. Through false blurred eyes, Snake saw her watching the scene intently. One man pulled Snake up while the others searched and trashed his property. Snake fumbled in his pocket and pulled the six single-dollar bills and 30¢ he had.

"This is all I have," Snake pleaded. One of the guys made a call.

"It's an old bum who thinks we're trying to rob him."

Snake didn't catch what was said on the other line. They released him and left. Snake picked up his cans and placed them back in the cart. He fixed his temporary home up. The lady smoothly put the cigarette out and went in. She walked like she was in the military. There was no feminine posture about her. Snake hated women. Women who thought they were men were women he hated the most.

*****

Before taking the girls somewhere he wanted to share with them, Sincere stopped at Miami Sub and placed an order for all four of them. He let the girls control the music in the car. In the back seat, they rapped and sang like they were auditioning to sign to a record label. It was nice to hear laughter and joy from them for a change. That was a rarity. Sincere ended up at a place in Miami Lakes with a great hilltop that sat right up under the moon. They made the incline climb, and Sincere laid a couple of blankets on the ground for them to sit on.

"This is a real beautiful view," Lisa said, admiring what she was looking at.

"The moon looks so huge from where we're at," Monica said.

"This is real sweet. But what's the purpose of bringing us here?" Sandra asked.

Sincere gave this some thought. Opening up to the three people that actually made him happy and not think of the pain felt right. Revealing things to people you hardly know wasn't always good. His parents were dead. There was no changing that. He wasn't gonna go into details about their death. But it's something he felt the need to open up to someone about. He needed therapy. Sandra, Monica, and Lisa, for the time being, were therapists.

"When I left New York, my mother and father were killed. They were basically the only family I had. I carried a lot of pain within me when I first came here. The pain is still and will always be there. I come here sometimes to think. This is like my place of escape. It's a place I felt the need to share with the three of you. Since we've met, my mind has been clear of things that had me grieving before. You three eased and subtracted my sadness. You three are like blankets that keep me warm when I'm cold. I really wanna thank each of you for sharing pieces of yourselves with me. I don't want y'all fighting or competing for me anymore. I can never just choose one of you. Doing so will only hurt the other two. So I'm extending my hands of friendship. It's all I can give any of you."

Lisa and Sandra had tears coming down their faces, messing up their makeup. Monica laid her head on Sincere's shoulder. There was no animosity or tension in the air. The girls felt sympathetic and were sincerely concerned. After apologizing for his loss and thanking him for opening up, Sincere and the girls had a great time together. No arguments. No sideway glances. Just high fives and a whole lot of compliments and smiles.

At 3:00 a.m., Sincere dropped all three girls at Monica's house. He wasn't giving anybody an upper hand. No one questioned his decision. All three kissed him in their own way, giggling like little girls after doing so. They attempted to convince him to go inside.

"I basically have the house to myself the rest of the weekend," Monica hinted with a seductive smile.

"I'm pretty sure Monica's got some games that we can play," Sandra suggested, grinning at Monica.

"Even if she doesn't, I'm pretty sure we can find something to do," Lisa added in.

Sincere could barely keep up with Monica. Adding two more girls wasn't something he was ready for. Declining the invite was an easy choice to make. If the dance floor was an indication on how they would be all over him, he had to pass.

"It won't seem proper. If I ever have the chance to spend the night or day with any one of you alone, I'll do so. But I can't handle three of you. Good night."

CHAPTER 11

The place in Tenafly, New Jersey, was owned by a perverted guy who had two little girls hostaged in his basement. Three of The Source's men had the responsibility to check the place out: Devon, J Cash, and Noah. Devon was the one who noticed the girls. They were frightened when they saw him. Their faces were covered in blood. And they had an odor on them from not being able to bathe. Devon reassured them that he was there to help, and everything would be all right.

The pervert was in his tub with the radio blasting. He never heard the knocks or the door being kicked in. Noah wasted no time with him. He placed his big hands around the pervert's neck and choked him to death. Choking him was a lot better than shooting him. He deserved to know that he was dying. A quick death wasn't good enough for him.

When Devon set the girls free, he gave them some cash. J Cash quickly sanitized the place, wiping it off of possible prints. No matter what them girls testify in the court of law, the good deed would be overlooked. And the district attorney could easily charge each of them with the murder of the pervert. J Cash made sure that wasn't gonna happen.

*****

The Scientist figured it would be best for The Source to leave last. The Snake was somewhere. Where? He didn't know. Snake wasn't the type to let things go. A person couldn't get lax or complacent with him. He'll come when he doesn't expect him. He'll show up in places you'll never think he'll come in. The Scientist wasn't taking him lightly.

The Source didn't know that The Scientist was planning to follow him all the way until he was safe in Brockton. The Scientist left the warehouse and quickly changed cars two blocks away. He was now in a Toyota Camry. Once The Source was safe, The Scientist was gonna take a two-week trip to Berlin. It was a ritual of his to go on a spiritual journey at the end of May each year. Last year, he was in India. The year before, Greece. The two weeks was more than enough time for his people to have all the information he needed on Snake.

The Scientist couldn't help but watch how fast the homeless guy was walking all of a sudden. For someone who stayed drunk, his quick movements didn't match his appearance. The Source coming out of the warehouse could only mean one thing.

*****

Bernard and the lady were still in the warehouse. At the present moment, Snake felt real good. The getup as a homeless man worked. He had no doubt. He watched the lady jump in her Ford Focus and speed off. A part of him wanted to follow her. His motorcycle wasn't that far around the corner. Catching up to her was a long shot, though. Especially if she went east. Bernard was the one he wanted. Once he was out the way, that knife-throwing dude had to get it as well.

Twenty-five minutes later, Bernard stepped out in clothes he didn't wear while stepping in. Snake wasn't tricked by the smoke screen and misdirection. When the lady left, he knew Bernard was gonna follow suit soon. He anticipated it. He was no longer by the dumpster. He was on foot and on the move. His motorcycle was around the next corner covered up in a pile of branches. Snake quickly removed the branches and kicked the bike in gear. Bernard was about twenty seconds ahead. Catching up to him wasn't gonna be hard. There was no room for interrogation. A quick shot was his best option.

Snake was gaining on Bernard real quick. He was at least fifteen feet away from him. His .45 special was already out and in his hand. As Snake accelerated and pushed the bike forward from his peripheral vision, he saw a car speeding toward him. He had no time to dodge the blow that was inevitable. About seven-tenth of a second before the impact and collision happened, Snake jumped off his bike and flew over the edge of the road. The momentum and impact slugged his body. He suffered a big gash across his forehead when he stumbled on some rocks before falling into a creek. He nearly lost consciousness. He got back on dryer grounds and limped away as far as he could.

*****

The Scientist didn't feel like he was being played. If the situation were reversed, he would've come up with something similar. Snake was smart, and one who planned very well. The Scientist knew that he was a step ahead of him. He also knew that he had to keep it that way. He couldn't lose ground. He saw the pistol in Snake's hand. As Snake came closer to The Source's vehicle, The Scientist pressed his feet on the gas and rammed the Toyota into the motorcycle. Snake flipped in the air and went over the edge into a creek. The Scientist quickly got out, Bowie in hand, searching the area. The bike Snake was on was wrecked. The pistol he once held in his hand was not too far from the bike. The Scientist retrieved it. Snake was nowhere in sight. The hit had to injure him. The creek was only two feet deep. The Scientist knew he wasn't dead underwater. He was hiding or slowly getting away.

"Who the hell was that?" The Source asked with a pistol in his hand.

"Snake."

"He was on that bike following me. Is he dead?" The Source asked with a little alarm in his voice.

"I doubt it. I know I hit him. Get to where you need to go. I'm gonna be here for a while, searching the place," The Scientist said.

"Kill him."

"That's what I've been trying to do."

"If you stop carrying them damn knives and use guns for a change, he'll be dead by now." The Source snapped.

"If I wasn't here, you'll be dead by now. Don't ever tell me how to do my job."

The Source got into his vehicle and sped off.

For six hours, The Scientist searched the area. He went along the creek but nobody popped up. Certain areas had blood on the floor. The trail of it just happened to stop. Snake had disappeared again. If that guy didn't have rabbit luck, he was some kind of magician. There's no way he should've walked off after that hit.

*****

Montell just came from a storage room. It was a spot he kept his candy-apple-green seven trey. Two years ago, someone stole his rims while he was asleep. After that night, he never kept his car overnight at his residence. It wasn't safe there. Jackboys were always plotting and lurking. So he only brought it out when it was time to showcase.

Today was the beginning of a four-day Memorial weekend. A whole bunch of females were out and about exposing themselves for all to see in South Beach. South Beach happened to be one of the go-to spots this time of year in Miami.

Females all ages came to showcase their bodies. There's no other reason for a woman to walk down the street with a two-piece other than her seeking attention or trying to come up. Men were there to showcase their pretty cars or snatch a chick. Montell loved this time of year. It was easy for him to pick up females just by asking them to take a picture with him.

While heading back home, Montell stopped at a gas station to get some gas and back wood. A red BMW pulled up at the station next to him. Two gorgeous females came out wearing matching red bikinis. One went inside to pay for the gas. The other waited outside, holding the gas pump. Montell was a few steps ahead of the lady that was going in. He held the door for her to enter. After they both made their purchase, she returned the favor by holding the door for him.

Montell didn't say anything to either of the women. He didn't chase women when he brought out the seven trey. He was tempted to make an approach. But he stayed true to form.

On the road, the red beamer was following him. Inside he was smiling. He didn't even hit South Beach yet, and he already struck gold. Montell pulled up at a nearby park and got out of his vert. The two gorgeous women weren't too far behind.

"Y'all ladies going to the beach or coming from it?" Montell asked.

"We don't do beaches," Keisha said.

"And we are not gonna play any games," Brenda added.

"So what is it we're doing here?" Montell asked, impressed and delighted by the straightforwardness by the ladies.

"The people I'm in contact with, have reasons to believe that your nephew is in possession of something that doesn't belong to him," Keisha said.

"It's something of great value that needs to be returned immediately." Brenda put in.

"How did you know where to find me?" Montell had to ask

"There's no sense in wondering how we know what we know. Just know that it's in your best interest to cooperate and help us get what we need." Keisha stepped in.

"In my best interest. I know what's best for me, not you. And my nephew is just a kid on a brief trip down here. His hands aren't dirty or in anything that your contacts have involvement in."

"I beg to differ. Evidently you're unaware of the circumstances that brought your nephew to Miami. His father, Maurice, your brother, stole some materials that didn't belong to him. That thief resulted in his death. My contact is pretty certain that before his death, your nephew was given items as he fled down here," Brenda said, crossing a foot over the other.

Montell couldn't believe these two ladies. They took turns talking. A lame strategy to keep him off balance. They had to be fishing for something. The information they had wasn't enough. How did they know where to reach him? How did they know that Sincere was down here? Something was off but right at the same time. Maurice hasn't called or responded to any of his calls or texts since Sincere came down. Montell realized that he was probably communicating with people who played a role in his brother's death, or people who knew who did it. He'd be a damn fool to cooperate with the likes of these females.

"If you aid us in our search, you'll get $500,000," Keisha said, interrupting his chain of thoughts.

"Twenty percent of that up front." Brenda chipped in.

Montell was stunned for a minute—$500,000, that was a half-million. So much could be done with that kind of money. A hundred off top wasn't a bad deal. Not even thinking about the consequences or the destructive factors to the agreement, Montell anxiously asked, "What is it you need me to help you find?"

*****

Sincere thought of everything his dad told him. What stuck out the most now, how being happy could make him vulnerable. The past couple of months, he was really complacent. He was living life with no worries. He was actually living life the way he should—like a kid. He couldn't disregard the threat that was out there that his father told him about. He had to make some changes to his living location.

School was currently out. A few weeks would officially be summertime. From time to time, Sincere went to the local park to play basketball. Strolling the neighborhood this specific day, Sincere bumped into a middle-aged woman named Ms. Wright. He never looked at an older woman in any type of way, other than them being around his mother's age. This one looked really good. He found himself lusting and thinking about her every time he laid eyes on her. She had a sexual magnetic pull to her. From the way she walked to the way she talked, her entire aura shouted sex. Sincere's very first encounter with her, she stopped him and inquired about her daughter. At the time, he had no idea who her daughter was. She happened to be a year older than him.

After that first encounter with Ms. Wright, every time she saw him, she flirted with him and even went so far to speaking about raping him one day. Technically it would be rape since he was underage. But what boy in his right mind would report having sex with a sexy older woman?

"One of these days, I'm gonna take you to my house and teach you a few tricks these young little girls you play with haven't learned yet," Ms. Wright teased.

"Is that so?"

Sincere enjoyed kicking it with Ms. Wright. He just didn't get her daughter when he finally realized who she was. One night, while thinking of his father's advice, a place. That night, Sincere went to her place, hoping to catch her. Her daughter answered the door.

"What do you want?" she asked with her face all screwed up.

"Is your mother home? I really need to speak to her." The girl just rolled her eyes and sucked her teeth. "Why the attitude?" Sincere went on to say. "I never did or say anything to disrespect you. Yet every time I see you, your face is balled up. What's up with that?"

"My mom is not here."

"There you go again with the attitude." Sincere pointed out.

"Truth be told, I don't like you."

"I can clearly see that. But why?" Sincere could've sworn her face softened.

"I just don't. My mom should be back shortly. You might as well wait inside."

Sincere saw through her facade. If she really didn't like him, she wouldn't have invited him in. Were all females crazy? They were all puzzles. He wasn't gonna even try to pick up the pieces and put them together. It was a headache.

While entering her home, he had to brush his body on her. She purposely didn't move, eyeing him like a hawk the whole time. She then sucked her teeth again and walked off somewhere. Sincere took a seat on the couch and waited. The girl came back with a drink that Sincere gladly took.

"Thanks. What's your name?"

"Now you wanna ask. Amanda."

Amanda walked off again, rolling her eyes. She had problems, Sincere thought. Halfway into his drink, his eyes couldn't stay open. Not even knowing what was going on, he fell asleep.

*****

Snake was inside of a log. He lost a lot of blood and really didn't have the strength to take too many steps. His current position had to do. This could very much be the end for him. He lost his pistol. He didn't have the energy for hand-to-hand combat. He needed a weapon. If someone came after him and found him, he was gonna be a goner.

Snake could barely keep his eyes open. All those days and nights without sleep was catching up to him. Normally his body was immune to restless days and nights, but the loss of all that blood weakened him. He did his best to cover his trail. It wasn't sloppy, yet it was far from his best. Hopefully it was good enough.

*****

Sincere woke up hearing Ms. Wright chastising Amanda. Her voice was filled with anger.

"What you did was low and sick. I didn't raise you like that. You think I'm stupid? You left the boy's damn zippers down."

"You did worse. So who are you to judge?" Sincere heard a loud slap.

"You have no right to talk to me like that. Take your tail to your room!" Ms. Wright screamed.

Sincere looked down and fixed his pants. He couldn't remember when he fell asleep or what took place last night. It was already 10:00 a.m. How long did he sleep, he thought. When Ms. Wright came in his presence, he asked, "What's going on?"

"You overslept. What is it that you wanted to see me about?" Ms. Wright said, covering up for her daughter.

"What did your daughter do to me? I still feel drowsy."

"She didn't tell me."

Ms. Wright was avoiding answering the question. Sincere knew she was lying for Amanda. She didn't get slapped for no reason. Whatever sick stuff Amanda did, her mother was riding with her. She may not like what she had done, but she wasn't throwing her child under the bus. Sincere respected that. Ever since Amanda gave him that drink, he passed out. She had to have slipped something in it.

His father's words came crashing into his skull, *Never accept or drink out of a glass or cup that someone you don't know or trust makes. If the container or bottle isn't sealed, anyone can slip something in it, and never leave your drink unattended. Remember how they did Diamond in* The Players Club. *That can be done to anyone.*

It made sense now. Amanda spiked his drink with some sporadic or gang date drug. She had to have done something to him while he was asleep. Males used roofies to have sex with females without their consent. Why would Amanda even think of drugging him. Nothing will ever change his mind about a female's sanity. Some of them really had psychological problems.

"It's good of you to stick by your daughter's side. You know she was wrong for drugging me. So you owe me."

"Me, owe you. Look, sweetie, I'm not the one who did anything to you—if in fact anything was actually done to you. But if it's in my power to appease you, I'll help."

"I need you to rent an apartment under your name for me," Sincere said without hesitation.

"Tired of sleeping under your parents' roof. I would let you stay with me, but I don't need the Department of Children and Family being sent to me."

"No one's gonna do that. My parents are dead. I have been living alone for three months now. I just wanna move."

"How do you pay rent?" Ms. Wright asked, fishing.

"The same way you and everybody else pay it. I'll give you $500 to do this for me."

"Boy! I don't need your money. You selling drugs or something?"

"Of course not." Sincere was surprised that she even asked him that.

"This place is going under my name. Convince me why I should do this for you."

"Honestly, I'm afraid. My parents were killed. Whoever killed them could be looking for me. The apartment is under my father's name."

"I would ask you for more details, but that's none of my business. I'm gonna take a chance. Don't mess my name up. Do you have a place in mind?" Ms. Wright asked.

"This building looks fine to me."

"Everything's two-bedroom." Ms. Wright pointed out.

"That's perfect."

"Down payment is $1,500, $800 for the monthly rent."

"I'll bring the money for you tomorrow."

"How old are you again?" Ms. Wright asked.

"I'll be fourteen next week."

Sincere was familiar with some of the look Ms. Wright was giving him. If she really wanted to have sex with him, he considered that a fair exchange. Another three months, he planned on moving to a whole new area. In fact, it would be best for him to do that before the school year starts.

CHAPTER 12

Snake watched the lady that was in the warehouse searching through the area. Seeing her didn't come as a surprise to him. His gut told him a lot to do with what was going on. What really caught his attention was the knife the lady was holding in her hand. Snake wasn't one to believe in coincidence or happenstance.

What're the odds of two people chasing him with knives instead of guns? A slim chance to none. One plus one equals two every single time. Snake thought of the person's demeanor, walk, and stance while she was at the warehouse—all masculine. With a better look at the person, Snake smiled and then passed out. Before losing consciousness, he realized, the lady wasn't a woman at all. It was the knife-thrower.

Snake woke up with no idea of what day or time it was. He didn't know how long he was knocked out. The hit to the forehead wasn't the most excruciating. A rusty piece of metal that was on the side of his abdominal was causing the real pain. He had to get the piece out correctly and insides clean before the infection or bleeding worsened. It took him almost an hour to get to the side of a road. Before the car he saw from a distance cut to him, he passed out again.

*****

Alexis was surprised that Gregory hadn't reported to work for the past couple of days. It was unlike him. He never missed work. Since his tenure at the company, he only requested a day off once. Something wasn't right.

"Yolanda, I need to see you in my office," she said over the phone.

Alexis didn't like how things were turning out with her and Yolanda. She cared for her and wanted the best for her, but Yolanda was becoming an emotional wreck.

Outside of sex, there was no real connection. It's like Yolanda trapped herself in a place of sorrow. Every day her mind was consumed and possessed with grief. Alexis didn't have the time or energy to babysit a grown woman. She had a company to run. Alexis had been where Yolanda was. She was molested and raped before. Granted everyone handles problems differently. That experience can be traumatizing. Alexis didn't have the patience or will to tend to a crying shoulder every day. It was becoming too exhausting. She knew what she had to do. She didn't like it, yet it had to be done.

"Yolanda, have you heard from your friend Gregory? He hasn't been coming to work."

"It's not my job to keep up with people that don't show up," Yolanda said.

That's the other thing. Alexis didn't like it. Yolanda's mouth done became really salty. She had every right to be upset. She shouldn't shift or direct her anger to everybody else. Especially those that were trying to help her. That was plain out wrong.

"First, you need to watch your tone with me. Secondly, I asked you because of your recommendation, he got this job. So have you heard from him lately?"

Pouting now, Yolanda shook her head no. Alexis didn't have time for a woman to be throwing these tantrums and having these childish mood swings.

"I think it will be best for you to take some time off," Alexis said.

"Remember what happened the last time you told me that."

Alexis couldn't believe Yolanda just said that. Did she really expect her to feel guilty about that horrific incident? She must be out of her mind. Alexis ignored the statement.

"I have a round-trip ticket for you to take a break and regroup in the Bahamas. Try clearing your mind and getting back focus."

"You're trying to push me away." Yolanda started with tears in her eyes. "I had a feeling all along you were using me. I don't need your ticket." Yolanda stormed out of the office and out of the building. Alexis didn't try to stop her. Yolanda was starting to get out of control.

*****

Snake woke up in someone's bed. He tried to get to his feet. But his legs couldn't carry his weight.

"My mother said you need to rest. The medicine she gave you is gonna help you get better. She also said don't try to leave. You need rest to gain your strength back."

The girl helped Snake back in the bed. He instantly went back to sleep. The next time he woke up, a lady was placing a plate on the cabinet by the side of his bed. Snake wasn't the sentimental type. Yet he was thankful for the helping hand he received from this woman.

"Thanks for patching me back up," Snake said slowly.

"You're finally up. Are you hungry?" the lady asked, knowing that he was.

"I'm famished." She walked over and placed the plate in his hands.

"How does your body feel?"

"It's getting better. Why am I always sleepy?" Snake had to be sleeping at least eighteen to twenty hours a day.

"It's the medication I gave you. Your body needed to fight the infection inside of you. The more rest you have, the better."

"I take it that you're a doctor."

"I was a doctor."

"Was? You don't have to work at a hospital or wait for someone to give you that title to be one," Snake said, not knowing the compliment he was giving.

"Thanks. That title was bringing in a lot of money."

Snake ate his food and didn't say anything else. He liked the fact that the lady he now knew as Paulette didn't pry or ask him any questions besides his name, which he actually gave her. She didn't interrogate him. She didn't report the incident to the police or anything. What civilian does that? After eating his food, he went back to sleep.

*****

Yolanda had a blade in her hand while she was lying in the bubble-filled tub. The thought of suicide had been heavily on her mind since Corey violated her. Alexis brought comfort to her at times. So she never acted on those thoughts. Now the one person she was counting on to hold her up and keep her together acted like she didn't care. That really hurt. It was like Alexis was intentionally twisting the knife, that was already planted in her heart, harder and harder. Yolanda felt used. She opened herself up to Alexis in more ways than one, and Alexis didn't appreciate it. She was ungrateful.

As Yolanda was sticking the razor in the veins of her wrist, she was startled by the sound of her phone. If there was any interruption while she was attempting to take her life, it was a sign for her not to do it.

The phone call was the sign. She went to her room to answer it.

"Hello."

"Hey, sis! Sorry I haven't called. Been tied up. You okay over there?" Hot Rod asked.

"I'm surviving."

"If you need anything, you already know, it doesn't matter what it is. I could make it happen," Hot Rod answered her.

Yolanda thought of Alexis and how funny she was acting. She had to be cheating on her. Why else would she try to send her away? Alexis needed to feel the way she was feeling.

"Can you have your friends come see me? I need to send someone a message," Yolanda said with a smile on her face.

"Enough said."

*****

Paulette Smith Jones was a former doctor and a widow with a fifteen-year-old daughter. She lost her license due to malpractice.

One night while doing surgery on a patient, she told a nurse she was really comfortable with increasing the dosage of medicine the patient was taking. The nurse accidentally gave the patient more than she should, which led to the patient's death. Paulette took responsibility and got fired. The patient's family also filed a lawsuit, which she was still currently fighting legally.

Three months before the accident at the hospital, she lost her husband in a plane crash. Things had been going downhill for her ever since. The house she momentarily owned had to be sold soon. She also had to find some kind of work to generate income.

Paulette never thought she would do any real medical work ever again. The guy she picked up six nights ago named Quincy almost died. It was great to know that she could still save lives. Not once did she probe or question Quincy. Something in her heart pulled her to the stranger. Looking into his eyes, she saw a lot of darkness. She saw a man who been through things she probably could never imagine. Nonetheless, she helped him. Not just because it was the right thing to do, she felt some kind of connection between them.

*****

Montell was beside himself when he went to Sincere's apartment and found out it was vacant. Where did he move to? Why didn't he contact him? That little boy had brains like his father, and that wasn't a good thing for him. Sitting in the parking lot inside of his car, Montell finally cooled down and got his thoughts together. He was banking on Sincere going to the high school that was near the middle school. He needed someone to register him in. Montell was expecting a call from him soon.

Montell had $400,000 riding on Sincere to give him what the pretty ladies needed. Montell had no intentions of returning the $100,000 back if Sincere was in the blind. He robbed females before. This would be no different. He started his car and drove off. Before bending a third corner, he saw Sincere walking with a pretty older lady. Montell couldn't help but smile. The kid probably moved in with someone. That someone could very much be her. Montell parked his car and followed them on foot. When he was led to some apartment they entered, he was satisfied. Now it was about finding out what floor and room number he stayed in.

*****

Brenda and Keisha were inside Alexis's house. Getting in was easy. Yolanda gave them the code. Keisha couldn't understand why a woman wanted her significant other or lover to be raped, let alone with a gun. This girl Yolanda's screws had to be loose in her head. Why would you want someone you're with to feel that kind of pain? People had some really strange ways.

Keisha and Brenda wore push-up bras to suppress their breasts. Brenda had fake dreads on her head, and Keisha had a mouth full of plated golds in her mouth. The false identity was to put the police on a wild goose chase. When Alexis came home, Brenda wasted no time. She hit her with the pistol, demanding to know where her husband was. They knew she wasn't married. Just another wrong lead for the detectives to follow. Keisha tied Alexis's hands and feet, then placed tape over her mouth. Within minutes, Brenda was pushing the gun up Alexis's vagina. Alexis blacked out. Keisha and Brenda were out the door minutes later.

*****

Paulette's fifteen-year-old daughter quickly took a liking to Quincy. As he was recovering, they played chess, scrabble, and pinochle. She never saw her daughter so alive. Never saw her so happy since her father died. Maybe Quincy was a blessing in disguise. Maybe the Lord was putting him in their life to help with the grief. Life has been dim ever since her husband died. They needed some form of light to get through the dark days.

Paulette stepped out to go to the store. She didn't know why she was doing it, but she wanted to give Quincy a gift. She wanted to show her appreciation for the joy he was bringing to her daughter. She didn't know what he liked. She hoped she ended up picking up a likable gift.

On the fourteenth day, Snake was on his feet. He wasn't at full strength, but he was no longer handicapped. Paulette nursed him back into shape. The past couple weeks, she cooked for him. She cleaned him. Helped him to the bathroom. He could never remember relying on someone for so much help. Even as an infant, he had it rougher. Paulette was a kind and extraordinary woman. She spoke of her history as a child and adulthood. When Snake never answered a question about his personal life, she changed the subject and spoke of something else. She never tried to fish or trick him into speaking of something he didn't wanna talk about.

One day, while changing the bandage and wrapping around his wounds, she brushed her fingers along his chest. It wasn't sexual or intimate. The touch was normal, but for the first time in a long time, Snake craved to have sex with a woman. That thought alone helped him to decide to leave the following day. He didn't need no woman clouding his thoughts. A very low percentage of him entertained the thought of killing Paulette and Pamela. They gave him no reason to do that.

On the day Snake was leaving, Paulette went shopping. Pam was downstairs watching TV. He didn't wanna sneak out or leave a note. They deserved better than that.

"Hey, Pam! I gotta go. There's a few things I need to take care of."

"Are you coming back?" she asked, trying to look and be strong.

"I don't know. The work I do is dangerous."

"If you live through it, please come back." Pam gave Snake a big strong hug." I'm gonna miss you, Quincy."

Snake didn't know what to say. He couldn't remember the last time he received or gave someone a hug. This was unfamiliar territory for him.

"I won't forget about you," Snake said.

"No one uses my dad's car. You can leave with it and bring it back after you're done doing bad things," Pam said, giving him her little smile.

"Trying to make sure I come back, huh."

"Yep, and my dad has a gun inside of his stereo system. Mom doesn't know. If you're out doing dangerous things, you're gonna need protection."

"Thanks." Surprisingly, Snake hugged the girl and made his way out the door.

Snake never considered or thought of retiring. He never thought of being a family man. Deep down, he wanted more and a better life. He couldn't keep going on killing people. Eventually someone was gonna kill him. Paulette and Pam showed him what he could have. They knew that he did things that were bad. They didn't pull away from him. They embraced and welcomed him.

*****

When Alexis woke up, her entire body was sore. She was no longer tied up. She was hoping it was a terrible dream. The pain she felt erased that possibility. The two guys that were in her house humiliated her and showed no respect for decency when they did what they did to her. One of them even threatened to pull the trigger while jamming it inside of her. How could someone do something so foul? How could she be mistaken for a drug dealer's wife? Alexis crawled to the phone and called Yolanda.

Yolanda took Alexis to the hospital, then waited in the waiting room. Six hours later, Alexis came out with a detective by her side. The detective handed her a card and promised to stay in contact. Several officers were at Alexis's home, looking for any evidence that could help them find the two predators. Going back to Alexis's place wasn't an option. So they went to Yolanda's home.

Yolanda had Alexis wrapped up under her arms. No words were needed. They understood each other. They suffered and felt the same pain. Alexis wasn't going anywhere. She also wasn't gonna push Yolanda away. Yolanda was doing cartwheels inside. She wasn't supposed to be this happy. If it took for another person to feel what she felt to make her feel better, she had to bring others pain more.

*****

Back in high school, when Snake was in the tenth grade, his name was ringing on every level. He and Hot Rod had the streets on lock. He had street cred, money, cars, females, and sports rank, the typical honors that elevated a person's status. He was an exceptional cornerback, but he refused to play organized football. Females from all grades flocked toward him. Snake knew he was a cut below average-looking guy, far from being a *GQ* or top-notch male model that embodies the pretty boy or handsome look. Money always had a way of changing people's perception and outlook of things. Snake knew that most of the attention and love he got wasn't genuine. It was out of fear and power that money generated.

Snake always had his eyes on this one particular female named Jessica. She was two years older than him and breathtaking. It's like everything stopped when she entered a room. Her beauty and elegance demanded respect and recognition. She was classy, well dressed, smart, and the top-rated point guard in the state of New York. Word around school was no one had a chance with her. Since she was in the eighth grade, she had been dating this big-time drug dealer, five years her senior, named Fresh. Fresh kept Jessica laced up in designer clothes and shoes. She wasn't in need of any money. Fresh kept her straight.

One day, while Snake was attending one of Jessica's basketball games, she asked him for a ride home. Snake never knew that Fresh set the whole thing up. Jessica was a queen making power moves. She was well aware of Snake's interest in her. So she and her king formulated a plan. That very first night, while staying up in front of her porch, talking for hours, Snake fell in love with Jessica. Having sex with her five days later had him all twisted and gushy with emotions. Snake didn't realize his juice was being taken away. Or better yet, she weakened his flavor. Like coffee that used to be hard and strong, she softened it with milk, creamer, sugar, and ice to make it weak. For the very first time, Snake was gone in the head about a female.

During Jessica's prom night, Snake decided to introduce Jessica to his mother. The date was scheduled weeks in advance. While they were in the living room, Fresh and two other dudes, Snake and Hot Rod robbed before, came in with guns drawn. It broke Snake's heart to see Jessica leave his side and give Fresh a kiss as she walked out the door. The $58,000 he lost was nothing compared to Jessica's betrayal. Snake slipped up and let a female seduce and trick him. That was the lowest point in his life, and it happened to be one of his greatest experiences. He never allowed another woman to get close to him. He never saw Fresh or Jessica again. Blue and Rob, the ones that helped with the robbery, quickly became old news.

Snake was reminiscing about that time. Paulette couldn't be placed in the same category as Jessica. Paulette literally saved his life. She had no reason to deceive him. She hardly even knew him. Snake haven't dealt with every woman. Being realistic, he knew there were good women out there. But how can one tell? In a book Snake read a long time ago, he remembered it saying, "Shaitan says to a woman. 'You represent half of my army. You are my arrow which I throw and never miss. You are the place of my secret, and you are the messenger of my affairs.'" Women were cunning and deceitful. Jessica taught him that. Paulette might not just be different in every way. Snake wasn't ready to take that chance.

*****

Paulette was saddened when her daughter told her Quincy had left. Eventually she knew it would come to that. She never met a man who was so distant and disengaged. Quincy put on a good front when it came to his anger. He worked in a funeral home. Who in their right mind would actually work there? Someone had to. He just didn't look like the type that would do so. A part of Paulette wished she was there to tell him goodbye and give him the farewell gift. A part of her also believed that he was gonna return. Her daughter was very confident that he would. She knew something that she didn't.

Unlike many men she met, Quincy was a gentleman. He didn't misinterpret her touches or helping hand. Not once did he make a move physically or make a suggestion or impression to do so verbally. When it came to trying to make a connection, Quincy did his best to disconnect the lines of communication. Paulette knew it had something to do with his past. She also knew if given the chance, she had what it took to help him overcome whatever it was he was struggling with.

CHAPTER 13

The Source just had an interesting meeting with Hot Rod. He offered Hot Rod $10 million for the undisclosed information of Snake. Like a money-greedy man without loyalty, he needed time to think about it. The Source gave him twenty-four hours to make a decision. In any group, clique, gang, or organization, no matter the number or power, there's always a weak link. There's always someone who wasn't fully solid. Someone who would tell and sink the whole ship for money or to save himself from death or prison time. It never fails. The Source knew the same thing applied to those who were around him. Truth of the matter is, in the game, whether it's street, politics, or corporate, it was hard to trust anyone. Friends, females, and family members even leave you out to dry.

Hot Rod was gonna give him what he needed. He was, in fact, a businessman. The Source presented a good business proposal that he couldn't refuse. Once Snake was finally out of the picture, Hot Rod was not in line. People like him didn't deserve to live.

*****

Monica, Sandra, and Lisa didn't like the fact that Sincere was avoiding them. He occasionally spoke to them over the phone, but they all wanted to see him. He denied them that privilege. Monica was the least fooled by his actions.

"Another girl got his attention," Monica said, brushing her hair.

"What makes you think that?" Lisa asked.

"She's right. Think about it. We're all beautiful. What boy wouldn't wanna hunt us down and spend time with us?" Sandra put in.

"Whoever she is, is gonna get a beat down," Lisa said, balling up her fist.

"Amen to that," Monica agreed.

"It's gotta be someone who stays around his house." Sandra added

"Y'all down to take a trip to his neighborhood?" Monica asked.

"Let's do this," Lisa said.

Sandra and Lisa tied their hair in ponytails. They were ready to get their hands dirty. Whoever the female was, she had to get dealt with. She interrupted what they had going on. That was a big no-no.

*****

The Scientist was at a masjid in Berlin. He was listening to a Muslim brother given a sermon about mannerism. The thing the brother said made a lot of sense. He was speaking of a guy in the Koran named Lukman. Someone asked Lukman one day, how he has great manners and good characteristics. Lukman said he looks at others and sees who he doesn't wanna be. The Scientist liked that. It's a lot a person can learn from watching another individual. You could see a person walking with his pants down and be like, I don't wanna be seen like that. As the Muslims gathered up to pray, The Scientist left the masjid.

Over the years, The Scientist listened to Buddhism, Christianity, Judaism, Islam, atheism, and Scientology. He learned something from each walk of life. The Muslims had something in the Koran that stated, "There's no compulsion in religion."

That statement was true. The Scientist believed that there was only one God. He also believed that every religion had some contradiction to it because of the confusion men put in the Scriptures.

The Scientist was a person that believed violence was necessary. There was seldom a time for peace. He didn't believe in turning the other cheek. Maybe one day, he will ask the Lord for forgiveness and change his ways, but why do it now, when he had no plans of changing?

*****

Before going to Miami, Snake felt the need to do two things. He first was gonna take care of the family that had a lawsuit on Paulette. She didn't need the added stress and pressure. So he had to *X* all five of them out. It was only fair. Snake had always been an attentive listener. Paulette vented her frustration about the lawsuit and lack of money she had. Clearly it wasn't her fault the person she operated on died. The other family was just looking for a quick check.

Snake knocked on the family's door without anything covering his face. The area the family stayed in was deep in the woods. The next neighbor was probably two miles out. Snake didn't understand how people could live in these types of areas. It was a death trap. Nowhere to go. Nowhere to run. A young kid answered the door and just invited Snake in. The entire family was at the table eating dinner. No one was surprised to see him. It's like they were expecting him.

"You must be the paralegal Mr. Stevenson was telling us about." Snake gave the man a false smile and played along.

"Is the whole family down here? We have some important stuff to discuss."

"Yes, everyone's down here except the younglings."

"I think it would be best for everyone to see the settlement," Snake said.

One of the men rushed to get the two little kids. When everyone was seated, there were nine people in total. Snake had a .380 that held ten bullets. If anyone ran when he started shooting, he would have a problem. So he had a solution for that.

"Come over here." Snake motioned for the two youngest kids who had to be three or four years old. Everyone in the family was smiling, thinking a payday was coming their way. Those smiles quickly evaporated when they saw the gun.

"Who are you?" one man asked.

"Here's the deal. Only two of you get to have the money. If anyone do anything stupid, one or both these kids will die." Everyone nodded in agreement. Snake told everyone to close their eyes. "When someone dies, whoever opens their eyes will die too."

One by one, Snake killed every member of the family. All nine of them. Even the kids. That's a problem Paulette no longer had to deal with.

The second thing Snake did, he had someone wire Paulette $150,000 in her account. That should be enough to keep her afloat for a while. Now he had to make some stops to get some weapons. Then he was heading to Miami to get the kid.

*****

Montell jumped in his car and noticed a manila envelope on the windshield. It's not something that he had placed there. Someone had to be in his vehicle. He grabbed the envelope and pulled out the content. There were ten different pictures of the mother of his daughter doing sexual things to a group of men. What was more disturbing, his two-year-old daughter was included in every picture, watching someone he never saw was holding his daughter. Montell's phone rang.

"I see you got the pictures."

"Who's this?" Montell yelled into the phone.

"You know who this is. Don't think we won't kill you and your whole family. Get us what we need," the female said as the phone clicked.

Montell was furious. They forced his daughter to watch his fiancée having sex. He started to regret his decision to accept the deal. The more money he was associated with, the bigger the problem. Sincere better have what they needed.

*****

Lisa, Sandra, and Monica were inside of Monica's father's car. They did some investigation and found out from Chris what neighborhood Sincere stayed in. Riding around the blocks, it didn't take them long to find him. He was walking out of the park with a nobody none of them even recognized. Not knowing if the girl was related to him, Monica parked the car. Lisa and Sandra quickly ran up on the girl and started jumping her. They didn't beat her up as bad as they wanted. She fought back like a cat, and Sincere was protecting her.

"Stop hitting her." Sincere pushed Sandra and pulled Lisa off the girl. Monica couldn't believe he was on the other girl's side.

"She's the reason you've been avoiding us?" Sandra asked, giving the girl she didn't know a dirty look.

"You girls need to go home," Sincere said.

"So it's like that. You choose her over us," Monica said.

"What!" Sincere asked in confusion. What was wrong with these girls, he thought. They acted like he wasn't allowed to speak to another female without their consent. They were insane. "Y'all not gonna pick and choose who I speak to."

"This ain't over with, hoe," Lisa said to Tamika. The three girls stormed off.

"You okay?" Sincere asked Tamika, a girl he just played basketball with.

"Your groupies, huh?"

"Not quite. I'll speak to them and make sure they leave you alone."

"I can hold my own. Those girls need to fall back. Which one are you dating?" Tamika asked with a grin.

"They're all just friends."

"Acting like that, you must have sex with all of them."

"Friends don't have sex."

"You are not fooling anybody. Especially not me. I saw how they all were looking at you. It must have been that good," Tamika teased.

"All you girls are crazy," Sincere said, walking off the other way.

"You're not gonna keep running from me. I always get what I want."

*****

Li'l Gangsta got word that Ghost was dead weeks ago. He never knew that Ghost and The Source was plotting to have him killed. This new information from Hot Rod was suspect at first. Ghost's wife, Veronica, confirmed what Ghost and The Source was up to. L. G. couldn't let that slide. L. G. had to set an example. No one put a hit on his head and lived to see many days. The Source went after the wrong target. L. G. knew he had to get rid of Veronica. Her loyalty was to no one but money. She didn't care about who she set up or who she got killed. L. G. had no intentions of being on the wrong side of any stick.

That Friday night, L. G. went to Passion. He did his usual: paid for a section, got some bottles, and got freaky with a couple of dancers. Not once did Veronica come to his table to greet him or give him a dance. Something fishy was in the air. Anything that was outside of what was normal had to be questioned. Veronica was up to something. L. G. discreetly watched her speak to a group of three men who had their eyes locked in on him. How many sides was she playing? L. G. had to get up out of the club. Going back to his car wasn't even a thought. There's no telling who was outside lurking. L. G. called one of the bouncers over and slipped him $200. That was the fee to take a dancer to the green room. The green room was a place people had sex in. L. G. normally did that wherever he was in the club. He knew it was a side exit by the green room. He took two dancers with him.

"Listen, here's $400. Split it. All I need y'all to do is stay here for about five minutes."

"So you are not trying to get some?" one of the dancers asked.

"Not tonight. Five minutes, okay."

"Whatever."

L. G. peeked out the door and calmly left. If someone was watching the side exit, he was out of there. He abandoned his car and made a call.

"Son, pull up at the used dealership by Passion."

"Give me ten minutes."

When Rick came through, L. G. got into his car, and they parked in the club's parking lot. Rick made his way inside of Passion. L. G. stayed put in the car. Thirty minutes later, Rick jumped in L. G.'s car and sped off. No one followed him. Two hours later, Veronica was leaving the club alone. L. G. never saw the three guys again. They must've left when he was waiting on Rick.

Veronica was heading straight to her place. L. G. could tell by the route she was taking. It was a route she instructed him to take before. L. G. sped ahead of her since he knew her destination. He waited in his car for her to arrive. At 4:16 a.m., she got out of her vehicle. Three shots hit her. She was dead before she hit the floor. She never knew who killed her. Never saw it coming. Never again would she make money off men.

*****

Paulette and Pamela were in front of the TV looking at the local news. The news anchor reported nine people dead, children being among them, in gruesome fashion. All victims took one bullet to the head. Paulette felt sorry for the family. Even if they tried to sue her.

They didn't deserve that. How can people be so heartless? How can people show no sympathy for human life? The world had to be coming to an end, she thought. The story didn't come as a surprise to her daughter.

"Now we don't have to worry about that lawsuit," Pamela said, nonchalant.

"Are you serious? Nine people are dead. Including three children. That doesn't affect you in any way?"

"I don't know them. I could care less."

"Get out of my face. I can't believe you. What's got into you?"

"Whatever." Pamela left and went to her room.

Paulette didn't know what was going on with her daughter. When did she get so hard and cold? Paulette had to get a drink. She stepped outside and went to the closest ATM machine to get some cash. She checked her account three different times. Each time it said she had a total balance of $168,000. Where did the extra money come from? This couldn't be an error. No one had her bank account information. Paulette rushed home and shared the news with her daughter.

"Pam! Pam! Get down here!"

"What's wrong? You okay?"

"Yes, we're okay. Look at this." Pam looked at the receipt and smiled.

"It's gotta be Quincy," Pam said.

"That's far-fetched."

"Who else could it be?" Paulette was silent. She did save his life. Was he also behind those deaths? Paulette didn't wanna think about that. She had a lot to ask him if he ever came back. She wasn't letting him off the hook. He had some explaining to do.

CHAPTER 14

MR. MALLORY

Mr. Mallory was a former army guy now teaching ninth grade. He made sure his students stayed in compliance with his rules. There were no cell phones, food, talking, playing, or passing notes in his classroom. He didn't even allow his students to have restroom breaks. Mr. Mallory was being paid to teach. He didn't have time to babysit or train his students. Most people said he took life too seriously. That he did. How else was he supposed to take it? Life wasn't a cartoon. It wasn't fun and games, and it wasn't filled with Mickey Mouse stuff. There were people starving. People dying. People at war.

Mr. Mallory wished he had the power to take a few of these kids to Iran to a concentration camp they had set up. Especially that fast no-good tease Cindy. She was always flaunting her boobs in a braless top, showing way too much cleavage. Then there was April with her tight skirts. At times, she purposely wore things that were see-through, just to let people know she was pantiless. It's a shame how at a young age, these girls can be such sluts, he thought. How can any parent allow their child to walk out of the house dressed like that?

There was also Sarah, Felicia, Barbara, and Melissa. Damn near all of those little tramps were hot and fast. The boys loved it. Every young boy entertained the girls. Every kid except this one boy who never smiled. He knew what life was about. He always came to class prepared and with a purpose. He was focused, and he listened tentatively to instructions. He wasn't one to suck his teeth or get discouraged by the assignment or what was being taught. The kid never attempted to befriend anyone. He ignored those sluts like they were flies on poop. At his young age, he knew what life was about. Mr. Mallory thought it was impossible, but after a week of observation, Sincere was the only student he ever took a liking to. The kid had a heart of the street. A mind of a general. His eyes had this seriousness to it. He knew pain. Real pain, and he knew how to deal with it.

Fresh off a five-day suspension for breaking a boy's nose during summer school, Bobby walked in the spill out with his eyes fixed. Everyone in school knew he was in charge. Bobby was a nineteen-year-old eleventh grader that stood at 6'3", weighing a bulky 235 pounds. He was looking for the new kid that read faster than anyone else in class. Who the hell did the chump thought he was, showing off and making everybody look slow? He had some nerve to mock everyone. He had to be taught a lesson.

Bobby searched the spill out, but he didn't see the kid. He left the area, not knowing if he would've waited another minute, Sincere would've walked right in his path.

The following day, in culinary class. Bobby was happy to see Sincere. So far they shared both of their alternative classes together.

"Hey, you sitting in my seat!" Bobby said to Sincere, trying to put down on him.

"I'm sorry, bruh, I don't want any problems," Sincere said as he moved to another seat.

Bobby tapped him on the shoulder as soon as he sat down. "That's my seat too!"

Sincere looked at Bobby and almost said something slick. He knew this dude was gonna eventually be a problem. Bullies don't understand peace. Hurting them was the only comprehension they understood. Sincere rose to his feet and thought of kicking Bobby in his groin, but a pretty girl got between them.

"Hey, I'm Sierra. You can sit in my seat," The pretty girl said, giving Bobby a mean look.

The pretty girl, Sierra, walked Sincere to her seat, then took the first desk.

Bobby made Sincere leave the vacant. Evidently Booby was heated. Sierra was his girlfriend. Why was she getting in his way?

Why was she helping someone beside him? She never did that before. Bobby wanted to crush the chump's skull open. His time was coming, and it was gonna come fast.

Sincere knew, more than ever, that Bobby had to be dealt with. Not only because he was testing his manhood but also because Sierra, his girlfriend, had stood up for him. Which apparently was an ego-crusher. Sincere's father taught him a long time ago that jealousy makes a man do foolish things.

His dad's exact words were, "Don't ever underestimate someone who is scared or jealous. Especially a man that's jealous because of a woman. A jealous man can become very dangerous. He doesn't think with logic. He only acts off emotions."

Sincere wasn't trying to end up on the wrong side of things. He did nothing to trigger the way Bobby was acting toward him. A thought occurred to him on how to handle the situation while working on his assignment.

*****

Susan just walked out of the corner store after purchasing a loaf of bread, gallon of milk, and a carton of eggs for her mother. It was a little after eight o'clock, and the darkness of the sky was starting to fill in. As Susan strolled down the alley, she bumped into Bobby the bruiser. His attempted to grab her and pull her toward him, but it was futile. She resisted his advances.

"Why are you tripping? You know you want me," Bobby said firmly; he could get whatever and whenever he wanted.

"Boy, please! You better go to your girlfriend and leave me alone." Susan snapped.

Bobby ignored her and grabbed her with more force this time, trying to kiss her and touch her in places he had no business touching her in.

"I always get what I want. Right now, I want you," Bobby said as he kissed her against her will.

"Let me go, you're hurting me," Susan begged.

As the words left her mouth, some metallic object hit Bobby across his head, and he fell to the floor. Out of shock, Susan dropped the items she was holding in her hands. The boy that saved her repeatedly punched Bobby in his face with so much force. Her legs couldn't move as she looked in awe. The face of the attacker, her savior, was the quiet kid in one of her classes named Sincere. Susan watched in amazement as Sincere took a steel and slammed it hard on Bobby's kneecap. She heard the crack of what must be broken bones from where she stood. Bobby hollered in pain. Sincere dropped the steel and casually walked toward her.

"Hey, Susan, are you okay?"

Susan couldn't speak. It wasn't fear she felt. She was excited. Her small nipples hardened against her shirt. She was in a daze. Sincere looked at her quizzically and gave her $10. He picked the bag of broken eggs and spilled milk and walked off with words she couldn't hear. When did she become deaf? When Susan finally came back to earth, her first thought was, he remembered her name. She gathered herself, took the loaf of bread, and skipped by a moaning Bobby without a glance or care about his conditions. She repurchased the milk and eggs and some Skittles and chips with the money Sincere gave her. What a sweetheart he was, she thought as she headed home.

After dumping the bags in the trash can, Sincere walked to where his car was parked and went home. A week ago, while riding around certain neighborhoods, Sincere peeped where some of the kids at his school hung out at. Bobby was a small-time weed pusher around his way. He stood out. Following him wasn't hard.

Early the next morning, Susan was in front of six girls replaying every detail that took place the previous night. Most of the girls didn't believe a word she was saying; Bobby the bruiser wasn't one to fall so easily to the likes of a well-mannered kid like Sincere. It was possible but unlikely to happen. Everyone knows that Suzie gets high. It wouldn't be the first time she told a fib. She had the hots for Sincere. The first day she saw him, she let it be known that her canon was open, waiting for him to drop a load in it.

"You know, y'all think Suzie is lying, but last school year, I watched that boy beat Chris up. He's not as sweet as y'all think. He's like a bomb waiting to get lit up," Nicole said.

"So you believe me?" Debbie pointed out as all the girls got silent.

Sincere walked calmly by them without a glance. He didn't have the slightest idea that he was the topic of their conversation. Susan left her friends and started walking beside him.

"Hey, good morning. I never got to thank you last night."

"You cool. He deserved what came his way," Sincere said, now looking at all the girls who were watching him.

"I brought you something with the money you gave me." Everyone watched Susan dig inside of her purse to retrieve a pack of Skittles. "It's my favorite. I brought you a pack," she said, smiling.

"Thanks," Sincere said as he accepted the candy. "See you around."

Susan skipped toward her friends with a huge smile on her face. No one doubted what she said now.

"I think I'm gonna ask him out," Susan said cheerfully.

"I called dibs on him first," Jackie said.

"That you did, but all you do is freeze up when you see him," Tiffany reminded her.

"Go for it, Suzie," Debbie encouraged her.

*****

Snake thought it was best for Hot Rod to send two of his female workers to Miami. Don't get it twisted, Snake didn't trust them. He just knew how easier it can be for a woman to deceive and manipulate a man. Men don't look at women as potential threats or killers. Men are always blinded by the visual. A pretty face, to most, is not something to be intimidated or threatened by. Women that are trained can be the best killers. A woman doesn't make a person tense or afraid. A woman's background or career is hardly questioned. The way a woman presents herself, whether it's classy, slutty, professional, or typical, it's not out of the norm. Even with women who are aggressive, they don't exude fear in people. And to Snake, it was a great trap until he arrived.

*****

During Mr. Mallory's class, Susan dropped a piece of paper in front of Sincere's desk. Mr. Mallory didn't miss it. He was watching the whole play.

He waited to see how the kid was gonna handle the situation. Surprisingly the kid picked the note up, and that disappointed him momentarily. Disappointment turned to approval as Sincere walked to the garbage can and shredded the paper. The kid walked back to his seat and resumed his work as if it never happened. The looks on those sluts' faces were remarkable, Mr. Mallory thought.

While in the spill out, Sierra approached Sincere with two of her friends. Sincere didn't know if she felt some type of way for what he did to her boyfriend. After what she did, that wasn't the case. She handed him a paper.

"That's my number. Make sure you use it soon," Sierra said while her friends were smiling.

Sincere got none of these girls. He sent Sierra's boyfriend to the hospital, and she didn't appear to be angered by it. It's like she was happy. Once again, he thought of what his father once said, "It's hard to understand the ways of a female. They're gonna do a lot of stuff that's gonna confuse you. There's good girls out there, but some girls will do their best to destroy you without you knowing it."

Sincere wondered what Sierra was up to. While looking at the piece of paper she handed him, Susan came toward him with a group of four.

"Why did you throw my letter in the trash but keep hers?" Susan asked bashfully while her friends sized him up.

"You know the class rules. You could've given me that letter anywhere outside of the classroom. I respect Mr. Mallory. So I won't break his rules."

"Everybody doesn't see it that way."

"Apparently. I'm not everybody." Sincere shot back.

Susan didn't like his tone. It made her angry in a way. It also was turning her on. This boy had her perplexed.

"What was in the letter?" She heard him asking. Words couldn't form in her mouth. When did she become so shy?"

"I have to pee," Susan said and took off. Her friends weren't too far behind her.

*****

Mr. Mallory felt the need to have a dialogue with Sincere. Everything he was hearing about the kid was something he wouldn't turn his nose up to. When he told the kid he needed to speak to him after school, the kid didn't do what most kids would do and ask why. He just said, "Okay, sir." The kid had respect. Whoever his parents were, they raised him properly.

With his hands to his side, looking Mr. Mallory dead in the eyes with a stare that was unreadable, The kid said, "Yes, sir. You asked for me?"

The kid was unlike that bully he summoned last week. The kid showed respect, and he held eye contact. The makings of a good solid man.

"You know, kids talk a lot. Too much, if you ask me. I don't know your story, but that was a nice whopping you put on Bobby the other day."

Sincere didn't respond. Mr. Mallory admired him even more. The boy wasn't one to gloat or boast. That was smart. Boasting about doing something wrong is an admission to the wrong act. That can come with consequences sometimes.

"Listen, Mr. Williams. I really wanna thank you for coming to class and doing what's required of you every day."

"You're welcome, sir. School is for learning. Life is too short to be toying around and playing all day," Sincere said. A smile crept on Mr. Mallory's face.

"You couldn't have said it any better."

*****

Brenda and Keisha knew they had to let Montell know the seriousness of the situation. He thought it was a game. The pictures of his fiancée and little girl really got his attention. If it became necessary, he would lose his family in a heartbeat. They watched as he pulled into his nephew's apartment. Keisha has been watching the place the past week. The little boy seemed to be close with a lady that also stayed in that apartment. If Montell didn't get any results, it may be in their best interest to use the lady as some kind of leverage.

Snake was in Miami, going to see Brenda and Keisha. He already had things mapped out. For one, there were too many people involved. That had to change immediately. In Snake's assessment, it was never smart to have several individuals on a single assignment. Snake was never the one to look at things from an optimistic point of view. He always focused on what could happen if things went wrong. He always thought of the consequences. Loose lips, blackmailing, greed, those were always factored in when dealing with other people.

As soon as Snake met Brenda and Keisha, he had to make certain things clear. People had to get eliminated.

"If the kid's uncle doesn't have anything for us by tomorrow, kill him. Keisha, see what the lady knows. Kill her and her daughter, if she doesn't cooperate. Brenda, get rid of the white girl and Yolanda," Snake instructed after they updated him on the events that took place since they arrived.

"Yolanda's the boss's sister," Brenda complained.

"She has information on you that she shouldn't have."

"I can't take that order," Brenda said firmly.

That's another thing Snake hated about women. They didn't like to listen. This woman Yolanda could implicate them in their criminal activities. The white girl, Katherine, could easily cut a deal with the state. They had no business of being alive. Brenda and Keisha should've known better.

"I'll figure it out. Meet me here in two days," Snake said, already knowing what he had to do.

Snake hated dealing with other people. Eventually he was gonna end up killing Brenda and Keisha. They knew way too much. They did a good job. It just wasn't good enough. Snake watched from a distance, on foot, as things unfolded.

Brenda and Keisha were inside of a Lincoln town car watching Montell climb Sincere's balcony. He tried the doors, then checked the windows. They both were locked. He knocked on the door and then left when no one responded. Montell didn't even know he had eight separate eyes watching him.

*****

Mr. Mallory had followed Sincere home one day. He wanted to see if the boy was involved in some illegal activities. On this particular day, a guy was in the kid's balcony, checking the windows and doors. It wasn't the only thing that caught his attention. There was a car that was parked three spots from him thirty minutes ago. No one came out of the vehicle. Once the guy left, the Lincoln town car pulled off minutes later. The kid had to be in some deep waters. Was he even aware of what was going on? Mr. Mallory left the area, not knowing he too was being watched by a pair of eyes.

*****

Sincere was inside Ms. Wright's house, watching TV with Amanda. He already spent more time there than his own place. Amanda apologized to him for what she did. They now had a sexual understanding. Sincere grew up thinking that males were the ones who wanted sex more than females. That couldn't be true. Almost every female that was interested in him, all they wanted was sex. Over half the girls in school seemed to be addicted to sex. It was all they cared to do. That was crazy.

"I saw your uncle again today. Why are you avoiding him?"

"I don't want him to know where I stay," Sincere said, not really trying to get in a conversation about it.

"It's too late for that. He was on your balcony."

Sincere knew his uncle was up to something. How did his uncle know where he stayed? The past two months, his uncle didn't make one attempt to reach out to him. These weekly checks have stopped coming in. Not that Sincere was depending on it. He had to find out what was going on. He couldn't avoid his father's words in one of his letters. About how Montell couldn't be trusted and how anyone can be brought.

*****

Snake wanted to know who was in the Dodge truck. His timing couldn't be more perfect. A couple of crackheads were beside Snake, oblivious to his purpose of being there. The person in the Dodge truck could easily be anybody: a friend of Montell, a friend of the ladies, a detective. Not knowing didn't bother him at all. The truck would reappear. When it did, he knew exactly what needed to be done.

Snake left his spot and went to his hotel room. Yolanda had to be dealt with after Brenda and Keisha were dead. They all were living on borrowed time. Before crashing and going to sleep, he thought of Paulette and Pamela.

*****

There was something fishy going on with Yolanda. Almost every other night, she was sneaking out, doing God knows what. One night, Yolanda brought company to her place. Alexis never saw the person's face. She did overhear Yolanda telling the person she wanted a gun rammed up a woman's vagina like last time. Alexis almost fainted when she heard that. Did Yolanda have something to do with her being raped? She had to. Was she trying to have her raped again? Ever since that night, Yolanda wasn't the same. She was more energized and happy, and given the circumstances, that was strange.

Yolanda slipped into the bed with Alexis. Alexis pretended to be asleep. Yolanda wrapped her arms around her. Alexis never felt a touch so cold. She never felt fear as she felt now. Who was Yolanda really? What type of people was she dealing with? And how can she gather evidence against her?

CHAPTER 15

Alexis remembered how she once wanted to be a forensic worker or pathologist. She thought of all the crime shows she watched on the justice station. She decided to watch a program called *Deadly Wives* on the crime station. A scene from the show put an idea in her head. She didn't have sufficient evidence to report to the police about her suspicion of Yolanda. This was personal. This had to be done by her. Many times, the police let people off the hook if evidence wasn't concrete. Substantial evidence wasn't gonna work in this situation. So Alexis knew she had to do this herself.

Having money made getting her hands on certain things a lot easier. Dressed like a cowgirl, Alexis went to a ranch in South Miami. Her whole purpose was to get a tranquilizer which was used to calm horses but was deadly if placed in a human. After leaving the ranch, Alexis went to Walgreens to get a syringe. After some heavy thinking, she knew she couldn't just stick the needle in Yolanda. A few minutes of brainstorming, she got a Visine bottle, emptied it out, and placed the poison inside of it. The next time Yolanda slept over, Alexis had a surprise for her.

*****

Hot Rod decided to turn on Snake. They had a good run. All good runs eventually come to an end. Nothing in life lasts forever. Snake and he really had nothing in common. The more they aged, the more their differences showed. Snake had no interest in business or making money. All he cared about was killing. That came as an advantage at times. Everything in life had to be balanced out, though. There was a time for peace and a time for violence. Snake didn't know the definition of peace. This was the time for peace. It was an election year. Hot Rod didn't need the unnecessary heat. What he needed was Snake getting them drives from that kid.

Once those drives were safely in his hands, he was gonna collect that ten mil. Life couldn't be any sweeter than that. Who needs friends when you have money.

*****

Mr. Mallory was studying Sincere during the entire class period. He knew when someone was being watched or about to be attacked. Something familiar about his own son drew him to the kid, so he was gonna help him. When class ended, Mr. Mallory stopped Sincere at the door.

"We need to talk."

Susan and all the other girls looked back, wondering what was going on. Just like girls, they didn't know how to mind their business. After the students finally left the classroom, Mr. Mallory got right to it.

"I don't know what you're into, but several people have been following you and trying to break into your house," Mr. Mallory said. The kid didn't look surprised.

"So you've been following me?" The kid was right on that.

"I had my doubts about what you were into. It doesn't justify what I did, but I'm glad I did it. I think you're in danger."

Mr. Mallory was someone Sincere respected. If he happened to be in danger, what was next? In his heart, he knew whoever killed his parents would eventually come after him. What exactly was inside the backpack?

"Listen, kid. If you want me out of your business, I'll stay out of it, but it looks like you're gonna need some help."

"I don't even know who is after me," Sincere said.

Sincere ended up telling Mr. Mallory everything that led him to being here in Miami. Sincere didn't know if that was a mistake or not, but it felt like the right thing to do. In life, he knew what appeared or what felt good doesn't constitute being good.

"I think it's best for you to relocate. I got a place you can stay at until we can figure what's going on."

"Thanks. Why are you doing this?" Sincere asked.

"When I was in the service, my son was around your age. You remind me of him," Mr. Mallory said.

"How old is he? What happened to him?" Sincere asked with concern in his voice.

"All I know, he hung with the wrong crowd. The facts of his death are iffy. He ended up getting shot. Maybe it was due to a mistake of identity. Maybe it was off of something he did. No one really knows. No one got arrested. That was twenty years ago."

*****

Keisha followed Ms. Wright right to her front door. Ms. Wright was startled when she saw her.

"Do you have any idea where my nephew Sincere's at?" Keisha said, pretending to be Sincere's auntie.

"He never told me anything of him having a family down here," Ms. Wright said. She really wanted to ask, *How did you know to come here?* But she had a role to play.

"My sister. His mother died before he came to Florida," Keisha lied.

"I'm sorry to hear that. Amanda, honey, we have company. Get something to drink for me as our guest," Ms. Wright told her daughter, then said to the lady. "Come on in. He should be back any minute."

Keisha entered the apartment and stood by the window. She declined to take a seat. She also didn't drink the beverage that was given to her. Keisha thought of questioning the females. But there was no sense in doing that. If the kid was gonna be here any minute, she had to hurry up and get rid of the females. She smiled as they came out of the living room and headed to the kitchen.

*****

Mr. Mallory noticed the Lincoln town car in the parking lot once again. If they knew about Sincere and wanted him as bad he thought they did, they or that one person would try to attack or confront who Sincere was in contact with on the regular. Sincere and Mr. Mallory explained the situation to Ms. Wright and Amanda. Instead of running away and being afraid, they both were looking forward to acting out their roles. They didn't care if it was dangerous. Females, at times, never knew what troubles they actually put themselves in.

Mr. Mallory was in Amanda's room, looking at the camera he had set up in the house. He watched the woman who had claimed to be Sincere's auntie.

Ms. Wright had a wire on her, so he was able to hear the conversation. When Ms. Wright and her daughter were going toward the kitchen. The lady reached in her purse and pulled out a gun. Mr. Mallory expected some kind of twist. He swiftly rushed out the room without making a sound. The silencer was already placed on his Berretta. Before the lady entered the door way of the kitchen. He let off two quick shots that hit the lady on the opposite shoulders. The impact of the bullets caused the lady to drop the gun and fall to the floor. Ms. Wright and Amanda's eyes were wide with shock. They understood how close they were to death.

Mr. Mallory didn't wanna kill the lady right away. He needed answers. Turning her into the police would make matters worse. That would give her time to contact people she knows that was a part of this.

Picking up the lady's gun, he asked, "What are you doing here? And what do you want with the kid?"

The lady didn't say anything. Mr. Mallory applied pressure on her gun wounds to add to the pain that she was already feeling. "Talk!" he yelled. The lady just grunted.

"You don't have to hurt her." Ms. Wright intervened.

Mr. Mallory couldn't believe what he was hearing. This lady was on the verge of killing her and her daughter, and she had the audacity to tell him not to hurt the lady after he literally saved their lives. That was mind-blowing. He had to take the lady to one of his places. It was obvious; he wasn't gonna get anything done here. Question was, how would he get her out?

*****

Katherine wanted to go to the police and make a confession about everything. She couldn't do so if she didn't have any information to incriminate Brenda's actions. There was no way she was gonna allow her to continue to extort her. Even if she had to suffer for killing Gregory.

Brenda was secretive with everything she did. Katherine knew nothing of the people she stayed in contact with. Brenda hardly stayed on the phone over twenty seconds. Almost every time she got a call or made one, she left. Catching her slipping might be hard.

Unbeknownst to Katherine at the moment, she caught that slight break when she noticed Brenda speaking to Yolanda during lunch break. How did they meet? Were they dating? Did Brenda have something over Yolanda's head too? As soon as Brenda pulled off from the Inc., Katherine made her way toward Yolanda.

"I see you know Krystal too," Katherine said.

"Krystal?" Yolanda asked, raising an eyebrow. "I know her as Nancy."

"Nancy, huh." Katherine wasn't surprised. She was positively sure neither was her actual name. "Are you two seeing each other or something?" That question threw Yolanda off. It was evident on her facial expression.

"What makes you ask that?"

"She's into females, just like you." Katherine put out there, knowing Yolanda and Alexis had something going on between them that was more than just business.

"You don't know what I'm into," Yolanda said defensively. "You need to mind your business and stay in your place before you get put in your place."

Not one for confrontation, Katherine left. Obviously she made Yolanda upset. That was nowhere near the plan.

Yolanda was a little heated by the trailer trash white girl speculating and fishing on what or who she was into. She had to be taught a lesson. So she called one of the ladies for another favor. She wanted the trailer trash to feel what Alexis felt. It was only right.

*****

Snake witnessed the well-shaped black man placing what appeared to be laundry in his truck. He had two bags full. Snake knew whoever this guy was, he wasn't a tenant to any of the rooms in the apartment building. His actions confirmed that he wasn't part of any agency or department. Finding out who he was, was gonna be important. It was evident now that he was helping the kid.

Keisha went in over an hour ago. The job should've been done by now. Killing someone is not hard. Getting away with it is hard. Snake knew something was foul. He had no intentions of going inside the lady's house. He already had a feeling what to expect. He would pay the family of two a visit later on. It was important to know who this man was and what exactly he had in them bags.

*****

Katherine was out in the lobby at the Inc. when Alexis approached her.

"I've observed you and Gregory taking lunch breaks together. Do you know anything of his whereabouts? I'm about to replace him," Alexis said.

"He took his clothes out of my house weeks ago. I haven't heard from him or seen him since. I went to his place, and it was empty. Apparently he moved out."

"That makes no sense."

"I said the same thing. Can I help you with anything else?" Katherine asked, ready to change the subject.

"I got two o'clock. I don't know where Yolanda went. I need you to cover for her until I get back," Alexis said.

"Sure," Katherine replied, wondering if Brenda was in the midst of Yolanda leaving.

Alexis found the way Katherine was looking at her to be uncomfortable. Was she starting to trip and assume that everyone wanted to forcefully do something to her sexually? She couldn't stop thinking of the guy's threat. That incident did change Yolanda's behavior toward her. She was more of herself and very supportive. Her entire attitude flipped. Alexis wasn't buying the act anymore.

*****

Brenda didn't know why the guy wanted Katherine and Yolanda dead. Montell, that was understood. She also didn't like the fact he wanted the mother and her daughter dead. The guy probably had something against women, she thought. Her boss, Hot Rod, told her they needed more than one set of eyes and ears at the Inc. The guy didn't call the shots or even the plays. When the boss said something, it was final.

Brenda just got through speaking to Yolanda in person, and the woman wanted to meet up again. The boss already told her and Keisha to give or help Yolanda with whatever it was that she wanted or needed done. After their meeting, Brenda was at a loss of words. Yolanda wanted Katherine to experience the same treatment as her lover. Something was really wrong with Yolanda.

How does anyone getting raped by a gun bring you pleasure? It was something Keisha had to do. It wasn't smart for Brenda to do it herself. She would if she had to, but Keisha was the best option, and the best option hadn't been picking up her phone for the past four hours. Ever since Keisha went to that lady's house, they lost contact. It was unlike Keisha to not check in every hour on the hour, if she wasn't asleep. Brenda tried not to think about it, but she felt something was wrong.

*****

The Scientist didn't like The Source's idea of falling back for the moment. When you had your enemies up against the ropes, you don't stop throwing punches. You don't give your opposition time to adjust or regroup. You go in for the kill. The Source was making a huge mistake. The Scientist had nothing of importance to handle in the US of A. If The Source didn't want him to put out the fire, he wasn't gonna be anywhere near when the fire erupted. The Source probably had something up his sleeves. Whatever it was, it better be deadly because sooner or later, Snake was coming.

*****

Before going anywhere he planned on being at for more than thirty minutes, Mr. Mallory had a habit of circling the block at least three times. It was his way of checking his surroundings. His way of making sure he wasn't being followed. His way of seeing if something was out of the ordinary.

Mr. Mallory first circled the block. A car made two right turns with him but eventually made a left on the third turn. Mr. Mallory circled a second and third time around. Everything seemed to be in place. He drove about three minutes to get to where he needed to be.

Mr. Mallory pulled inside of his garage and took the bag that had the lady in it, out. He made sure to tie her up and punch big enough holes to give her breathing room. He untied the lady and made her sit on a chair.

"You're a pretty woman. Whoever you're doing this for is not worth the trouble. Tell me what's going on and what do you want from the kid."

The lady kept her mouth tight and shut. She really thought she was tough. Mr. Mallory knew no matter how hard or tough a person was, they could be broken. There's only so much pain a person could take. Even if a person trained themselves to get used to the feeling—losing body parts, losing blood, getting burned or electrocuted for hours, and days without food and water was unbearable—sooner than later, that person would be praying for a quick death.

"Don't make this hard on yourself. I'm gonna give you one more chance to kill this tough-girl stuff and save yourself." To his surprise, the lady spit on him. Mr. Mallory tied her to the chair and taped her mouth shut. He pulled out a sharp six-inch blade while standing behind her. He quickly took one of her ears off. He didn't wait to see her face before taking the second ear off.

Mr. Mallory knew from experience, women took pain far worse than men. After five minutes, he took the tape out of her mouth. Before he could ask a question, she was telling him everything she knew.

*****

Brenda had a ski mask on waiting for Katherine to come in her room. The quicker she did this, the quicker she would have that crazy Yolanda off her back. This was the last time she was doing something like this. It was far better to just kill someone. Brenda still didn't hear from Keisha. That bothered her a lot.

When Katherine came into the room, Brenda didn't say a word. She crept up behind her and hit her as hard as she could with the butt of the pistol. Brenda pinned Katherine on the bed and tore the silk gown she had on right up off her. Every time Katherine tried to resist, she got hit with the pistol. After the fourth hit, she accepted the abuse.

*****

Snake followed the guy in the Dodge truck. A couple of turns he took made Snake change his course and go the opposite direction. Whoever this guy was, he was good. He was trying to make out a tail. Snake used the same strategy on numerous occasions. Going around a circle can help you determine if you're being pursued by someone. It also can help you better dissect the area. Snake didn't know if the guy made him. He wasn't taking any chances. Following him was gonna be difficult. He had to find a way to catch him when he was on the ground again. Snake decided to pay the family of two a visit.

They had some answers he was looking for. It was time to apply pressure.

*****

Katherine was one of Alexis's top workers. Her not showing up to work was a big deal. It didn't compare to Gregory's disappearing act. Something in the air was smelling real funky. Alexis needed Katherine. So she went to her home to see if she could find out what was going on. When she arrived at Katherine's place, she was all bloodied up. Her lips and eyes were busted. Her clothes were torn.

"What happened?" Alexis asked, pulling out her phone and immediately calling to get some medical attention.

"Someone came and raped me. He raped me with a gun," she said in between sniffles.

Alexis's entire thoughts and body shut down momentarily. She was no longer in the room with Katherine. She was back in her room being manhandled by the assailant. The people had to be the same. Two same incidents, weeks apart, incidents that were extremely unheard of. Forget rare. Alexis didn't have anything to say. All she could think about was, who was behind this?

They rode to the hospital in silence. When Katherine filed a report with the detective, it happened to be the same detective that was investigating her case.

"Do you know anyone in your company that would want to hurt you?" the detective asked.

Apparently he thought someone at the Inc. had something to do with it. In a way, it made sense because both of them worked there. The detective had Gregory as his prime suspect. His criminal history didn't do him any justice. Since no one knew where he was at, that didn't go in his favor. Not that it mattered; Katherine strongly felt as if Gregory had nothing to do with it. She was very adamant in her argument with the detective about that.

*****

Montell was starting to feel a lot of pressure. He underestimated the people that gave him what he considered, at the time, a good deal. He could no longer keep his family around. It was too dangerous. His fiancée was a totally different person after what happened to her. He didn't know if she would ever forgive him about that.

Montell had $148,000. He gave $125,000 of those to his fiancée. He advised her to go stay with her sister in Orlando while he searched for the person that did that to her. Montell didn't know that one of the ladies told his fiancée about the deal they had. Montell also didn't know he wasn't gonna see his daughter or fiancée anymore.

Montell wished he would've thought things through. Jumping to accept the money was a terrible choice. Probably the worst he ever made. He had to get in contact with Sincere. He had to find a way to help his nephew escape. Even if it meant the death of him.

*****

Alexis checked Katherine in a hotel. The doctors told Katherine she could stay in the hospital for a couple of days, but it wasn't necessary. Katherine declined the offer and left. Alexis offered her to take two weeks off, yet she insisted on working.

The next morning, Alexis went to pick Katherine up so she could gather some clothes at her place. Katherine told Alexis to park on the side of a van so they could watch her place.

"What's wrong?" Alexis asked, not knowing what was going on.

"Just keep an eye on my house."

For ten minutes, that's exactly what they did without speaking. Alexis was starting to feel that Katherine was delirious, but when she witnessed Yolanda coming out with an unknown female, she was confused.

"What's going on that you're not telling me?" Alexis asked.

"I'm trying to figure out how Yolanda fits in all of this."

Alexis didn't know what to say. Who was the woman she was with? What did Katherine mean by her last statement? What was Yolanda doing at Katherine's house? Alexis thought of the conversation she overheard from Yolanda with the anonymous person. Could that person be the woman she was with?

"Katherine, this might help the both of us figure out what's going on. Almost two weeks ago, someone did to me what they just did to you, the same way," Alexis admitted it.

"That monster. I knew it."

"What! Who are you talking about?" Alexis asked in confusion.

"That lady with Yolanda has her hands all over this."

"If that's so, Yolanda has her prints in it too."

"So what do we do?" Katherine asked.

"I don't know. We gotta do something."

Alexis wasn't gonna tell Katherine what she intended to do to Yolanda tonight. It's something she intended to take to the grave with her. If she had to, she would work with Katherine to handle the other girl. Alexis couldn't overlook the fact that it was two people with male voices that attacked her.

CHAPTER 16

Detective Strong was trying to put the pieces together. Something about what Katherine said made him doubt his suspicion on Gregory Black. If—a big if—Gregory Black wasn't involved, who else to look for? Outside of Mr. Black, no one else stood out. Either he did it or someone else was setting him up to take the fall. Where was he? A person doesn't just vanish without a trace. Unless they were running from something, hiding from something, or buried in something, finding him and questioning him would give him more than he had now.

Detective Strong knew the woman wasn't being straightforward with him. He always had a knack of knowing when a person was lying or hiding something. The two women were clearly hiding something, and that something had to be out of fear.

Strong was keeping a keen eye on Katherine's place. He observed a green Nissan Altima parked by a van. Grabbing his binoculars, he immediately noticed the two women who were sexually abused. He stayed in his car, wondering what they were up to. When two other women walked out of Katherine's home, Detective Strong's antennae rose. If Alexis and Katherine didn't greet these two, that said something. They knew those two women were in the house. Yet they stayed in the car. This was a lead that he had to follow. He quickly took pictures of the two mysterious women. He then left when Alexis and Katherine entered the house.

*****

Snake went back to the home that the family of two resided in. He softly tapped on the door and waited for a response. A fairly attractive woman opened the door. It amazed Snake how stupid people were. Not even knowing who was on the other side of the door, people just had a habit of giving people access to their homes, not realizing the possible danger in that. Snake already had his .45 Magnum out and on the side of his hip. The pretty-faced lady's eyes widened when he started to raise it.

"Calm down and don't make a scene," Snake said as she backed up, giving him room to enter. "Take a seat and call your daughter," Snake instructed.

The lady did as she was told. Seconds later, her daughter came to the living room. She dropped the plate she was holding when she saw the man with the gun. Snake motioned for her to sit by her mother.

"I really dislike asking questions twice. One lie, one misleading information, and I'm gonna automatically kill one of you. Understand?" Both females rapidly said yes. "A man left here like an hour ago with two bags. Who is he? And what were in those bags?" Snake purposely left out Keisha's entrance. It was to test the female's honesty."

"The man is a teacher at North Miami Beach Senior High School named Mr. Mallory. That's all that we really know about him. He just came to our home three days ago," the attractive lady said.

"And the bags?"

"A lady we never saw came to our home and tried to harm us. Mr. Mallory shot her and placed her in the bag and left."

Snake partially got the truth. The lady left out some important information. Information he never inquired about. Technically the attractive-looking lady never lied. She never even mentioned the boy.

"What about the boy?"

The two females looked at each other and put their heads down.

Snake meant every word he said. A single bullet hit the lady's daughter on her forehead. Her mother started to scream, then instantly lunged forward to attack Snake. Two quick shots dropped her to the floor. The woman had some fire in her, Snake thought.

He was taught a long time ago to never stay close to someone you planned to hurt. Doing so could easily put you at risk.

It was visible that the females didn't wanna give up the kid. That was cool. He now knew where to find the enigmatic man. He would eventually lead him to the kid.

*****

Sincere couldn't stay cooped up in Mr. Mallory's shack doing nothing. Getting out for some air and to do something normally felt good. While walking around, absorbed in deep thought, he bumped into Tamika, the female that used to date Bobby the bruiser. She wasn't someone he expected to see. Sincere still didn't know her objective. He never knew her angle.

"Hey, Sincere! I didn't know you stayed around here," Tamika said, giving him a friendly hug as if they were on those terms. "What's wrong? I feel your tightness. Loosen up a bit. I'm not trying to bite you," she joked, giving him a huge smile.

"I'm actually visiting a friend. Didn't think his place would be so dull."

"Well then. It's a great thing we ran into each other. If you like, we can go watch a movie," she suggested, thinking he was gonna take her up on the offer.

"I'm not in the mood for that."

"What exactly are you in the mood for?" she asked with a grin.

Sincere couldn't grasp the meaning behind the question. It was more than one way to take it. "Honestly I just wanna clear my mind up."

"I know the right place for that." Tamika grabbed Sincere's hand, and he reluctantly followed her to wherever she was taking him. "It's not that far. Trust me. You'll love it."

Trust was a very strong word people tend to throw around. They underestimated the depth and meaning of the word. Sincere didn't even know this girl, and she was telling him to trust her. He couldn't help but shake his head. Females.

Ten minutes later, they were sitting on a bench in front of a small fountain and memorial he couldn't place. Absolutely no one walked on the path.

"I love this place because it's peaceful." Tamika started. "There's the sound of nature. Birds chirping. The soft breeze from the wind. Nobody here to distract you. No disturbance whatsoever. Just calmness."

"It's a good place of escape. What exactly are you escaping from?" Sincere asked. Tamika looked at Sincere, considering whether or not she should open up.

"Bobby used to beat me up on a regular when I didn't do what he wanted. One day after a beating, I was just walking and came across this place. I walked past the street up ahead a million times, and I always passed this spot. Now anytime I just wanna free my mind of all the troubles in life, I find myself sitting here."

For some odd reason, Sincere felt a connection with Tamika after she shared that. He watched her as she closed her eyes and went into her zone. He did the same. For thirty minutes, they sat there in silence. Sincere liked the fact that Tamika didn't ask him what was bothering or troubling him. She understood. If he wanted her to know anything, he would tell her.

The entire trip, while walking Tamika home, they were in a friendly argument about who was the best basketball player of all time, among Jordan, LeBron, and Kobe.

"Jordan got six rings. He never lost in a final, unlike LeBron and Kobe," Tamika said.

"If your argument is based on rings, Bill Russell got eleven. Robert Horry got seven. Statistically no one's better than LeBron."

"He has a losing record in the finals. He shouldn't even be mentioned as one of the greats. He's overrated."

"Jerry West lost eight out of nine finals he went to. I think he was the only player to win finals MVP on a losing team, and he's on the logo. No one's throwing shade at him," Sincere said.

"I don't care for him. LeBron is trash."

"You a hater," Sincere joked. Tamika pushed Sincere lightly as they shared a laugh together.

At the foot of Tamika's doorsteps, Sincere was expecting to get another friendly hug. Tamika surprised him by not giving him anything.

"Hope your thoughts are better than they were before. See you around, Sincere."

"It's like that. I can't get a hug?" Sincere asked.

"Maybe another day."

Just like that, she walked in her home, leaving him hanging. Why was he eager to feel her touch? Was she stringing him along? Sincere didn't have room to occupy his thoughts with her. He didn't need the distraction. Under different circumstances, he would've probably pursued her. Under different circumstances, he would've taken charge and gotten a kiss, but things were the way they were. Sincere headed back to the shack. Mr. Mallory was sitting on a chair, waiting for him.

*****

Montell was inside of an interrogation room, speaking to a couple of detectives about most of the things that took place since he met the ladies. He lied about several things and didn't mention the money. It was obvious to Montell that the detectives weren't taking him seriously. He really had nothing for the detectives to go off of. He didn't know the females' names, address, or anything. He had no proof they did something wrong. It was basically his words, which didn't look believable. Montell walked out the police station in anger. He had to be thankful for something.

Happening without Montell's knowledge was a third detective taking notes in another room. He observed Montell from the one-way mirror. The description he gave of one of the ladies could be what he needed information on. As Montell left, Detective Strong wasn't that far behind.

"Mr. Williams, I would like you to go through some photos and tell me if one of the females you see are the one you described."

Montell reentered the police station and went inside another room. The detective pulled out about thirty pictures. He scanned through most of them without a second glance. He finally landed on one of the women he recognized. He immediately pointed her out to the detective.

"That one right there is one of the girls, "Montell said, pointing vigorously at the photo.

"Calm down. Tell me everything that's really going on, and not that BS you gave the other two guys.

*****

Brenda watched as Montell was leaving the police station. It didn't take a rocket scientist to figure out what he was doing there. He had to be mouthing off in ways that could put someone in danger with the law. That someone could very much be her. The guy with death in his eyes alerted her that Keisha was shot and got kidnapped. With the way Yolanda and Katherine had been acting, the guy's suggestion of killing the four females and Montell was something they shouldn't have brushed off. He obviously knew what he was talking about. It didn't matter what Montell was speaking to the police about. He had nothing on her. A rat had no place on this earth. The future was very short for Montell.

*****

Mr. Mallory placed himself in a catch-22. He wasn't one who considered going to the authorities for anything. The fact that he shot and cut the pretty woman's ears off had him facing attempted murder. You could also add kidnapping to that. Going to the police was a no-no. Releasing her wasn't a good idea either. How did helping a kid out result in him committing these types of females?

Mr. Mallory had no sympathy for the pretty woman. The nature of law was on his side. The woman was a cold-blooded, calculated, and meticulous killer.

The best thing to do was kill her. He would be saving lives by doing so. After chopping her up to pieces, he burned parts of her bodies deep in the woods and fed the rest to the sharks. Mr. Mallory headed to the shack and was surprised that the kid wasn't there. Sincere left a note stating he was going out for a walk and will return back shortly. When the kid finally returned, Mr. Mallory got right to it.

"Things are a lot worse than I thought. I spoke with a hired lady who was trained to kill. She came down here with another female to get some disc or drive from you. Word is before your parents died, your father gave you something, which led to you coming down here. Whatever that something is, now I have an assassin after us. After gathering all the information I can from this female, I went to warn Ms. Wright and Amanda about our perilous situation. It saddens me to say both of them are dead now. We should've never gotten them involved in this."

Mr. Mallory was astonished by the kid's demeanor. His facial expression stayed the same. He didn't even react to hearing about the deaths. The kid acted like his heart was carved up in stone. The kid had to level with him about everything. He was basically putting his life on the line to help him.

"Do you know anything about this disc?" Mr. Mallory asked.

"No, but it must be in the backpack that my father gave me before he got killed."

"That's a start. Let's go get it."

"I'm going alone. I'll be back in about an hour."

Sincere thought of what his father had once told him about putting his trust in people.

"You'll never fully know who you can trust. Even with someone you knew for twenty years or since childhood. Circumstances change things quickly. People will let you down. They will disappoint, but a select few will show their loyalty and go out of their way and beyond to be true to you. Everything is based on the situation. You can determine who is who when you're down or in danger. Even with that, circumstances can easily change things."

Mr. Mallory didn't have to do anything that he was doing. Sincere was gonna trust him. He had to trust somebody in this situation.

*****

The energy Brenda was getting from Katherine before and especially after her being abused was full of questionable contingencies. Brenda didn't feel at ease in any way around Katherine. Her body language and attitude was open to skepticism. Brenda wasn't the kind of person who lacked a good sense of judgment. There was unseen pressure that she was starting to feel. Keisha was more than likely dead. Montell was talking to the police. Her natural aptitude was telling her it was time to flee. Nothing good can come out of staying.

Financially Brenda was very disciplined when it came to saving. She had more than enough to live off and start a legitimate career with. The signs couldn't be ignored. Instead of heading to Katherine's house to spend the night, Brenda got on I-95 and headed north, right out of the state of Florida.

*****

Detective Strong enjoyed his conversation with Montell. He acquired a lot from it. What was given couldn't be revealed to anyone else. There was a lot of money involved in what they had, money he had to get his hands on. Officers across the nation didn't get paid enough for all the risk they took. If an opportunity was presented for Strong to get some extra change, he would cash in.

Strong gave Montell an order to determine the site of his nephew and get his hands on the drive. Once it was in their possession, he planned to secretly apprehend the two females and demand the remainder of the money for recovering the disc. As soon as they made the exchange, he knew disposing the bodies of Montell and the women would be very important.

*****

Sincere went to the safe house for the second time since his arrival in Miami. He had no reason to be there before. He pulled the backpack out of the wall, emptied out the money, and went back to the shack.

Mr. Mallory opened up the backpack and searched through it. He noticed a concealed compartment at the bottom of the backpack. He pulled out a blade and cut the bottom open. Mr. Mallory discovered a small disc.

"Let's see what all the fuss is about."

CHAPTER 17

THE DISC

Alexis was struggling with the idea of going through the actual action of killing Yolanda. It wasn't that simple. How could someone find the courage to take away what the good Lord created? Alexis just couldn't muster the strength to do such a thing. Never in her life had she reacted to a situation by acting out in violence. Although she was infuriated by what Yolanda arranged, she was smart enough not to take action and do something that could potentially end her career.

Alexis knew Katherine had her own agenda. Together they could possibly work on unfolding things Yolanda was keeping hidden and who she was working with to have that heinous act done to them.

*****

Snake received a call of great significance from Brenda; her taking herself out of the picture was a move of wisdom. Snake hated operating with the involvement of others. True enough, he was the one who implied and recommended for the ladies to accumulate information until he arrived. They added too much intricacy. They shouldn't have intruded in what Shadow had going on with the blond-head white girl. Snake regarded it as a dumb move that could come with unforeseen effects. Whenever an assignment was in progress, there should be no detours. Besides the uncharacteristic blunder by Brenda, her alerting him of her departure and warning of Montell's brief visit with the local authorities, was appreciated.

Montell was now a source of vexation. He had to go. Killing him would probably make the people of law be on the lookout more. But it had to be done. Snake had to move quickly. Rushing things normally can lead to mistakes, but he was no rookie at this. Prolonging Montell's death would only make his task harder.

During Snake's initial encounter with Brenda and Keisha, he collected every fact and data about Katherine, Yolanda, and Montell. Those collections were of great value. He always did his best to know as much as he can about people who can impose to be a possible threat. Hot Rod never mentioned having a sister. What he didn't know, he couldn't be blamed for. Snake discovered that every other weekend, Montell went to his mechanic who had a strange room where he kept one of his cars. Montell always went there a little after noon.

That Friday, Snake waited for Montell to exchange cars. After he did so, Snake followed him. Unlike the man Snake was pursuing in the truck, Montell didn't have the slightest clue. He was oblivious of what was yet to come. Anyone who spoke to the law and crossed someone for money was headed for destruction.

*****

Mr. Mallory and Sincere watched what was on the drive in silence. To Sincere, it was just a sex tape. Mr. Mallory knew better than that. There's always things behind the scenes that the naked eye doesn't see. The two people, or one of the people, he was watching had to be someone of importance. It's unlikely that killers were on the loose to obtain something of no value. Whoever was on the screen or whoever filmed it didn't want those images to come out.

"Do you recognize anyone on the screen?" Mr. Mallory asked the kid.

"No."

"Stay here. I'm gonna see what I can find out. I'll be back in about an hour."

Mr. Mallory went to the home of a friend who thought he breathed, lived, and knew everything there was to know about New

York. It was clear to Mr. Mallory that the people on the screen had to be from the same place as Sincere.

"What's going on, Todd?"

"Yo, my dude Joe. What brings you by?"

"I'm in a tight spot right now and having difficulties putting some pieces together. You're a certified New Yorker, who knows almost everybody there is to know. I'm gonna run a video by you that's filled with a lot of sexual content. Tell me if you recognize anyone."

"Let me see what you got," Todd eagerly said.

Within seconds, Todd catches a visual of the two individuals. He pulled a chair and sat down. He ran his fingers through his hair and started shaking his head, muttering something Mr. Mallory couldn't catch.

"How in the world did this get in your possession!" Todd asked with concern in his voice now.

"That's beside the point. Who is on the film?"

"Besides the point on my tail, these are big-time people."

"I'll let you know once I know what's going on. Work with me here." Mr. Mallory pushed. Shaking his head, Todd started.

"The female is New York's mayor's wife. The guy is one of his biggest endorsers named Rodney, a.k.a. Hot Rod. He's nothing but trouble. Don't know how the mayor got mixed up with the likes of him."

"So this Rodney guy is not by the books." Mr. Mallory pointed out.

"By the books. This guy is a hoodlum. He owns many businesses that he washes up his street money with. There's a Bronx tale that's him, the mayor, and another guy no one seems to know now used to wreak havoc in their heydays."

"What's up with the wife?" Mr. Mallory asked, trying to see how she fit in all of this.

"She's a woman that comes from wealth. Don't know how she's involved with Rodney."

"One last question. If this footage surfaced, who will it affect more?"

"I can't really say. It's gonna hurt everyone. It's easy to say the mayor because of his political status. His wife is considered a sweetheart. That will change. But if the mayor is not the mayor of New York anymore, a lot of heat would come down on Rodney. The mayor's brother is the police commissioner in Brooklyn. Those cops are the dirtiest of them all. So imagine how things can be."

"I owe you for this one," Mr. Mallory said, preparing to leave.

"Just keep me informed. I want details."

"Give me forty-eight hours, and I'll be back. In the meantime, dig up everything you can on all three parties."

"I'm on it."

"Thanks, Todd."

"Be safe, my dude."

*****

Detective Strong had a lengthy session of questions with Katherine and Alexis. It appeared that things started to go haywire once Yolanda was raped. Alexis's admission to that caught Katherine by surprise.

"I need you two to help in locating Yolanda's companion. It's actually two of them. They are wanted for multiple murders, kidnapping, armed robberies, and extortion, among other things," Detective Strong lied.

Strong was fishing and trying to see what he could find. Two people were involved in Alexis's abuse. He didn't think Yolanda played a part in the act. It had to be the other woman Montell mentioned. What was startling, Alexis said she heard the voices of men. Were these women smart enough to alter their voice? Doing so wasn't hard. Strong had to speak to Yolanda. He had to rattle her to see what she was gonna admit to. People always folded under pressure. Strong knew exactly how to apply it.

While heading to pay Yolanda a visit, Detective Strong received a call on his radio.

"Dispatch to one on one. What is your location?"

"I'm on Ives Dairy Road."

"Smitty needs back up at Washington Park. A man has been shot."

*****

Montell had made three stops. All stops were in public, all around a large crowd. He was the typical showman. His first stop was at a Walmart. Then he lingered at a mall. He never got out of his vehicle. He came to this center of population just so the masses could acknowledge his existence. It's something he found off of Montell's third and final stop was at a crowded park. People were just randomly gathered there. Men came to showcase their vehicles. Women came to showcase their bodies.

As Snake walked by, no one paid him any attention. He wasn't laced up in designer gear or dripped up in jewelry. To them, he was a nobody. Someone without any validation or status. Someone that was being overlooked. Snake loved the lack of attention. He couldn't understand why someone would crave attention or want to be seen when they were doing dirt. That was a recipe for disaster.

Snake knew exactly what he had to do. The Montell show had to come to an end. Creating an alibi wasn't necessary. All he needed to create was confusion. A simple gunfire would do the trick to make people scatter. Snake let off two gunshots in the air with one of the games he held. While everyone bolted and ran for cover, his second gun silently did the job. Hitting Montell across his chest and slumping him to the ground. A couple of females saw the blood and screamed. Most people kept it moving, doing their best to leave the scene. Evidently no one wanted to be around when the law came. Snake ran in fright like the others. Although that mission was complete, things were gonna become more problematic if he didn't get to the kid.

*****

Yolanda tried contacting the two females, but it was to no avail. Alexis had been spending a lot of time with that trailer trash. They were never friendly before. Now they acted as if they were besties. Yolanda was sick to her stomach, seeing them together. It was like a slap to the face. What made matters worse, Alexis had replaced Yolanda as her secretary and put Katherine in that situation. That move really pushed her over the edge.

"I can't get in touch with none of the girls. I need something handled now," Yolanda ordered.

"Let me see what I can do."

"Get me some help ASAP." Yolanda snapped, then hung up the phone.

*****

Sincere elected to leave the shack again. He was forced to be confined in one particular spot with nothing to do. He needed an outlet, not necessarily a place to vent, just someone to unload and discharge on. He wasn't in the mood for playing basketball or watching any films. He wasn't in the mood for conversation. He could only think of one person who was very much the same. Someone who he considered to have a temporary remedy. Someone who had the energy to keep him occupied for hours.

"What's up, Monica? You busy?" Sincere asked.

"Not really."

"Can I come over?" Sincere asked with no intentions of prolonging the conversation.

"Sorry, I told you I was gonna do it, Mommy. My friends are here now. I'll tell them goodbye and call you right back."

Sincere smiled when the phone clicked. Monica had to be with Lisa and Sandra. She obviously didn't want them to know that he was on the phone. That was very smart of her. When she called back, she told him her parents weren't coming back home until Tuesday. So they would have the house all to themselves. Sincere liked the sound of that.

*****

Alexis placed Yolanda back as a receptionist. That move emotionally and mentally disturbed Yolanda. Detective Strong came up with the idea. He wanted Yolanda to be out of her element and off balance. Alexis really didn't know if the detective's strategy was going to work as planned. In hindsight, it did. Yolanda was erratically becoming a huge disturbance at work. Her hair was in disarray. Her clothes were wrinkled and sour. She either gave people, who came to the front desk, attitude, or she flat out ignored them. Alexis could no longer allow her to cause uproar at her place of business. She had to put an end to her chaotic behavior.

"Yolanda, is everything all right with you?" Alexis asked in a firm voice.

"Why do you care?" Yolanda yelled back, causing people to stop and look in their direction.

"You're not displaying the right kind of mental capacity right now. I'm gonna have to ask you to leave these premises. You can't work here in your current state."

"Leave the premises. I can't. What. Wait, I have to be here. Who's gonna take the calls? Who's gonna greet the people that come in?" Yolanda asked calmly.

Alexis couldn't fathom how Yolanda's posture and mental position did an about-face. She would go from deranged and widely impractical to calm and rational in a matter of seconds. She had never seen anything like it.

"Katherine will fill in while you're gone."

"That trailer trash slut. How dare you? First my secretarial job, now my receptionist job. Where is she?"

Yolanda got off of her feet and started screaming for Katherine. The security guards were alerted in an attempt to unruffle the situation. When Yolanda caught a glimpse of Katherine, she ran at full speed in her direction.

"I'm gonna kill you!" she yelled with fury in her eyes.

Before Yolanda could reach Katherine, she was seized by a couple of guards. Due to her illness, she had to be restrained. Yolanda's refusal to comply forced Alexis to call Detective Strong on speed dial. Other officers were already en route from a previous call by an employee.

*****

Detective Strong got a call from Alexis about Yolanda's crazy behavior. He couldn't be at two places at once. He called another detective he was real close with and told him to check out the shooting at Washington Park for him. He had to follow his instincts. Something was going on with Yolanda that he had to find out. The shooting at the park probably had something to do with gang members. Most shooting in black neighborhoods were either gang or drug related.

*****

Monica wasn't apprehensive or doubtful in any way about why Sincere called. He knew she wasn't the talking type. He called her for one reason and one reason only—he was thirsty. She was delighted that out of every female he knew or could've called, he called her. It meant something. He wanted to be pleased by her. She was gonna give him something that would never leave his memory.

Monica didn't have sex since the last time she did it with Sincere. She no longer had any interest or desire for sex with any other males.

The only person she craved was Sincere. It was good to know that he was on his way.

*****

Alexis couldn't believe the way Yolanda was behaving. It's like she was possessed by an unknown force. Alexis was in awe as she witnessed Yolanda's transformation when the police officers arrived. Her resistance immediately ceased. Her eyes were no longer dark and angry. They were soft and sad. A security guard and several employees related to the officers the events that took place.

"Do you want us to take her in for trespassing?" a lady officer asked.

"Trespassing?" Alexis didn't understand how a person can get arrested for trespassing at her own workplace.

"Apparently that's the only thing she broke. You're the owner of this company. So this is your property. Once you told her to leave and she refused, her remaining here became an unlawful act."

"No, no. I don't want her arrested," Alexis said, not meaning it.

Detective Strong was entering the building. Alexis brought him up to speed with everything that happened.

"Something's totally wrong with her. In fifteen minutes, it's like I saw four different people. I had never seen someone make a transition like that before."

"She seems perfectly fine to me," Detective Strong said, looking at a now-tearful Yolanda.

"Let me show you the cameras," Alexis said.

"Hold on."

Detective Strong showed the other officers his credentials and placed hand restraints on Yolanda. He told them to keep an eye on her until he came back. Alexis showed him the footage of what was recorded. Detective Strong saw what Alexis was talking about. Yolanda's temperament kept being replaced with another simultaneously.

When they got to the lobby, there was a huge commotion. An officer was bleeding and holding his left ear, while another officer was Tasing Yolanda.

"What happened!" Detective Strong asked when he reached them.

"This witch bit my ear off," the bleeding officer complained in disbelief.

Detective Strong shook his head in disappointment. Yolanda had an expression of pure evil on her face. She licked the blood that was around her mouth, then she went into a blank state, staring at the ceiling.

"Yolanda, you are under arrest for the battery of a law enforcement officer. You have the right to remain silent. Anything you say or do can be used against you in the court of law. You have the right to an attorney. If you cannot afford one, one will be appointed to you."

After Detective Strong read Yolanda her rights, He took her into custody. She had a look of innocence now on her face as she stared Alexis down.

*****

Mr. Mallory came back to an empty shack. What bothered him the most, there was no note like last time. He started to worry about Sincere's whereabouts. His vehicle wasn't in the parking lot across the street. Maybe he forgot to leave a note.

His doubt got put to rest when he received a call from the kid.

"I forgot to leave a note. I'll see you in class on Monday."

"All right."

At the end of the day, Mr. Mallory knew Sincere was gonna make his own choices. He couldn't keep him sheltered. He wasn't his guardian. It probably was a good thing the kid was away. Todd would have more information in two days.

CHAPTER 18

GOING CRAZY

L. G. found himself in Jersey City, sitting in front of The Source's mother's house. For the past week, he had surveyed a dozen of The Source's Known businesses, and he was always a no-show. Places he would normally check up on, at least once a week, he also stayed away from these spots. That's what led L. G. to where he was at now.

Four years prior to this dry. Li'l Gangsta was a young lieutenant trying to put himself in position. He was given the duty to escort The Source to his mother's house on her birthday night. L. G. smiled at the opportunity back then. It will prove to be a fatal mistake by The Source. There's certain things only those that are real to you should know in most cases. There's things no one should know. L. G. would never let one of his bottom workers know where his mother stayed, let alone someone from the top. True enough, some of the most loyal dudes came from the bottom. L. G. also knew that's where the most treacherous dudes came from as well. It's not always easy to determine who is who at times.

L. G.'s mind was already made up once he set out to do something. Absolutely nothing could derail him from it. A turtle's head stays inside his shell when he's in danger. The Source was hiding from someone. He hasn't been seen or heard from in weeks. Like a bird having to come back to feed and tend to her chick, killing his mother will definitely bring him back to the birdhouse. It will have him vulnerable and open. It will indeed lead him to his death.

*****

Nicole Newman Cohen has been living a lavish life since she was a toddler. Marrying Vincent wasn't a move of love or status. She did it for the sole purpose of putting her true love, Rodney White, in a better position. Vincent had been infatuated with her since day one. To him, it was love at first sight. Nicole didn't believe a foolish thing like that existed. It's impossible to love someone totally off looks alone. Many things and feelings had to be explored and discovered, but Vincent was convinced that the very first time he saw her, he was hooked.

Vincent was a sophomore at the University of Syracuse during her freshman year. That's when she was first approached by him. She rejected all his advances and ignored his compliments. No matter how many times she did it, he was always persistent, never one to give up. She told her secret boyfriend at the time about Vincent. Instead of confronting him, he came up with a plan. It was a plan she was against, but she did it to prove her love and loyalty.

Ten years later, she was trapped in a marriage she didn't wanna be in. Stuck with a man she didn't love. This wasn't the way she envisioned her life. She was basically living a nightmare, waiting to wake up.

Nicole was born in wealth, married to a man with money. The man she loved had money and gave her whatever she wanted. Nicole knew that money didn't equal the happiness and joy that love brought. Some would choose money over love in a heartbeat. True enough, money made things easier, but it was a complicated and stressful side to what money brings. That people didn't see. True friends or people cannot be determined by a huge bank account. Money wasn't what Nicole needed. The lack of true love and loneliness could be overwhelming. Nicole knew of this from experience.

She would trade everything she had for love in a second. Love superseded everything else to her.

*****

Detective Strong was bewildered when he heard about the death of Montell. Unlike the lead detective in the case, Strong didn't believe his death had anything to do with drugs, debt, gang affiliations, popularity, or females. Everything pointed to the women Montell told him about. Once the other two detectives who interviewed him at the police station got a wind of his death, they'll know or assume that his conversation with them was a warning of what was to come for him.

Detective Strong had to find the kid. He couldn't let $400,000 slip out of his hands like that. The best way to catch the kid was to get him at school. All kids go to school. Especially the ones that are not in the streets.

Little did Detective Strong know he was on a wild goose chase. He was literally relying on a ghost. He was unaware of Keisha's death and Brenda's disappearance. Sincere knew nothing about the money and who was after him. All Detective Strong was doing was putting his life in jeopardy. That was, in fact, part of his dues but was signing up for death.

*****

Mr. Mallory was back at Todd's house going through the files that he just received. He couldn't understand the information that was given. It was no help.

"From my sources, which, as you know, is the best of the best, the mayor's wife is not really happy with her husband." Todd started.

"I can be careless about that. What's the deal on the other two?" Mr. Mallory asked.

"Everything that's going on with the other two have a lot to do with the wife, but since you think this wife is not a factor, there's a small rumor that the upcoming election is gonna be rigged."

"Elections are never rigged," Mr. Mallory stated flatly.

"This is not your field, Joe. When you don't know something, it's good to just listen," Todd said with a grin. "My inside source told me the mayor is gonna intentionally lose the election. Word is, he wanna focus more on his marriage and children."

"That makes no sense. Why not just not run at all?"

"His hands are tied up to some people on the streets, Rodney being one of them. A friend of the mayor's wife told my source that the wife is secretly in love with Rodney."

"Does the mayor know anything about this?" Mr. Mallory asked, surprised by the new revelation.

"Of course not. I think Rodney had that film recorded, but I won't put anything past that wife of his."

Mr. Mallory knew more than he knew before about the people in New York. He told Todd about the kid. He also revealed what took place at Ms. Wright's house. Todd and he had a lot of history. They did a lot of unwritten things that weren't on the right side of the law. Todd was a standup guy and true friend. He also happened to be one of the few people he trusted. So telling him the details of things really had no harm in it.

What to do with the disc was the unanswered question. Mr. Mallory already made a duplicate for safekeeping. Keeping the kid safe was the problem. Mr. Mallory questioned himself at times and wondered if what he was doing was worth all the trouble. At the end of all of this, he and the kid could easily end up dead. He didn't wanna live his life looking over his shoulders all the time. He also knew he couldn't go back and change his decisions. It's something he had to live with. Once he put himself in it, there was no turning back.

*****

Samantha Dixon was a lawyer that Rodney knew in Miami. She had represented Gregory Black on his direct appeal. So Rodney hired her to help his sister. Ms. Dixon knew that Yolanda was on the psych floor at the women county jail in downtown Miami. Yolanda's court date was arranged for Monday. Ms. Dixon already knew which direction to take with the case. It was obvious that her client was mentally disable and incompetent. Everything depended on whether the police officer or the state would go forward and press charges. It really didn't make a difference. Ms. Dixon was confident that she would get Yolanda released within a month. Her brief visit with Yolanda didn't tell her much about her client. The visit was shortened due to a stabbing that placed the facility on temporary lockdown. Ms. Dixon was going to pick Yolanda's brains out tomorrow before her court appointment.

Samantha Dixon was proud to be a lawyer. It's a job she enjoyed. She worked at a black-owned firm that represented only black clients. She knew firsthand how difficult it was for incarcerated individuals, especially the black race. The system was designed and rigged up to be against them. The men had it hard, but people always overlooked the struggles of the black incarcerated women. So many women got locked up for their loyalty to a man, and those same men leave the woman dead with no support.

Samantha knew the black race was dysfunctional and out of sync. Nonetheless, it wasn't gonna stop her from trying to make a change.

*****

Sincere didn't feel like going to school anymore. Too many unknown factors were bothering his thought process. He knew he wouldn't fully be able to concentrate on schoolwork. The news he received about his uncle's death while watching the local news scared him to death. Whoever was after him was starting to have no regard for consequences. They, he, or she were clearly getting their point across. The disc already caused three people he knew to die. Who would be next? Going back to school would be a real stupid thing to do. That's the first place the person would go to, to try to find him. Sincere smiled at the thought of how proud his father would be of him for thinking the way that he was thinking.

"Under extreme pressure, it takes a strong mind and a strong man to think straight and make wise decisions. People normally fold under pressure. The mental distress and irony of things are too much for most people to handle. During pressure moments, when you have time, think things through. If time is not on your side, you better be quick on your feet. It could be the difference between life and death," Maurice had once told him.

School was no longer an option. Sincere needed a place to stay. Once he came up with where he would go, he would eventually leave Miami. He could no longer stay in the city. The heat was on. Staying in it was gonna get him burned. The best thing for him to do was relocate.

"When is the next time your parents are gonna be out again?" Sincere asked a jubilant Monica.

"More than likely, Friday. The past four months, it's been clockwork that they leave on Thursday or Friday and come back on Tuesday. Why do you ask?"

"My uncle just died. I'm gonna need somewhere to stay," Sincere said.

Monica wrapped her arms around Sincere and expressed her sympathetic sorrow for his loss. She assured him that she would be there for him any way that she could.

"You can stay here with me as long as you want. My parents never come to my room. It's like I don't even exist. They don't even care who I invite inside the house. If they're here, and we're here, I'll just tell them you're my boyfriend," Monica stated excitedly.

"So you and your parents are not close, I assume."

"They both wish they had a boy," Monica said sadly and walked out to get a drink.

Sincere didn't understand how her parents can be so inactive in her life. That had to be the reason she used sex for. It was her tool and place of escape. It's wrong for a parent to constantly leave their child at home unattended. How could they not love their daughter? And what kind of parent had no care of who their daughter let in the house? Monica's parents were not fit to have a girl. It benefited him, but it saddened him because he knew deep down inside, Monica was hurting.

*****

Yolanda was standing at her door, waiting for the guards on the night shift to do their fifteen-minute rounds. The correctional officers made a huge mistake when they placed another individual in her room last night. She was supposed to be in a one-female cell. Instead from everybody else. Unfortunately a dozen females declared a psychological emergency over the weekends, which filled the psych floor up, past its capacity. So it forced some females to share a room.

Yolanda didn't like anything about her bunkie. She reminded her too much of Alexis. She was pretty like her. That irritated the hell out of her. What made matters worse, she snored just like that backstabbing cunt. Yolanda could no longer take it. The sound of her driving was crazy. As soon as the officer did her checkups, Yolanda strangled her bunkmate to death. After doing so, she ran her head against the wall, knocking herself out.

*****

Monica was flooded with joy; after a wonderful weekend with Sincere, she was on cloud nine. She became a sexual gymnast and did the performance of her life, the past forty-eight hours, for her extraordinary acts. He wanted to spend more time with her.

He had to be sprung since he didn't wanna leave the house. That wasn't a problem. She was sprung as well. Sincere had her open in all types of ways. She did something she never did with anyone before. She took off her mask and showed him who she truly was. It felt real good doing so. She was tired of putting up a front. Pretending to be happy was getting played out. She was emotionally wounded. Those scars came from the lack of love she received from her parents. She expressed that to Sincere, and he said all of the right things. For the very first time, Monica knew what it felt like to be in love.

After another round of sexual exercise, Monica thought of her time with a former dope boy she used to date. She remembered how he used to act when he was on the run. He stayed at her house a lot to duck off until he could figure things out. She wondered if Sincere was running from something. He didn't go to school with her today. She never knew him to miss a day. He practically loved going to school. Monica wasn't slow or lame. There was something going on with Sincere that he wasn't telling her. He was someone she cared for deeply. Someone she loved. She had to put her nose in the mix of things. It was only right.

"I'm not your ordinary female from the block. I see things most people don't recognize. You may not want me all in your business, but I wanna be here for you through and through. That's through the good and the bad. I know there's a lot you have on your mind. A lot that you're going through that I don't know anything about. I just need you to know, if you need me to do anything for you, I mean anything, don't hesitate to ask me," Monica said, surprising herself that she really felt that way.

"It's nice to hear a female say that. I'll keep you in mind when I'm in need."

Monica was a bit disappointed by Sincere's response. She wanted more. She wanted him to be able to count on her. She wanted him to trust and believe her. He probably had his reasons for having his doubts. In due time, she would gain his trust and prove to him that she was the right one to be on his side.

*****

Yolanda woke up and found herself hog-tied to a chair. Everyone was looking at her as if she was crazy. She couldn't remember what happened the previous night or why her head was throbbing.

"Why am I tied up?" Yolanda asked one of the guards politely.

"I don't have time to play this game with you. Your lawyer will be here shortly to see you," the guard said and walked off.

Yolanda didn't understand what game the lady didn't have time to play. Or if she ever played a game with her. And what lawyer was she talking about? Did someone in her family die? Was this lawyer coming to talk about what they left for her? Why was her head hurting? And why the hell did she have a straitjacket on?

An hour later, a fairly attractive woman pulled up a chair and sat beside her. The woman looked familiar to Yolanda. She wondered if this woman was the same lady she saw at the mall yesterday. Was that yesterday? Her mind was foggy.

"Hey, Yolanda! How are you doing? I leave you for less than forty hours, and I'm being told that you murdered your cellmate."

Murder. Yolanda couldn't believe what she was hearing. She finally looked around and paid attention to her surroundings. She wasn't at a carnival like she thought at first. She was in one of those scary houses with ghosts. She hated ghosts. When she saw one walking by, she passed out.

CHAPTER 19

GETTING GHOST

The Scientist was back in Rosedale, Maryland, teaching class. His trip to Morocco was wonderful. The thought of staying there permanently weighed heavily on his mind. The culture, environment, and livelihood out east was far better than what he was accustomed to in the United States of America. The Scientist didn't know how or why the United States was considered as the land of the free or the best country in the world. Statistics didn't show them to be that all. The numbers and high percentage of abortion, prostitution, incarceration, rape, sexual assault, robberies, murderers, strip clubs passed other countries by rates that were astounding. The United States of America was a land of corruption and the home of thieves. Travelling allowed him to see that.

The Scientist loved teaching the young kids and being a mentor to them. In a way, it would sadden him to leave them, but he couldn't stay. Life was far better for him on the other side of the ocean. Staying in America would only get him killed. True enough, there was violence everywhere. He just knew, life would be shorter for him in America.

The Scientist threw a farewell party for his students on his last day, the day before he turned in his resignation paper to the principal. It was against school policy to throw a party without the consent of administration. He was clearly out the door now. The kids deserved every right to have fun and be happy on his last day.

The Scientist already had his things packed. The thought of moving out east had been on his mind for a while now. A woman, of all people, he met in Morocco last month helped him make the decision. It had nothing to do with affection or love. It was more so her way of life and how peaceful she seemed to be. He wanted what she had. She was willing to teach him how to get it. With all the traveling and exploring The Scientist had been doing, he knew all along; he was just searching for inner peace.

The Source looked at his phone and saw an incoming call from The Scientist. Anything involving him was never good. The Source knew the best thing for him to do was to ignore the call. Yet he seldom did what was best for him. Anytime The Scientist called him, that meant he was in trouble. The Source always said he wasn't gonna help The Scientist anymore. But The Scientist saved his life. How can you ever turn your back on someone that did that?

"What's up?"

"He killed my mother, man! She's dead!" The Scientist frantically said over the phone.

"Where are you?"

"Jersey City. He killed her, man."

"I'll be there tomorrow."

*****

Snake was the third car that parked in the North Miami Beach teachers' parking lot. From a distance, he watched the janitor and the PE coach park before him. The eighth car that arrived happened to be the mysterious man. Going into the school and following him was pointless. Snake knew exactly where he would be for the next eight to ten hours. Searching for the kid among hundreds of others was a lost cause. He had to count on the mysterious man to lead him to the kid. Snake pulled the recliner on the seat back and got comfortable as he waited.

*****

Detective Strong arrived at North Miami Beach Senior High School a little after 9:00 a.m. He lied to the principal and told her he needed to speak to Sincere Williams involving some information he withheld in the investigation of his uncle's death. Getting their cooperation wasn't hard from there. They printed out his class schedule. He immediately went to where he thought he would find him. To his surprise, Sincere wasn't in the building. After questioning all of his teachers about the kid's attendance, it was the first time he hadn't showed up for any of his classes. Word was he had been missing in action for the past three days. Somebody had sounded the alarm. Where could the kid be? Detective Strong didn't know where he was staying. Montell was dead. He was nowhere near in finding the two females. The money he thought he was bound to collect was getting away from him.

*****

L. G. was lying low inside of a rental, scoping the scene out. Police officers, coroners, and forensic people were going in and out of The Source's mother's house. The Source was currently inside as well. L. G. just waited. The Source was either angry or hurting. Both emotions were gonna play to L. G.'s advantage. Both conditions opened The Source up for attack. L. G. was ready to pounce.

L. G. waited four days for someone to make a report to the police. A woman in her fifties or sixties came on a Sunday, knocking on the door. After not getting an answer, she checked the door, which was unlocked. She then made her way in. Fifteen minutes later, the house was swarmed with EMTs and police. L. G. smiled the next day when The Source showed up.

After the police officers and the other crowd of people left, The Source remained inside of the house. L. G. decided to wait him out. It was a decision he regretted when he saw who came out the vehicle that just arrived.

*****

Mr. Mallory didn't trust the cop that left his classroom inquiring about Sincere. The tale he told about needing to speak to him for information linked to his uncle's death was straight BS. Sincere had no dealings with his uncle in any way. Mr. Mallory knew a fib when someone told one. This detective seemed too anxious. That was never a good sign. Now that the police were involved, Mr. Mallory wasn't so sure if that was a good thing. If the kid was to go up under protective custody, he probably would never get to live a normal child's life. Mr. Mallory really didn't know what was best for the kid. He just knew he wasn't secure from danger in Miami. The kid would have to move and change his identity to live anything remotely close to a regular life.

After school, Mr. Mallory was headed to the shack. Five minutes into his ride, he knew he was being followed. Whoever it was didn't try to conceal it. They stayed one-car length back. Mr. Mallory made a quick stop at a gas station, and the unmarked car sped off. Mr. Mallory had no doubt in his mind that it was the detective from earlier at the school. Out of every teacher he spoke to today, why follow him? Either Mr. Mallory had it wrong, or things were heating up.

Sincere was sitting on the couch when Mr. Mallory stepped inside of the shack. Seeing him was something he expected.

"I had a gut feeling that you would be here today. We have another problem."

"You're not gonna ask me where I've been?" Sincere asked.

"If you wanted me to know, you would tell me. I'm just glad that you haven't been coming to school."

"I'll be a damn fool to go there," Sincere quickly said.

"Why do you say that?" Mr. Mallory asked.

"If someone is trying to find me, that'll be one of the first places they'll go to."

Mr. Mallory was impressed. The kid's natural aptitude to think things was unlike anything he saw in a person his age. The kid was far from dumb. He adapted to the danger of his situation quite well.

"Wise of you. The police came around sniffing about you. A Detective Strong claims he needs to ask you questions about your uncle. I doubt if it has anything to do with your uncle in the ways he want us to think."

"Why not speak to his fiancée? Why me? It makes no sense."

"It makes a lot of sense. If this cop wants you that badly, he could very much be dirty." Mr. Mallory pointed out.

"I can't stay in this city anymore. I have to go somewhere. But I don't know where to go," Sincere admitted.

"It's hard for you to just up and leave. Being underage works against you. You have to be with an adult to make certain things happen."

"I'll give you $50,000 to get me set up in Georgia, South Carolina, or Louisiana. I can't stay here."

"I don't need your money, kid. How are you gonna keep up with your rent? How are you gonna make money? This is something you have to think through."

"I know. That's why I'm here. I need your help to leave. I can't do this on my own. Money is not a problem. If I stay here, they will kill me too."

Mr. Mallory knew the kid was right. Staying would only bring him closer to his death. He had to get him out of the state. The kid really had no one to go to for help. Mr. Mallory knew just the right person who wouldn't mind helping.

"I have a niece who stays in a small spot in Georgia called Peachtree City. Let me see if I can make something happen for you."

"Thanks a lot. I'll come by tomorrow."

The kid got up and left. Mr. Mallory didn't try to stop him. No one knew the kid had a car. If someone was following him. They would've abducted him or killed him. He replayed their conversation. He couldn't get over the fact that the kid offered him $50,000, then said money wasn't a problem. The kid was unpredictable in a good way. He couldn't help but wonder if the killers were trying to get the money from the kid as well.

*****

Samantha had her hands full with Yolanda. Bail was set for the battery on a law enforcement officer. But it ended up getting revoked as the extra charge of first-degree murder had been introduced in her files. Samantha never saw a person exhibiting serious and debilitating mental disorder as she saw with Yolanda. The girl was really a nutcase. It wasn't an act or role she was playing to get a good deal in the courtroom. The girl was officially crazy.

Yolanda was currently on suicide watch in an empty cell with nothing but a turtle suit on. There was no mattress, sheets, blanket, or pillow in the cell. The room was empty of any possession. It was just her in the toilet. To make matters worse, the room was extremely cold. Samantha was totally against a person living in these conditions, but with Yolanda's mind frame, it was understandable. Every seventy-two hours, Yolanda was gonna be evaluated by the psychiatric doctor. Samantha received word that Yolanda hadn't eaten or drunk anything in two days. She wasn't even speaking to anyone.

The officers on the floor handcuffed Yolanda and placed shackles around her ankles. Samantha observed all of this in the small room she was in. When Yolanda entered the room. She gave Samantha a friendly smile.

"Where's my kids?" Yolanda asked, looking surprised that there were no kids in the room.

"Kids?" Samantha didn't understand where she was coming from.

"I told you last night to bring my girls. Why are you always trying to keep my children away from me, Trish? Lawyer! Did something happen to my kids?" Yolanda asked, raising her voice.

"Calm down, Yolanda. You don't have any kids."

"My kids are dead! No! No! No!"

Yolanda went into all kinds of fits of rage by kicking and screaming. She continued her outburst and tried to get herself free. All she was doing was causing more pain to her wrist and ankles. Samantha tried to calm her down and explain that no kids were dead, but Yolanda wasn't having it. Mentally she was far gone. The commotion caused the guards to end the visit. They placed Yolanda back in the isolation room. All her years of representing someone, Samantha never saw anything like that before. How in the world did Yolanda get to that point? There were a few people she had to take deposition on. People that can at least give her an understanding on what was going on because she was lost.

*****

Snake drove by the gas station and quickly parked around the corner. He then jumped in the Uber that he paid to stay three-car lengths behind him, in the Crown Victoria that he was in. When the mysterious guy got back on the road. Snake instructed the driver to stay right behind him. For ten minutes, they were basically going in circles. Snake was hoping his tactics would rattle the guy. Only a police officer was bold enough to let someone know that they were being followed. A police officer could easily find out where someone stayed. The guy probably wasn't dumb enough to lead him there, but Snake was pretty sure that the guy's walls would eventually start to crack.

Snake gave up on the joy ride and made the Uber driver bring him back to his vehicle. If things didn't progress in a more advanced stage in finding the kid in forty-eight hours, Snake was just gonna kidnap the guy and force him to talk.

*****

L. G. didn't like seeing The Scientist coming to The Source's aid. He kind of liked The Scientist. He picked a real bad time to pop up. When it came down to it, The Scientist was loyal to no one but The Source. L. G. knew what it was; both of them had to go.

L. G. didn't think it would be wise to follow then. If he wasn't able to plug The Source now, another opportunity may not be presented to him. L. G. didn't wanna do anything suicidal just to kill The Source. It wasn't that serious; nonetheless, it was a must that The Source died. L. G. wasn't sure if any officers were watching the house. He doubted that they were. What he was about to do was risky and a bit desperate. That's why he had Rick in the cuts. He was all in.

The Scientist was out the door six hours later. He entered his car and stayed there. L. G. already had the engine in his vehicle running. When he saw The Source coming out, he put his car into gear, then sped directly toward The Source. The Scientist didn't miss nothing. He cranked his car and drove it towards L. G. The Source saw everything. Yet he didn't even try to run or get away from the oncoming car. L. G. wasn't expecting to hit him, but he did. The Scientist's car hit L. G.'s passenger side real hard. It caused L. G. to hit his head on the side window, which shattered and put a nasty gash on the side of his face. L. G. opened the door and stumbled to the floor. Instead of getting up, he stayed where he was at, gun in hand, waiting to see some movement. None came. Until The Scientist fell from the top of the car with a gun wound to his head. Rick emerged from the corner.

"Let's go, kid!"

L. G. got up and passed by The Source. His eyes were fixed. They ran around the corner to where Rick had parked his vehicle.

L. G. had a feeling he wasn't gonna be able to do this on his own. He needed some help. The decision to let Rick in the play practically saved his life. He had no idea that The Scientist was on top of the vehicle getting ready to put a knife in him. The job was done. Now it was time to get ghost.

*****

Mr. Mallory had gotten in contact with his niece in Georgia. Speaking to her about bringing Sincere over to stay temporarily was a win-win for them both. She was dying for some company, and Sincere needed to get out of the city.

Bernice Mallory was a thirty-year-old single woman. She had been a loner damn near all her life. After a miscarriage she had when she was sixteen, she was no longer able to conceive or have a child. She was really looking forward to having a teenage boy staying with her. She always wanted a son. The idea excited her so much that she made the decision to go down to Miami tomorrow to go and pick him up.

CHAPTER 20

TAKEN

It was the end of the school week, and Monica decided not to go to school today. Sincere, the love of her life, just informed her that it was a strong possibility that he would be moving to another state real soon. How could he just up and leave her like that? She had to find a way to convince him that she should go with him. Only one thing came to mind. It was a bit scandalous, but a girl had to do what a girl had to do. She hooked up with one of her exes for a quickie. She felt dirty and ashamed afterward. She had to get this done. Next month, she will be good and pregnant. That's a damn good reason for her to go with him to wherever he planned on going. A damn good reason.

*****

Hot Rod was just informed about the death of Bernard and Samuel. There was only one person he could think of who had the guts to go after them two. Hot Rod was a bit shaken up. The possibility of Snake being aware of his betrayal was probable, but then again, Snake did not have any proof that a conversation between them two existed. If The Source ran his mouth, one way or another, Hot Rod, still felt that Snake had to get eliminated. Snake was extremely great at what he did, but he was thoughtless. He lacked emotions and didn't take orders from anyone. If Hot Rod was still heavy on the streets, he and Snake would make war with anybody who was in violation. When money increases and a person reaches a certain status financially, certain lifestyles are not necessary. And where Hot Rod stood now, having Snake as a partner wasn't worth it.

Hot Rod was relaxing in his office when the knock came. He didn't schedule to see anyone nor was he expecting someone. Only a select few came to his office unannounced. He panicked for a second when he thought of Snake. Glad that the door was locked, he put his pistol off of safety.

"Who's there?" he asked, trying to sound calm.

"It's Brenda. Open up."

Hot Rod unlocked the door and slowly opened it. There stood Brenda. The fact that she came alone was a problem. Ever since he met her three years back, there were only two other occasions that she came without Keisha. Once was when Keisha had gotten shot during an assignment that almost went south. And the other time was when she was arrested and taken in for a murder charge. Seeing Brenda alone meant that things weren't going right in Miami.

*****

Samantha just got through the deposition of Alexis and Katherine. According to Alexis, Yolanda was the type of person that anyone would love to be around. She was easygoing, a great listener, relatable, funny, caring, compassionate, friendly. She was just an all-around cool person. Until she got raped two months ago. Everything about her changed after that incident. She became distant and cold, and her eyes were always filled with rage. Alexis also told her she didn't witness any personality changes until the day she got arrested.

The information she received about Yolanda's rape was what was triggering her behavior. With the judge being a female and a former rape victim as a child, she can sympathize with her client. But then again, she could very much be hard on her for using that harsh experience as an excuse. You never know which way the judge is gonna lean.

Samantha was in Miami-Dade County courtroom waiting on the guards to escort her client in. She didn't know what to expect when she saw Yolanda. That last visit they had didn't go as well.

Hopefully things would be different now. Yolanda wasn't allowed to wear any regular outfit since she was still on suicide watch. She was garbed in a green turtle suit, the issued color and outfit for psych inmates. Samantha didn't like the outfit. Seeing Yolanda surprised her. There was no unruffleness in her.

"Good morning, Yolanda. How are you feeling?"

"I'm feeling great. Things could always be worse. So I'm thankful for what I've been blessed with."

Was this actually the same girl? Or was she in one of her characters? As much as Samantha liked this new Yolanda, this wasn't the time or place for her to get her act together.

Everyone rose to their feet when the judge entered the courtroom. After about fifteen minutes of hearing other cases, Yolanda's case number got called out. Everything went in slow motion from there. As Yolanda stood up, she looked to the side and saw Alexis and Katherine coming in. Yolanda whispered something, then as fast as a cat tried her best to reach the two women. With amazing speed, she leaped across the bench that separated the inmates from civilians. Before she was able to reach the women, she was tackled by the guards. Instead of submitting, Yolanda resisted and tried to break free. Chemical agents had to be placed on her, which cleared out the entire courtroom.

The corporals and lieutenants of the facility were contacted immediately after the chaos subsided.

"The one thing I would like to know, why in the hell she didn't have any leg restraints on?" Lieutenant Fletcher asked in disgust.

"I thought those weren't allowed in the courtroom," a young officer who escorted Yolanda said.

"When a person is in green or red, anytime he or she leaves their room, they should have wrist and ankle restraints on."

"I didn't know, sir," the young officer said.

"Get your bags and go home. Corporal Durant, write her up for this."

"I'm on it, Lieutenant."

Lieutenant Fletcher took a look at the woman who caused all the ruckus. The woman looked terrified. He wasn't fooled by her act. He saw her type come in and out of the system.

"I hope when you get your day in court, they bury you, bitch."

Suddenly the look that was just filled with terror moments ago turned into a look of anger. The lieutenant smiled. "Get this mutt back inside of her cage."

*****

Early the next morning, Snake was waiting for the mysterious guy in the teachers' parking lot. Snake knew he had to be more aggressive and make things happen off the muscle. Time wasn't on his side. This guy didn't seem like the type to just slip up. Snake had to force him into a corner. He came prepared, just in case the guy didn't wanna cooperate.

Around the same time the day before, the mysterious guy pulled up in the parking lot, going to his designated parking spot. When the guy cut his engine off and stepped out of his vehicle, Snake hit the gas and parked right behind the guy's car and came out with his pistol drawn.

"Put these on," Snake said, throwing him a set of handcuffs.

"What am I being arrested for?" the guy asked.

Snake cocked his gun back and aimed it at the guy's kneecap. Reluctantly the guy did as he was told. Snake hit him with a tranquilizer that was sedated with chemicals to put a person to sleep. He checked the cuffs, then double locked it. Next he placed the guy in the back of the van, tied his legs up real tight. Then he drove off.

*****

Hot Rod didn't like the information that was given to him by Brenda. If Snake didn't get his hands on that drive, it could very much derail everything he had going on. He couldn't grasp how a young teenager and a teacher can outmaneuver people that were trained. The job was supposed to be simple. An in-and-out operation, but the little brat was becoming a headache, just like his father.

"You got your money in advance already. Law low. Enjoy yourself. If I need you, I'll contact you," Hot Rod told Brenda.

Immediately after Brenda left, Hot Rod picked up his phone. He had a real important call he had to make.

"Nikki. We may have a problem. Meet me at that spot we were at last week. Make sure you're not being followed, and come in disguise."

*****

Yolanda was back in her cell. Her skin and entire body was on fire from the mace the guard sprayed on her in the courtroom. The guards refused to let her take a cold shower. Their job was custody, care, and control. The only thing they cared about was control. Yolanda got on her knees by the toilet and used the toilet water to wash out the pepper spray that was in her stinging eyes. While doing so, a female guard walked by and laughed. Yolanda took note of everybody who antagonized and made fun of her. When the time came, she promised herself that she would kill them all.

When Yolanda's vision was no longer blurry. She took a dump on the floor. After doing so. She picked up her own feces and spread it over the window of her cell. She was hoping the lady who made the last round came running inside.

*****

Mr. Mallory was up about thirty minutes ago. His body felt real weak. Besides being in the back of a van, he had no idea where he was. The van was not moving and whoever kidnapped him was sitting near him. Whoever this person was, he knew damn well it wasn't a cop. Police didn't instruct anyone to handcuff themselves. That just wasn't happening. This had Sincere written all over it. Before he could process what he was thinking to do, the guy turned around and faced him.

"I know you're up. No need to keep playing possum. What I put in your system was a small dose that didn't last over an hour. I gave you enough time to think things through. Introductions are not needed. I know you're a trained man. It don't matter what field you were in, but I know you know your stuff. Don't toy with me. I'll cut you in pieces if I have to. If you don't fluke up and escape, know this, you're gonna die. That death could be a real quick one, or…we can drag it out for days or weeks. I'm pretty sure you're familiar with the drill," the man said, then turned his back to him.

Mr. Mallory knew this guy was serious. The intense look in his eyes said it all. If the guy never would've spoken, Mr. Mallory was convinced that the guy was not someone to be taken lightly. It was inevitable that he was gonna die. No matter how tough he or anyone was, he knew there was only so much pain a person could take. The more it's inflicted, the weaker the mind and body got. Everyone could be broken. He wasn't excluded in that statement. Whether he said something now or later, it all boiled down to him doing it. It would be real stupid of him to get chopped up in pieces and lose blood, only to give up information anyways.

Mr. Mallory saw the equipment inside a cart the man intended to use. Some of it were items he was familiar with. The guy grabbed what seemed to be a replica blade that he used on the lady he killed.

"I'm not a man of many words. I said enough as it is. Where's the kid?" the man asked.

"He should be at one of my houses later on today."

The guy just nodded and then asked for the address. Mr. Mallory gave him the address to the shack. He hoped his niece already came and left, but knowing her, she wouldn't leave without seeing him.

*****

Nicole was tired. Tired of pretending to be in love with someone she didn't love. A part of her wanted the tape to come out or whatever it was Rodney was making a fuss about. She didn't care about the backlash. She didn't care about the supposed humiliation. Everything she did was to please Rodney. She didn't know how much longer she could go on pretending, though. At some point, she would have to set the terms. Either she and Rodney would officially be together, or they weren't. She had no desire to continue this farce with the mayor. It was getting played out, and it was already mentally and emotionally draining.

On her way to her rendezvous with Rodney, Nicole really started to think and wonder how someone was able to record her and Rodney having sex. None of her close friends were bold enough to do such an act. The one friend she had who knew all about Rodney and her wouldn't dare make an attempt. The party had to come through Rodney. It may just be something he had planned. It's a question she wanted the answer to. Why would he record them? Why do so without her permission?

*****

"Hey!"

"Are you looking for someone, ma'am?" the boy asked politely.

"*Ma'am*! I'm not that old. Don't ever use that word with me again. I'm Bernice, Joe's niece."

"Okay. I'm Sincere. Thanks for helping out."

"No prob. Where's my uncle?"

"He won't be back for hours. Are you ready to leave?" Sincere asked, ready to go.

"Why are you in such a hurry? I wanna see my uncle before I go."

"It's best if we leave now. He'll be over to visit next weekend."

"That's a bummer. You got everything you need?"

"Yes, ma'am," Sincere said with a slight grin on his face.

"You're gonna make me knock that grin right off your face," Bernice said, thinking of how good things may actually be.

*****

The Honorable Judge Rodriguez was sitting in her chambers, taking off her robe. Ten years of being a circuit court judge, she never witnessed a person, let alone a female, do what this Yolanda just did. Looking through the girl's files, she saw that prior to last week, she had a clean record; no citations, restraining orders, overdue tickets, criminal history.

"Ms. Dixon, this is not even your client's twenty-one-day arraignment. She was just making an appearance for her new charges, and I already deem her incompetent to be in my courtroom. I'm pretty sure the state won't drop the charges. Are you having a speedy or regular trail?"

"I haven't discussed that with her yet, but more than likely, speedy."

"I'm gonna have a psychologist interview her next week. If things don't go well, she will be placed in mental hospital."

"I understand, Your Honor. I will visit her to see how she's holding up."

"You know we're off the record, Sammie. What's wrong with her?"

"I think a switch got turned on when she got raped. From the information I collected, she was never like this."

"That's sad to hear. I'll help out any way I can."

CHAPTER 21

Feeling Pain

Sincere was more than happy to be getting away from Miami. If he had a choice in the matter, he would move as far as possible. Maybe to California, somewhere.

His dad told him once before, "Normally when things don't go as planned, or the way that it should, don't ever disregard or overlook the situation. Most times, it's nothing. A person forgot or lost track of time. Something came up. A person was distracted. Many non-threatening factors can cause a plan not to go through sometimes. Seldom it's something serious or life-threatening. Whenever you're in a situation where your life is in danger, always expect the worst. If someone doesn't come or call when they should, something went wrong. Don't ever think otherwise."

Mr. Mallory told Sincere that he would call him at 8:00 a.m. That call never came. Mr. Mallory's approximation on things like time were always on point. He was the kind of man to do what he said he was gonna do when he was gonna do it. If he didn't do it, it was because he couldn't. Circumstances that were pertaining to work couldn't be the reason why he didn't make that call. Students used their phones in most classrooms. Teachers occasionally texted or checked their messages. Mr. Mallory would have to step out of the classroom to use his phone. His students would probably make a big deal if they saw him using a phone. Stepping out for a mere minute wasn't difficult at all. Something wasn't right. He felt it.

The drive to Georgia was about a seventeen-hour ride. It probably would've been faster if Bernice decided to go over the speed limit.

"Why do you drive so slow?" Sincere asked.

"I'm not driving slow. I'm a little under the speed limit. Driving fast tend to draw attention."

"If we don't have anything illegal, what difference does it make?" Sincere said.

"It makes a big difference," Bernice replied. "Do you think having something illegal is the only thing to worry about?" she then asked.

Instead of answering her question, Sincere went back to a conversation he had with his father, the first day he was taking driving lessons from him.

"Always remember, it's wise to drive normally on the road. Only speed when it is necessary. Speeding just to be speeding could draw unwanted attention from the police. Doing that is never a good thing," his father said.

"But if I'm not doing anything wrong other than that, it's only a speeding ticket."

"It could be more than just that. Once you get stopped by the police, anything could happen."

"I don't understand, Daddy."

"You see what's going on in the news? With you being black, sometimes that can be a problem. So to avoid certain circumstances, drive the way you should on the road."

"Hello… Are you listening to me?" Bernice asked, bringing Sincere back to the present.

"You're right. I was just thinking of something my father said when I first started to drive. Avoid certain circumstances. Only speed when it is necessary were his exact words."

"Right he is. I thought you had a car," Bernice said.

"I do. I'll get it in a few days. Wanna settle down first and see how things are."

Sincere didn't think bringing all of his belongings, especially his money and guns, was a smart thing to do. With the exception of the $7,500 he brought with him. He kept the rest of the money in the safe house. He left his car at Monica's house. He struggled on whether or not he should take any of his guns with him. It didn't matter where he was at or who he was. Trouble always had a way of popping up.

The siren that was coming from his rear got his attention. He didn't know where in Georgia they were. He was mad at himself for that.

"Always know where you are. It's hard to get out if you don't know how you got in. It's easy to get lost. So whenever you're going somewhere you don't know, pay close attention to the roads and signs," his father said.

Sincere didn't know why they were being stopped by the police. While Bernice was pulling to the curve and keeping her eyes on the rearview mirror, Sincere put the money in his pocket, under his seat.

"Keep your hands on the dashboard. Let me do all the talking," Bernice said. Sincere just nodded his head. "Stay calm."

They both waited patiently as the officer took his time coming to their vehicle.

"What seems to be the problem, Officer?" Bernice asked politely.

"License and registration."

"Yes, sir." Bernice showed the officer what he asked for.

"Step out of the car, young man."

Bernice gave Sincere a look of concern. Sincere did what he was told nervously. This was his first encounter with the police. The officer patted him down, then told him to get back in the car.

"Most black folks should be like you two. Y'all are well trained. Carry on," the officer said as he went on his way.

Bernice was obviously angry about the encounter. It showed in the way she had her jaws set. Sincere realized leaving his guns behind was a great decision. One of them would've been on him.

"Are you okay?" Sincere asked Bernice.

"That man had no reason whatsoever to pull us over," Bernice responded in anger.

"We're black. That's more than enough reason."

"So you know how it is. What you put up under your seat?" Bernice asked, catching Sincere off guard.

"My money," Sincere replied while retrieving it.

"Looks like a lot for your age. Good that cop didn't see that on you."

Sincere was surprised that Bernice didn't question him further on the money. He wondered what she thought of him.

"Since I'm gonna be staying with you, we can take turns paying the rent."

"Boy, you better keep your money," Bernice said with a smile on her face.

"Yes, ma'am," Sincere purposely said, knocking that smile right off her face.

*****

Nicole was furious with Rodney at the moment. He showed a lack of concern or emotion for the way she felt and what she had to put up with over the years for him. It seemed as if all her sacrifices were being done in vain.

"What do you mean it's in everybody's best interest that I stay with him. What about me and what I want?" Nicole found herself pleading.

"What about you? I'm a businessman. You of all people should know that. Everything we got going on was never personal. It always was and always will be business. You know that," Rodney said.

"Busi—ness."

The word could barely come out of her mouth. Nicole was shocked. Nicole was hurt. Anger was the least of her emotions. Pain filled her heart. Pain flooded her thoughts. Pain covered her vision. Even through the pain, she could finally see things clearly. For so many years, she was living in denial. Now it was time to accept the truth; Rodney never loved her. He was only using her. Using her to make money. How didn't she see that?

"Don't make this more than what it is. Don't try to make us more than what we are. You know—"

Before Rodney could say another word, Nicole shot him. Rodney looked at the blood that was coming out of his shirt. Another shot hit him that sent him dropping to the floor.

"Nikki… What are you doing?"

"What I should've done a long time ago."

Nicole came closer and shot him in his stomach once more. Nicole turned her back to him as he coughed up blood. She knew he wasn't dead. No one was gonna come to help him. She was gonna watch him bleed to death.

*****

The kid wasn't at the shack. Nor did he ever show up. Snake knew the teacher was truthful about almost everything he said. The note his sister left confirmed what he told him.

"Call your niece now, to make sure all is well with her and the kid. Don't tip them off or say anything that can make you die a slow death." The teacher nodded, mouthed out the number, and waited. Snake put the phone on speaker.

"Hey, brother," a country-sounding lady said.

"Hey, sis! Did y'all have a safe drive?"

"Outside of being stopped by the police for driving while being black, everything is well," he heard his niece say.

"I wanted to see you before you left."

"Me too. Sincere really wanted to leave. He said you'll be coming up in a couple of days."

"I may not be able to make it. It's a long story. Where's Sincere?" the teacher asked.

"We're on speaker. He hears you."

"Sincere, take us off the speaker."

"What's up!" the kid said.

"The police grabbed me yesterday in school and interrogated me all day and night about Ms. Wright and her daughter. I don't have the slightest clue why they would even ask me about them or suspect that I was at their place," the teacher said.

"So that's why you didn't call."

"Yeah, I was at the police station."

Snake didn't like the conversation the teacher and kid was having. He wanted to disconnect the phone, but the teacher couldn't be that stupid to blatantly crash.

"That's better to hear. I thought something bad happened," the kid said.

"I'm good."

"You coming up soon?"

"It's too risky. Not trying to bring the heat to you. Just be easy, and I'll see you when I can," the teacher said. "I'll be down to get my car in a few days, okay?"

Snake saw the disappointment on the teacher's face. When the kid made that last statement, not once did he try to get the kid to come back down. It was obvious that he was trying to keep him from coming back down.

"What was that about with the police?" Snake asked.

"I had plans to call the kid at 8:00 a.m. yesterday. I wasn't able to do so. It was best for him to know why I didn't." Snake shook his hand and watched the guy. "Let the kid go. You can kill me and let things be."

"It's not about killing you or him," Snake said.

"I got the drive. I can give it to you since all of this is about that."

That statement got Snake's attention. He wondered what the guy was up to. If he knew this was about the drive all along, why prolong everything?

"How do you know about that?" Snake asked with his back turned to the guy.

"When I decided to help the kid. I didn't know how serious the situation was. Once people started dying, it wasn't hard to figure out that the kid had information or something of value. After speaking to the kid about what took place when he left New York, I searched his backpack and found the drive."

"So you know what's in it?" Snake asked.

"Yeah, I guess the people in it are important, if you and others are willing to go to the extreme to get it."

"Did the kid see what was in it?" Snake asked, already knowing the answer.

"No. He thought it was best if he didn't know what was in it."

Snake put a finger up to stop the teacher from talking. He was really disappointed in him. The teacher was cooperative the entire time, and now he decided to be untruthful.

"That's the first lie you told me. I hate when someone lies to me," Snake whispered.

Mr. Mallory never saw the blow coming. He didn't even know what hit him or how it got in the guy's hand. Mr. Mallory felt the blood coming down his chin. The entire left side of his face was on fire.

"It makes no sense to lie now. That drive could've been something the kid's father wanted him to see. Why wouldn't he wanna take a look at what was in it? I really thought you were smarter than that."

Mr. Mallory knew his mistakes. He still felt the need to see if he could keep the kid out of harm's way.

"We still don't know who is on the drive. I'll give it to you. Let the kid live his life."

"Or?" Snake asked, seeing if there was a stipulation that was beneficial to the teacher.

"There's no or. I know you'll find ways to make me give it to you anyways. I'm not trying to make this harder on myself, but the kid is a good kid," Mr. Mallory pleaded.

"Where's the drive?"

"Inside of the fish tank. It's wrapped up real good. So no need to worry about it getting damaged. Dig around the surface. You can't miss it."

Snake did just that and found it in seconds. Snake knew if he was in the teacher's position, he would've made an extra copy.

"Where's the copy?" Snake asked the surprised teacher.

Mr. Mallory didn't expect to hear that. The pain that he still felt across his left cheeks didn't make him hesitate with an answer.

"It's inside my tablet."

"Inside?"

"You have to get it open. Unloose the screws."

Mr. Mallory wondered if the guy would ask for another copy. He never did. The guy checked both drives and then sat on the couch with his eyes closed. Mr. Mallory knew the guy wasn't asleep. His eyes may very well be closed, but he knew the guy's ears were wide open.

*****

Hot Rod knew his life was coming to an end. He didn't expect anyone to come to his aid. Only he and Nicole were aware of their current location. It was unlikely that someone would come to his rescue. By the time someone arrived, it would be too late. He couldn't believe it; out of all people, it happened to be a woman that was gonna take his life. A woman he happened to know for years. As his life was draining away, he reflected back on what he could've done better to avoid his current fate. He went back to a conversation he had with Snake a while back.

"Kid, I'm telling you. This is the ultimate lick. Once Nikki gets in position, we're gonna be set," Hot Rod remembered saying.

"Everything good has a flip side to it," Snake replied.

"What do you mean?"

"This woman is in love with you, not him. How long do you expect her to keep this up and go through this?"

"As long as I tell her," Hot Rod had stated.

"I hope it doesn't come to it, but there could be a time that she's gonna want more. The part-time thing may not always be good enough."

"She knows this is business."

"For your sake, I hope she does. If you are smart, once you get what you need, get rid of her. She could be a problem," Snake said.

"Why are you so hard on women?" Hot Rod remembered asking, thinking Snake was crazy.

"They'll take your life without you seeing it coming."

Looking back, Hot Rod wished he would've taken Snake's advice. He never saw things coming. As he was getting ready to draw his last breath, he saw Nikki sitting on a chair, smoking a cigarette. When did she start smoking? She stared at him with a smile on her face. He had no strength to speak, no power to hold on. He welcomed death.

*****

Yolanda was in the back of her cell, waiting for the cell extraction team to come in. The guards were required to have face shields, a shield, and rubber boots on. It would've been hard for Yolanda to determine who Ms. Bush was. The day before, an extraction team ran up in a girl's room to take her out. While the guards were removing their face shields, Yolanda notice that Ms. Bush was the only one wearing black rubber boots. Everybody else had on powder blue. Getting Ms. Bush would be easy, Yolanda thought.

When the eruption and noise started, Yolanda was sitting in the corner. The noise indicated that the extraction team was there. When the group arrived at her door, everything got silent. Then Yolanda heard doors being kicked. She knew how dirty the officers played. While a group of guards were in front of her cell with a camera, a couple guards were down the wing kicking on the doors. It made it appear on camera that Yolanda was the one causing a disturbance.

"Inmate, I'm giving you a direct order to stop kicking on the door. Cease your disruptive behavior right now," a corporal said. The banging down the wing continued.

Yolanda knew it was pointless to argue her case. It was better for her to remain at the rear of her cell. Going to the door and pleading her case of not kicking on the door was what they wanted her to do. All the camera would show was a female starting trouble.

"Inmate, if you don't cease your disturbance of normal operation, we'll be forced to come in," the corporal said as the kicking never stopped.

Yolanda never knew how crooked most correctional officers were. They could literally kill someone, beat someone, and get away with it. It was wrong.

"This is your last and final warning. Stop kicking on the door," the corporal said again. The kicking continued.

Yolanda braced herself and got ready. It was good they weren't allowed to spray psych inmates in their cells anymore. That would've made it harder to get Ms. Bush. When they burst through the door, Yolanda was happy to see the black rubber boots up front. Before she had a chance to pounce on Ms. Bush and rip her face shield off and bite her nose, a big male guard pinned her to the ground, then drove his knees on her neck to hold her down.

"Stop resisting, inmate. Hold still," the big guard falsely said for the camera.

The black rubber boot kicked her in the stomach. Before Yolanda had a chance to scream in pain, another boot landed on top of her head.

*****

Sincere had doubts. Something about what Mr. Mallory said didn't sit well with him. He stated that it was too risky for him to make the trip up north. It was impossible for anyone to follow him on a short drive. A longer drive was not even a thought. There could be no risk in that. Unless there was something Mr. Mallory couldn't say. Nah, Sincere was overthinking things. Paranoia has been setting in a lot lately.

"I know we hardly know each other. Just to let you know, for the most part, I won't bother you. All I ask of you is…go to school. Don't bring that poison into my house, and you better not bring any fast girls in my room," Bernice said.

"I love school. So going is not a problem. Not only will I keep girls out of your room, none will be coming into our home, and what's this poison you're talking about?"

"Crack. Cocaine. Heroine."

"My dad told me a long time ago to stay far away from drugs," Sincere said.

"Great advice. Stay far away from it. On another note, if people ask, what am I gonna be to you?"

"You're the adult. That's for you to figure out," Sincere joked.

"How does Auntie B sound?"

"Never had one of those."

"You do now."

Sincere was aware that things were never the way it appeared to be. Things between him and Bernice can change drastically any minute. If—a big if—things stayed this way, it would be great.

CHAPTER 22

Bad and Good News

Nicole never left the apartment Rodney had rented in Staten Island. Her prints were all over the place. If she left now, questions may be asked later. It was in her best interest to get things cleaned up without any evidence leading back to her. Rodney told her they were the only two who knew about the place. At least that's what he claimed. His words couldn't be trusted anymore. After thinking over the matter, she came up with a great solution to the problem at hand and the possibility of problems that could arrive in the future.

From Nicole's recollection, Rodney seemed to be serious about that film of them having sex coming out. Nicole analyzed the situation, then came to the conclusion that the best thing she could do was tell her husband, Vincent, that she was forced and blackmailed to have sex with Rodney. Of course she would lie about the amount of years. She would tell him the blackmailing started last fall, when she was out with her friends. She had a bit too much to drink. Her friends left with random guys they met. She ran into Rodney. He was a gentleman and offered to take her home. She fell asleep in the car. The following morning when she woke up, he had all kinds of demands for her. The main one was trying to find out when the NYPD made a huge drug bust. That was also a lie. Nicole never really knew Rodney's main motive or objective. All she knew was enough was enough. She would no longer be enslaved to a man. She did what needed to be done, and that was killing Rodney.

*****

Yolanda woke up in the infirmary all bruised and battered up. The nurses refused to give her any medical attention. They walked by her bunk and didn't even acknowledge her calls or cries for assistance. She now knew firsthand that medical staff covered up the physical abuse the correctional officers handed out.

The whole system was corrupted. Ms. Owens, Ms. Walkins, Ms. Presley, and Ms. Bishop were added to the list of people she planned to kill. She would find out where each one of them stayed and track them down. But first and foremost, she had to find a way to get out of jail.

The next two days, Yolanda made no request or even bothered any of the officers or nurses. She stayed quiet and did everything they wanted her to do. On her third day in the infirmary, a nurse she never saw on the previous shifts allowed her to make a phone call. She used that call to schedule a visit with her lawyer. Evidently the new nurse, Ms. Dennis, was just doing her job properly, which would end up harming her coworkers.

*****

Sincere was back in Miami. Instead of stopping at the shack first, like Bernice insisted, he decided to go to Monica's place to get his vehicle.

"I'm gonna catch up with you later. Gotta say some goodbyes," Sincere said with a smile.

"Don't let them hold you too long." Bernice fired with a grin.

Sincere wasn't surprised at all to see that Monica had the house to herself. He thought she would be excited and full of joy to see him, but excitement wasn't the energy he was receiving from her.

"We need to talk," Was the first thing she said. No hug or kiss.

His mother once told him, when he had an argument with a girl in the fourth grade, "Anytime a girl or a woman tells you they need to talk, expect some bad news you probably wouldn't like, or she might have something serious, real serious, to talk to you about."

Sincere also remembered watching *Think Like a Man*, and something similar was said about them four dreaded words. Whatever the case may be, it couldn't be that serious, he thought.

"I'm pregnant," Monica said as she sat down. "No one knows but us. I don't even know if I should tell my parents."

Sincere was speechless. That's the last thing he expected. Him, at a young age, becoming a father, it's a responsibility he knew he couldn't shy away from.

"Son, in life, there's decisions we're gonna have to live with. Decisions we won't be able to take back or change. When I first got your mother pregnant, I didn't think I was ready to be a father. Having you was the best thing that happened to me. I would more than likely be dead now. Becoming a father made me better and gave me purpose. If you ever find yourself in that situation, you better man up," his father said.

"What if I don't love the girl, Daddy?"

"You don't have to love her. You respect her. It's the child that needs loving."

Sincere remembered that conversation with his father like it was yesterday. He made a promise to himself that very moment that if he ever got a girl pregnant, no matter what girl, he would do the right thing.

"Wow!" Sincere exclaimed.

"So you're not happy?" Monica said in disappointment.

"It's not that. I always wanted to be a father. This just came out of nowhere," Sincere said, scratching his head.

"When two people have unprotected sex as much as we did, it's highly possible that this would happen," Monica said shyly.

"This changes a lot," Sincere said, pacing the floor.

"What do you mean?" Monica asked out of curiosity.

"I can't stay down here in Miami. It won't be good for us."

"Wherever you go, we can go with you," Monica said with conviction.

"What would your parents say?"

"They wouldn't even know that I'm gone," Monica said with a forced laugh.

"Seriously."

"I'll just tell them the truth. That'll probably push me further away from them," Monica said with a pinch of sadness in her voice.

"Or it can bring you closer to them."

"I doubt it."

"Listen, Monica, I'll come back in a week to get you. We'll schedule a day for me to meet your parents. Break the news to them. Let's see how they'll take it."

"I won't be surprised if I'm on the streets before you get back," Monica said.

*****

Nicole was at home, in her husband's arms, crying. Vincent bought and sucked up everything she said. He didn't question or doubt a single word. The lies fell off her lips so easily. She told each one with persuasion. Vincent wiped her tears and assured her with soothing words.

"He can't hurt you no more," Vincent kept saying.

Before Nicole went to bed, Vincent asked for the location of the body. This was the whole purpose of telling him. She knew he would do anything to not have her implicated to the body. When Vincent left, Nicole smiled, then fell asleep. No nightmares came. Sleep came with ease. In fact, she slept like a baby.

*****

Samantha was heated when her client Yolanda lifted her shirt and showed her all the bruises around her stomach and back. She promised Yolanda that she would come back tomorrow to take pictures.

"How are you gonna do that?" Yolanda asked.

"Let me handle this. Just keep your mouth shut and don't talk to no one."

Yolanda seemed to have her head on straight, Samantha thought. Sneaking her phone in wasn't gonna be difficult. Every time she came in, they hardly searched her. So bringing it in was gonna be fairly easy. Once the pictures were taken, she would file a lawsuit for excessive abuse by a correctional officer and misconduct and malpractice by medical officials. This could turn up to be real good for Yolanda.

The following day, Samantha was inside Judge Rodriguez's chambers with the state prosecutor that was assigned to the Yolanda's case.

"They beat her up and got away with it," Samantha said.

"How did you get in possession of those photos?" the prosecutor asked.

"I took them with my phone."

"You know it's a crime to have any cellular device inside a correctional facility."

"Are you serious, Jackson? There's no audience or jury here. It's just us. There's no one here for you to impress. They've been beating her up for no reason." Samantha pointed out.

"That's less than what she deserves. This client of yours assaulted an officer and murdered her roommate."

"The department made a mistake by placing someone in her room. She was supposed to be housed alone."

"So that's the justification for killing someone," Jackson said.

"Jackson, please. We're not even here for that."

"You and I know this has everything to do with her charges."

"Your Honor, if the state wanna just focus on the criminal charges of my client, we are gonna press charges on every staff member who was involved in the abuse of my client. We are also gonna file a lawsuit," Samantha said.

"Is this what you want, Jackson?" the judge asked him.

"What is it that you're proposing, Ms. Dixon?" Jackson asked with a look of defiance on his face.

"Get rid of the murder rap and give her six months in a mental facility for the battery on a Leo."

"Are you crazy!" Jackson fired, jumping out of his seat.

"Look, Jackson. You've seen many cases with defendants that are incompetent. The most she'll probably get is ten years if we go along with this. Let's do both of us a favor for a change and save the paperwork." Samantha laid out.

"I want a five-year conviction for the murder."

"No deal, Jack."

"Eighteen mandatory and two-year papers. That's my last offer."

"Let me present the plea to my client," Samantha said.

"So if she takes the deal, the other case won't go civil?"

"That's part of the deal."

"Okay."

"Jackson, why are you protecting these officers?" Samantha asked.

"I could care less about them. One of the nurses involved is my sister-in-law."

"She needs to do her job correctly. Your Honor, for the safety of my client's life. I'm requesting that she be transferred to TGK with better treatment and supervision until her conviction."

"Is that all? Are you guys done here?"

"Yes, Your Honor," Jackson and Samantha said in unison.

*****

Sergeant Mc Knight got a call from the police chief to clean up a mess in Staten Island. Anytime the chief used the words *clean up* or *cleaners*, more times than not, a dead body was involved.

Mc Knight was the leader of the NYPD drug task force. He had a team of crooked cops who robbed, killed, and ran the streets of New York. Drug dealers made way more money than police officers. That was unfair. Officers took more risk and put their lives on the line every day, and they were underpaid. Mc Knight always liked the finer things in life. Since high school, he had lived a lavish life. With the internal affairs keeping a close eye on the department, he was no longer flashy or flamboyant. Nonetheless, he was making plenty of money.

When Mc Knight got to the address, his mouth dropped to the floor. Lying in front of him, in a pool of blood, was Hot Rod. He and Hot Rod were in business for ten years now. Hot Rod paid very well. Mc Knight didn't even wanna know what happened or who was involved. He went back to his van and took out the plastic and carpet. He wrapped Hot Rod up in it and left. He called the second team to let them know he was finished. Their job was to bleach and sanitize the place thoroughly.

After digging up the body, Mc Knight made the call he was contemplating about making.

"Speak."

"Don't question me about who, what, when, where, or how. Just know that this is facts. I'm sending you a picture just in case you have your doubts. I'm sorry, man," Mc Knight said and ended the call.

*****

Monica was delighted in so many ways. Her plan worked. Deep down, she knew was wrong for the deception, but she had no other choice. Moving away was perfect. It was nearly impossible for her lie to catch up with her. She would not do anything to make Sincere ever consider taking a paternity test. The problem she had was her parents. How would they accept the news? Would they really just let her pack her bags and leave? Where would she stay? Sincere will figure everything out eventually. In the meantime, she had to convince her parents that it was better for her to go away. The transition should make things better for everybody. Wherever her parents went every weekend, they could just stay there.

Right after Sincere left, Monica started to pack her clothes and other items that were valuable. The thought of calling and informing Sandra and Lisa never crossed her mind. All they would do is throw shade. Truth is, she didn't want either one of them being suspicious. By the time they found out, she would be long gone and at least six months pregnant.

Thinking back on the competition they had a few months ago, Monica was proud of herself. She knew all along, Sincere was gonna be hers. Now absolutely nothing could ever come between them. *Nothing.*

*****

"I got some good news for you," Samantha told Yolanda on their next visit.

"Spill it."

"The state is offering you eighteen months for everything. At the end of the day, you're gonna do what you want, but considering the circumstances, that's a great deal."

"I'm not supposed to be in jail. I have to get out. There's things that I really need to get done," Yolanda said with a blank stare.

"I'm gonna see what I can do. This prosecutor is hard."

"If he knows what's best for him, he better soften up, or he'll be on the list."

Samantha didn't understand what Yolanda was talking about. Knowing what she knew about Jackson's sister-in-law, she was confident that she could get Yolanda a sweeter deal. She may even be able to get her out before the year was out. Jackson would definitely hold a grudge about this, but she could care less how he felt in the matter.

CHAPTER 23

FALLING DOWN

A lady was knocking on the teacher's front door. Snake already knew who it was. She called earlier, stating that she would be arriving in a few hours. She then called back asking him why he left. Snake knew at the moment that the place they were currently in was probably an unlisted address. After giving the lady the address, they waited once again.

"Who all knows about this place?" Snake had to ask.

"Just a couple of people."

"The kid being one of them, right?"

"Yeah."

Twenty minutes later, after that first call, that knock came. Snake expected to see the kid with her, but he wasn't in sight.

"Tell her the door is open," Snake instructed the teacher. The teacher hesitated yet did as he was told.

"It's unlocked. Come in."

The lady took a few steps inside, then dropped her phone when Snake came into view with his gun in hand.

"Take a seat by your uncle and don't make a sound," Snake said.

"Bernice, do exactly what he tells you to do." The teacher chipped in.

"Where's the boy?" Snake asked.

"I dropped him off at one of his girls' houses," the lady replied with a look of confusion on her face.

"Will he be here shortly?"

"I don't know. He never said anything about that. What's up with all of the questions?"

Snake ignored the woman's attitude and sarcasm. Like most women, she didn't know better. Her life was in his hands, and she acted as if she was the one in control. Typical female behavior.

"Woman, don't lie to me and watch your tone." Snake hissed.

"B, just be honest with him. No matter how you try to protect him, it's gonna be fruitless," the teacher said, trying to ease the tension.

"Fruitless. Who is this guy anyway? What the hell does he want with us? We're not telling him anything."

Right when Snake decided to end the woman's life, his phone sounded. Only three people knew the number.

"Speak," Snake stated.

After gathering the information from the caller, Snake checked the screen and viewed the photo the caller sent.

Hot Rod was dead. The news happened to be a bit shocking to Snake. The timing of it was not something Snake could question. The hit could've come from anywhere. From anyone. Whoever had their hands in it, Snake would give them special attention. Being a loyal friend meant not letting the one you love die in vain. If he ever found out who did it, they would regret the day they were born.

Snake knew death was promised to everyone. This wasn't something he expected. Not Hot Rod. Snake didn't believe in coincidence. The timing of the call he just received when he was about to kill the lady didn't save her life. It only prolonged her death with Hot Rod being dead. It couldn't hurt him if the drive got in the wrong hands. Yet loyalty was everything. Snake told his friend he was gonna get the drive and get rid of the kid. He was halfway there.

"Is something wrong?" the teacher asked.

"Yeah." Snake fired a single shot that hit the lady in her right kneecap. "This lady has a slick mouth and doesn't seem to be taking me seriously? When will the boy get here?"

"Fuck you! I'm not a snitch. You're gonna have to kill me."

Snake looked at the woman and saw the fierce look in her eyes. She was definitely a strong woman. Nonetheless, there were still no exceptions. If he wanted to break her and make her talk, he could do that easily, but he didn't have the time. He shot her in her left kneecap.

"Please, man. Stop! Just take my life," the teacher said.

Without hesitation, Snake did just that. As the teacher's body slumped on the couch, Snake picked up the phone the lady previously dropped and tossed it to her.

"Tell the kid to get his ass over here," Snake demanded.

The lady stared at Snake in anger. Then instantly she reached for the phone the best way that she could.

"Sincere, run! Go back to my house. Don't come here!" The lady screamed into the phone.

Without a second thought, Snake ended her life with a single shot to the head.

*****

Detective Strong knew something was odd about one of the teachers he had spoken to. His demeanor was too calm compared to the other teachers he questioned. The fact that he didn't show up to work ever since Detective Strong paid the school a visit said a lot. This Mr. Mallory obviously knew more than he let on. Immediately after leaving the school, Strong made his way to Mr. Mallory's place of residence.

Detective Strong arrived at Mr. Mallory's address witnessing a man sneaking to the back of the house. He quickly pulled out his revolver and headed in the same direction he saw the unknown man go to. When Strong hit the corner with his gun drawn, the man he saw was trying to go inside the backdoor.

"Freeze! Put your hands in the air and stay still," Detective Strong said strongly. The man looked astonished to be caught in the act. He did as he was told, though.

"This is a mistake, sir. A friend of mine stays here," the unknown man said.

"That's a classic line. Tell that BS to someone else."

"Listen, asshole. Joe Mallory stays here. I haven't heard from him in a week. Something is wrong. That's why I'm checking his place," the guy said.

"You know Mr. Mallory?"

"Of course I do."

"Turn around and cuff up."

The unknown guy thought Detective Strong was born yesterday. Getting someone's name and address wasn't a tall task. These burglars really thought they were smart. Detective Strong wasn't gonna let him being disrespected slide either.

"You're making a huge mistake. By the way, let me see your badge," the unknown guy requested.

"Shut the *F* up. Before I shut you up."

Detective Strong handcuffed the guy and placed him in the back of his sedan. Instead of questioning the guy, Strong opted to check out the house. He went to the back of the house and picked the lock. After surveying the house and seeing that it was empty, he wondered where Mr. Mallory was. It didn't look like the house had someone in it in months. Heading back to his vehicle, Detective Strong was surprised to see the back seat vacant. Missing also from his vehicle was his police badge.

*****

The gunfire Sincere heard before the call went dead could only mean one thing—Bernice was dead, or she got shot, and more than likely, Mr. Mallory was in the same boat. It was evident that Bernice saved his life. He was minutes away from the shack that Mr. Mallory owned. Sincere made a U-turn and went back to the safe house.

Everyone who got too close to him and tried to help him got hurt or ended up dead. He could no longer be the cause of death to another individual. It just wasn't fair for people he hardly knew to make such a great sacrifice for him.

Contemplating about the entire situation that led up to this point, Sincere's thoughts kept drifting back to his time with Monica a while back. His father once said, "If you can't shake a thought, or if something keeps popping in your head for no apparent reason, revisit that entire situation and analyze it thoroughly. You could very much be missing or seeing through something that's important."

Sincere then thought of a conversation he had with his mother pertaining to pregnancy.

"Sincere, with these fast girls nowadays, you have to be extra careful. Females will lie to you in a heartbeat just to get their way. Don't ever fully trust a woman. It may hurt your girl's feelings, but always get a paternity test. One of these no-good girls may try to tie you down with a baby that's not even yours."

"Doesn't a paternity test have to be taken after the baby is born?"

"Yes, sweetie."

"How do girls know they are pregnant," Sincere remembered asking.

"They normally take a pregnancy test, but if a girl misses their period, more than likely, they are pregnant. Within a month, she should know."

Sincere started calculating the time frame when he started having sex with Monica. From what he recalled, they only had unprotected sex once, and that was two weeks ago, when he woke up to her riding him. Could that be the night she had gotten pregnant?

"Just because a girl is pregnant doesn't necessarily mean it's yours. A female can get anyone to cum in her," his mother said.

Sincere decided to pay Monica another visit. It was kind of crazy. Through the grief and pain and running from someone that was trying to take his life, he was thinking about a chick. Not on no emotional lovey-dovey tip but on some guarding-my-future tip, his mother warned him about females trying to tie him down. He wasn't going to put anything past Monica or no other girl. That seed of doubt that was planted in his thoughts about Monica's pregnancy had Sincere hoping Monica was being deceitful. He liked to be alone. Time would reveal the truth shortly, hopefully.

*****

Todd rushed to his home, changed his clothes, and quickly made his way to Joe's other home. After no one responded to his knocks on the door, he checked the knob, and it turned. He pushed the door open and fell to the floor when he saw the bodies in blood. He grabbed his phone and called the authorities to report the two deaths.

A detective took Todd to the police station for more questions. Three different officers asked him the same questions in different ways for the past thirty minutes. Now they have taken him to their turf, Todd didn't like that one bit. These other questions could've been asked anywhere but the police station. Cops had the tendency to take suspects in for questioning. But after seeing that asshole who placed cuffs on him earlier, with two women in suits, he knew this more than about Joe's and Bernice's death. One of the women placed the asshole in a separate room. After doing so, they both approached him.

"Were you apprehended by a detective earlier?" one of the ladies with a birthmark on her forehead asked.

"Yes. Why?"

"We are the ones who will be asking the questions. You understand that?" The prettier one jumped in.

"Yes."

"Did you steal the detective badge and escaped while in his custody?" Birthmark asked.

"Badge I know nothing about, and no one placed me in custody."

"Are you saying no one placed hand restraints on you?" The prettier one added.

"Yes. Look, I'm guilty of nothing. That asshole didn't read me my rights or show me any credentials. For all I know, I was being kidnapped," Todd stated.

"Why were you at Mr. Mallory's home?" the prettier one asked.

"He's a long-time friend. I haven't seen or heard from him in a week. So I was worried about him. I went to the first location and got no answer. That's when that asshole started harassing me, assuming I was some kind of thief."

"Where did you go after leaving his vehicle?" Birthmark asked.

"I went home to change and to get my gun. I have a permit for it."

"Why change clothes?" Birthmark asked.

"To conceal my weapon better."

"Where did you go next?" the prettier one asked.

"To my friend's second home. That's where I found the bodies."

"Can anyone support what you're saying?" Birthmark asked.

"Ask the neighbors."

"Which location?'

"Both of them."

Detective Strong didn't expect to see the unknown guy at the police station. Was he working with internal affairs? Was he at the teacher's house and plotted to set him up? Most importantly, how did they know about his involvement in the missing money that was confiscated six months ago from a drug bust?

"Mr. Strong, did you read Mr. Sorenson his rights?" Birthmark asked after she and her partner entered the room.

"I never had the chance to do so," Strong said, knowing that didn't sound right.

"Did you show your badge or let it be known that you were a detective?" Birthmark asked while her partner was taking notes.

"Not, but I—" He was cut off.

"Mr. Strong, did you alert or call for backup after placing Mr. Sorenson in the back of your vehicle when you went inside Mr. Mallory's home?"

"No."

"Did you have a warrant to go inside Mr. Mallory's home?"

As the question poured in, Detective Strong knew he was gonna be suspended or terminated. His badge being taken by that unknown guy was gonna result in his suspension. The missing money, if evidence led to him, would get him terminated.

As the unknown guy passed by the room, they locked eyes for a brief second. The guy had the nerve to smirk at him. Detective Strong got out of his seat and rushed the prick. No one even tried to stop him. It's like everything was staged. Strong lifted the guy off the floor and shoved him hard against the wall.

"You think this is funny! You think this is a game!" Strong yelled.

"Mr. Strong, release him, or I'll handcuff you myself," Birthmark stated.

Detective Strong let the unknown guy go and stormed out of the station. He ignored the calls from the ladies from the internal affairs to return. He and the female that was assigned to the property room had to get their stories right.

"Mr. Sorenson, you're free to leave. I do wanna know how you got out of these handcuffs," the prettier one asked.

"If I tell you, I would have to kill you," he said with a smile. "Seriously, when Joe and I were in the army, I specialized in picking and breaking through locks."

CHAPTER 24

THE ESCAPE

Snake didn't like the way he handled the situation with the teacher and his niece. When it came to taking someone's life, Snake did his best to take it with precision. Once he received the call from that NYPD cop that was under Hot Rod's payroll, he acted out of anger. He, of all people, knew the dangers of making choices without thought. Choices that were fueled by fury. He should've known better. It proved that he was human and had emotions like everyone else. The loss of Hot Rod hurt him deeply. Hot Rod was practically the only family he had left. The only person he gave his loyalty to. Now he had no one.

Snake went back to the place he was temporarily staying in. While cleaning it up, he felt highly disappointed in himself. Part of his job was to kill the kid. Now the kid was getting away scot-free for the moment. It was the first time he actually failed while doing an assignment. Snake had sources and plenty of money to track the kid down. It may take time. The desire was just no longer there. Every day Snake woke up with an itch. The thrill of living on the edge kept him focused. It gave his life purpose. Now that itch was gone. There was nothing to look forward to. A long time ago, Snake told himself the day he lost that itch was the day he was gonna pursue another lifestyle. Now the question was: how would he live his life?

*****

Lisa went to Monica's house to check up on her. It was unlike Monica to not pick up her phone or to not show up at a place or event she scheduled for them to meet since Lisa had known Monica. That never happened. So something was definitely wrong.

Lisa knew Monica had to be home. Seeing her father's car in the driveway was a good sign. With Monica's mother's car gone, that usually meant her parents weren't home. Monica answered the door on the first knock. Monica was either expecting her, or she was looking out for her widow.

"What are you doing here?" Monica asked Lisa in surprise.

"I should be asking you that."

Lisa noticed that Monica stood in the doorway, not giving her access to enter the house. The slut stood her up because she had a boy at her house. How could she?

"Who's in here with you?" Lisa asked, trying to look inside.

"No one. Why do you think someone's here?"

"You're blocking the doorway. It's obvious someone's in here."

"I'm home alone. Sorry. I have a lot on my mind. Come in… Oh shoot. We were supposed to do the photo shoots and audition today. I'm so sorry, Lisa," Monica stated.

"It's cool. Get fresh. We can still make it."

"I'm sorry, but my parents are sending me away to my aunt's house. They no longer want me to stay here. I have to finish packing up," Monica lied.

Lisa looked at Monica and didn't believe a word she was saying. Monica was hiding something. Being around someone for so long, there's things that just stick out, like Monica avoiding to make eye contact. If her parents were really sending her away, why not pick up the phone? Why not tell your friends? Lisa wasn't slow.

"That's BS. You were never good at trying to lie to me. I'm not Sandra, and you know that. So spill it," Lisa demanded.

Monica hesitated, then stated, "I'm pregnant."

"Oh my god! Who's the lucky man?" Lisa asked in excitement.

"Sincere."

The smile Lisa just had a second ago turned quickly into a frown.

*****

Detective Strong had been in the department long enough to know when the internal affairs had someone under investigation, they already had all the facts they needed. They took their time with each case because they knew, more times than not, the person they were investigating would incriminate himself/herself more. The department hardly ever charged one of their own for a crime. The worst they would do is fire him.

Strong was done with being underpaid and fighting a war that had no ending. In fact, the war on drugs and with criminals was overrated. Politicians and federal agencies were no different than those they were trying to incarcerate. They did their crimes on a higher scale. Everyone was a criminal, even the president. Strong had it with the good-versus-bad speeches. He had it with the Miami-Dade Police Department. He intended to book a ticket to Columbia first thing in the morning, online. With the amount of money he had in his possession, he could live life.

As Detective Strong was making preparations to go to bed, his first door get kicked in by a group of officers he never saw before.

"Lay your ass down. Don't do nothing stupid," a sergeant he wasn't familiar with, said.

The two ladies from earlier casually walked in with smiles on their face. Detective Strong regretted coming back home. He should've gone to a hotel. He had nothing of importance at his house.

"Mrs. Taylor, read Mr. Strong his rights," Birthmark said, widening her smile.

Taylor was the last person Strong expected to see. She was the one who inventoried all confiscated items. She was the only one who knew that he stole some of the money. Why did she wait all this time to turn on him? He should've killed her when he had a chance. Witnesses, no matter who they were, were never good. Another officer, Strong saw, read him his rights. They placed handcuffs on him and escorted him to one of the police cars.

*****

Sincere noticed Lisa's sister's car out front in Monica's driveway. Instead of pulling his car in front of her house, he parked it down the street and walked the rest of the way. Whoever entered the house last or departed from the door never closed it. Sincere walked in to two voices arguing.

"That's not Sincere's baby," Lisa said in anger.

"You're just jealous it wasn't you he chose." Monica shot back.

"You told me yourself during summer break, every time y'all had sex, he used a condom." Lisa pointed out.

"Sweetheart, that was during our challenge. For the past two weeks, why you think I've been avoiding y'all? All we've been doing is having unprotected sex," Monica lied.

Lisa got quiet for some reason. Sincere inched closer to where the sound of their voices were coming from. He now could see them. Monica held a smile of triumph on her face. At the moment, she really felt like she bested her friend. Then Lisa started shaking her head.

"You lying conniving whore," Lisa said out of nowhere.

"I am pregnant, and Sincere's the father."

"Our periods come two to five days apart every time, and it's not due until two weeks from now. So how do you even know you're pregnant?" Lisa pointed out, stating facts that Monica apparently overlooked.

"I know I'm pregnant for him," Monica stated as the tears started coming down her face.

"Why are you crying?"

"Because you don't believe me."

"You better tell me the truth, or I will call him now and tell him myself," Lisa said with a stern expression.

"He could be the father. I'm not sure," Monica slipped up and said.

"He either is or he isn't. You're not even positively sure that you are pregnant. Your period might still come." Lisa said. Monica wiped her eyes.

"Sincere and I are moving. It's best for you to stay out of my way and out of my business," Monica said, getting serious.

"Or else?" Lisa asked.

"Get out of my house!"

"I know every guy you slept with. Every single one. I will call all of them to see if you've been hoeing around. If so, Sincere will know what kind of slut you truly are," Lisa said, getting ready to leave.

Sincere quickly stepped back and was about to run out when he heard Monica's voice. He stayed still.

"I'll give you $5,000 right now if you don't say nothing. Please keep this between us."

Sincere couldn't believe his ears. He almost got tricked into believing he had a girl pregnant. Monica really had him fooled. If he never decided to ear hustle on the conversation Monica and Lisa were having, he would've stayed in the blind. Her plan would've worked. She would deny everything to the bus stop. The voice of his mother was loud and clear in his ears.

"Females can't be trusted. Trust me, I know. This is coming from one."

Even the advice and words from his father were ringing true once again. A month before his parents' death.

His father told him, "You can love a woman, but don't ever put all your trust in one. The way a female feels today can easily change tomorrow. Females live and make decisions by the moment. It's hard to understand why they do some of the stuff that they do. Never forget. Many men lost their life or their money for trusting a woman more than they should."

"You trust Mommy, don't you?" Sincere remembered asking.

"What part are you not listening to, son? I love your mom with all my heart, but my trust has its limit."

"I don't understand. You either trust her or you don't."

"When you get older, certain pictures will become a lot clearer to you. Just understand this. Females always do what's in their best interest, and what's best for them may just be something that will bring you pain."

Sincere was glad that the truth was out. He quietly walked out of Monica's house. There was no need to hear anymore. He went to his vehicle and headed back to the safe house. His mind was set on a plan for his escape to a better living.

*****

Yolanda accepted the deal at a mental rehabilitation center for some months. Before she got transferred, her lawyer told her about the death of her brother. It didn't bother her as much as Ms. Dixon thought it would. Her brother got everything he deserved. It was partially his fault that her life turned out the way that it did. He was never there to protect her. He wasn't even there recently. Yolanda, assumed Ms. Dixon, hardly knew her brother. He was basically a stranger that was trying to put on makeup for lost time. There was and will never be any tears about his death.

Yolanda intended to use her time to think of ways to get all the people that played a part in bringing her pain. She first had to find a way to not take the psych medication she was required to take. She wasn't trying to go crazy for real. She had everything under control. Only a fool took stuff that was created in a lab.

"Behave yourself. You will be out real soon, and I'll set you up with a job once you're released," Ms. Dixon stated.

"Thanks but I already have a profession. I will start taking it seriously after my release."

"Okay. You have my number if you need anything."

Yolanda went back to her cell. Four thousand three hundred and thirty hours from today, she would be free.

*****

Vincent was a bit upset that Rodney's body was found so quickly. In a sense, it didn't matter. Nothing was gonna trace the death to his wife. He made sure he had all corners covered. He would do any and everything to protect his wife from any harm as a husband. That was his duty and responsibility.

Vincent decided to leave his office early today. He had a special night planned for his wife. This was surely gonna be a night to remember. He had a limousine driver as a chaperone. A penthouse suite at the finest hotel in the city. Rose petals on the mattress, with Nicole's favorite appetizers on the cabinet. The room service woman already paid to serve their meals once they arrived and present Nicole with a $200,000 watch. Vincent was pulling all the strings to please the only woman he truly loved.

Vincent and Nicole were waiting out front of their home. Vincent didn't know what was taking the limo driver so long to come. He paid him to be here at 6:50 p.m. It was a little past 7:00 p.m. now. As soon as Vincent picked up his phone, the limo arrived. Vincent already had his mind up. He was gonna deduct the limo driver's payment. Not only for coming late but also for not coming out and opening the door for them. Being the mayor, he was due some respect. The limo driver had this coming. Once the night was over with, Vincent was gonna have him dealt with, but now, he would enjoy his time with his wife.

"This is so lovely, Vince. I have a feeling this is gonna be the best time of my life," Nicole stated as she read the card that was laid on the seat for her.

"Maybe not the best, but one of the best. I have something better in mind next week and the week after," Vincent said, turning up the charm.

"Love, I appreciate every—"

Nicole's words were covered up by her own moans. A television neither of them noticed at first came on, showing the footage of Nicole being pounded by Hot Rod and loving every minute of it. Vincent knew it wasn't an act, especially with her requesting more. Nicole tried her best to turn the TV off. The volume just kept getting louder and louder. Then it went on mute. Vincent just watched his beloved wife on the screen enjoying having sex with someone she claimed was blackmailing her. Someone she killed to hide the truth.

Vincent was heartbroken. He didn't know what to say. He couldn't believe what he was seeing.

"Baby, it's not what you think." Nicole started.

"Shut up and watch the film," Vincent said.

After watching the entire sexual act between his wife and Rodney, the volume came back on. Nicole tried to break the TV, but Vincent held her down as her voice filled the limo.

"When are you gonna take me away from him. You know it's you and only you I love," Nicole told Hot Rod.

"Just be patient. Things will work itself out during the next election."

"I'm tired of being with him. He's not half the man you are."

The TV went blank, and the window separating the driver to the back seat came down. A guy threw Vincent a gun. Nicole looked at the unknown guy as if she recognized who he was.

"You have the truth about your wife," the guy said and left.

Vincent picked up the gun and just looked at it. He would never kill or do anything to harm his wife. No matter what she did, he would always love her. The fact that she didn't share the same sentiment was extremely hurtful. He could not live knowing that the woman he gave his all to didn't love him. Vincent placed the gun to his temple and pulled the trigger. Nothing happened. He did it again and again.

"Stop it, baby. It's empty," Nicole said, wrapping her arms around him and consoling him.

"Why? I did everything for you." Vincent cried.

"I'm sorry, but we can start fresh," Nicole said.

Vincent continued to weep in his wife's arms. He didn't know how long he was crying, but when he reached for the door and tried to get out, it was locked and wouldn't open. He and Nicole tried breaking the widows, but it wasn't glass. Nicole spotted the fire heading their way, first on the ground. As Vincent looked, he saw the trail of gas the fire was following. Before he had a chance to tell his wife, he loved her, the limo blew up in flames.

CHAPTER 25

Loose Ends

Sincere had to get up out of the city. From the outside looking in, it may look simple. Just jump in your vehicle and leave. Yet Sincere knew, even with simplicity, complications and roadblocks were never that far. If he was to get pulled over, he couldn't explain why he was driving without a license. That alone would give the law to search his car. A trunk with a lot of money would be found, including guns. Sincere thought of this before speeding off. He had no guardian. Being stopped by the law will place him in a juvenile detention center first. Then a group home for kids under eighteen. It's a lot Sincere had to avoid. Being stopped by the police was the main thing.

Thinking back on one of the letters his father left him, Sincere knew he had to use his charms to get him out of the city. He didn't wanna deal with a complete stranger. At least with someone he knew of, if they did something foul, he could always find a way to get back at them. Dealing with someone he had no inside information on could leave him in a bad spot. He knew what he had to do. *Who* was the issue.

It didn't take Sincere long to think of a person. Better yet, a female to help him out. She had to be at least eighteen with a license. Lisa's sister was the only female that came to mind. Ms. Wright would've fit perfectly in this scenario, but she was no longer a part of this world. Sincere still felt bad about that.

Sincere didn't want Lisa or anybody else in on the loop. He didn't need no in-between person to make things happen. His father's messages and advice always helped him through.

"The right amount of money can get someone to do anything you want done. When it comes to money, the majority of people don't have any standards or morals. It doesn't matter if you know the person or not. For the right price, almost anyone can be bought. If you ever find yourself in a situation where you may have to pay for some help, a person who is familiar with you will always be the person that's best to deal with."

"What do you mean by familiar with?" Sincere remembered asking.

"Someone who doesn't necessarily know you, but they knew of you. Like you could be dating a girl, she has a friend that never met you, but she heard so much about you. It's better to deal with someone like that. A complete stranger or someone you know may try to get over. A complete stranger can run off without you knowing how to find them. Someone you know may try to be slick. Someone that knows of you, more than likely, heard good things about you. If they do pull a stunt, you know how to find them."

Sincere drove to Lisa's house, hoping her sister was there. He didn't even know the girl's name. It really didn't matter. She wasn't someone he was trying to get to know. Sincere wasn't expecting to see Lisa's sister's car. In fact, he was hoping it wasn't there. Not seeing it meant Lisa wasn't home yet. That was a good thing.

When Sincere arrived at Lisa's house, a car was parked in the driveway, but it wasn't one he recognized. Lisa's sister was standing on the front porch talking to some dude. Sincere could tell by her body language and posture that she was disengaged. A part of him didn't wanna disturb them, but he wasn't gonna wait like no sitting duck for them to leave. Sincere jumped out of his vehicle and approached them. Lisa's sister noticed him first and oddly met him halfway.

She gave him an intimate kiss and whispered in his ears, "Pretend that you're my boyfriend."

Sincere was caught off guard. He went along with it. It was actually developing to be a great opportunity for him to get what he wanted out of her. Once they were done acting, he didn't understand why it was so difficult for a female to be honest. It was nothing to tell someone it's not working out. Females will mislead a person until it's convenient for them to cut them off. That's flat out wrong. Sincere truly believed he would never understand the ways of a female. Trying to do so was futile.

Sincere walked up the porch holding this girl's hand he didn't even know. The guy didn't even look him in the eyes. Sincere respected that. He wasn't looking for a confrontation, especially about a female he didn't know, so he was glad this guy kept his problems with the girl.

"I love you, Lifa. You know I'll do anything for you. Just tell me what it is that I need to do," the guy said.

"My heart is not in it," Lifa started saying, until she was cut off by Sincere.

"Excuse me, but I'm gonna wait inside," Sincere said, walking in, not trying to hear the guy embarrass himself.

While sitting on the couch, Lisa's sister came in about two minutes behind him.

"Thanks a lot, Sincere. I had to get rid of him. He definitely wasn't my type," Lifa said, shaking her head.

If he wasn't her type, how did they end up together, Sincere wondered.

Reading his thoughts, Lifa said, "After I got to know him, the things that drew me to him ended up being an afterthought. It's strange how quickly a person's feelings can change."

"Differences and circumstances are the most common that I see," Sincere replied.

"That's true. From what my sister said, you have all the little girls chasing you," Lifa said with a knowing smile.

"No disrespect. I didn't come here for your sister or to make small talk. I came here to present a business proposition for you."

"I don't deal with drugs or anyone involved in that lifestyle," Lifa said, looking at him strangely now.

"Slow down. I'm not into that. I just need you to drive me to Georgia."

"Why can't you just drive up there yourself? You got your own car."

"I'm young. I don't have a license. If I get pulled over, they'll take my car and probably send me to jail," Sincere said.

"What do you think, I'm slow? I'm not one of these little girls you are running circles around. If the car is yours, why would you go to jail?" Lifa questioned.

Sincere didn't plan on telling her all the truth. No matter what he told her not to say, she was gonna run back and tell her sister. The less she knew, the better. Before Lifa could say anything else, Sincere pulled out his first offer from his pockets.

"I got $10,000 for you to take me to Georgia right now. I'll even pay for your fee to come back down. I promise you there's no drugs." Sincere offered with money in hand. Lifa accepted and took the money.

"Let me put my money up and grab a few things."

"Don't forget to grab your license. You're driving," Sincere said as Lifa went out of sight in a quickness.

*****

Snake wasn't that dumb to give the mayor a loaded gun before exiting out the limo. Even though the mayor didn't try to shoot him, he would never take a chance like that.

Pathetic wasn't even the word to describe what he was hearing. The mayor was a true sucker for love. Snake had an audio device installed inside the limo. The mayor actually tried to kill himself, and even after watching his wife have sex and profess her love to another man, he still wanted to be with her. Outside of money, women probably had the biggest influence in a man's life. He knew about that firsthand. That's why no women could be trusted.

After the limo exploded, Snake knew he had some legal work to do pertaining to Hot Rod's properties. He had no intentions of replacing his lost friend or running his businesses. Corporate life wasn't his style. Dealing with people wasn't something he was accustomed to doing. The world Hot Rod was living in wasn't gonna be a life he played a part of.

Once all his businesses were sold, and he cashed in, there was only one place Snake could see himself going to, but he had one unfinished business to settle.

*****

Li'l Gangsta was in Richmond, Virginia, terrorizing the streets. Ever since word got out that The Source was dead, and he was the one responsible for it, it added to the respect he was already getting and the fear he was placing in others. If it wasn't for his main man, Rick, things wouldn't be the way it was now. He could've easily got flipped. L. G. had to show Rick his appreciation.

"Hey, bruh, I gotta show you something."

Rick jumped in L. G.'s vehicle, and L. G. took him to a brand-new club that just got built. The inside was fixed. The only thing that was missing was a name and women to fill it up with.

"I know how much you wanted to get a nightclub, so I got this place for you," L. G. said, dapping Rick up. "I got a couple more lined up for you too."

"Thanks, kid. You don't have to do all that. This club right here is more than enough," Rick said.

"Always believe this. I take care of those who show their loyalty. You did that, and I appreciate you. For those who don't know better."

L. G. went up to a guy that just stepped out of his car. He whispered something into his ears, then put a couple of bullets in his guts. L. G. pushed the guy back inside of the car. Then the car sped off. The point he made was clear. It wasn't something he had to put emphasis on, but you could never be sure.

"That's what creep stuff gets anyone. Loyalty gets you love. Betrayal gets you death."

"That's understood," was all Rick said.

"I hope you know it's your job to find the dancers. I don't have time to search or interview any women," L. G. joked.

"Finding and getting females to work won't be a problem."

"What are you gonna name this joint?" L. G. asked.

"Sapphire."

"Isn't that… Never mind. Do as you see fit."

*****

Brenda was back at her hometown in Orchard, New York. She and Keisha had known each other since they were six. Their birthdays were two months apart. Their parents were extremely close. Brenda wasn't ready to tell them that Keisha was dead. She didn't wanna take the trip to Rikers Island to tell Keisha's father.

She didn't even know the facts of the situation. All she knows when a person doesn't get in contact with you after doing so every day for twenty-three years, something is wrong. Nothing can be right about that picture.

Looking back, life would've been a lot different if she and Keisha would've stayed at the University of Buffalo. Both of them left their freshman year. They were fascinated by the idea of being recruited for what was told to them at that time as "classified training." The first six months, they both made $50,000 each. They were getting paid at least two grand a week.

Their recruiter, a woman that went by the name Sam, first taught them how to get a man's attention without making it look obvious. Then it was how to follow someone and find out if you were being followed. They were then trained on how to seduce not only men but women as well. Next it was how to shoot and how to kill. Keisha was reluctant to do some of the training, but she went through it because Brenda was adamant on mastering the craft.

If they never met Sam, Keisha would still be here.

After telling Keisha's mom about her death, Brenda built the courage to go to Rikers Island Prison to break the news to Keisha's father. He was serving a twenty-five-year mandatory sentence for a murder his wife committed. Ten years ago, Karen accidentally shot a family member during a heated debate that led to a physical altercation. When Karen tried to remove a weapon from her cousin, the struggle ended up deadly. Keisha's father took the charge and confessed to the murder to free his wife.

Brenda hasn't been to prison in about five years. She knew Kevin was still there. She and Keisha had frequent talks of him. Brenda hated going to the prison. The hassle, excessive search, the wait could all be taxing sometimes. Some officers purposely did their best to discourage visitors from going. That in itself was really spiteful.

When Brenda walked inside the visiting room, Kevin kept looking behind her. Brenda knew whom he was looking for or hoping to see. This was the first time she came without Keisha. Before she had a chance to sit down and say hi, Kevin said, "What's wrong with my baby girl? You didn't come here all by yourself to give me some good news. So what's the deal?" Kevin asked.

During her time of training, Sam told her to never let a loss or death affect her or slow her down in any way. Brenda wasn't a robot. She had feelings. She had been trained for years to not act on emotions, to not acknowledge pain. Mentally Sam had changed her, but this loss was too personal. It was impossible for her to block the pain. No training could make her disregard or overlook this death.

"Key Key is dead," Brenda said, letting all the feelings she had bottled up inside, out. Kevin pulled her in and consoled her as she cried. "She's no longer…"

As Brenda let the tears fall, Kevin stayed silent. He didn't ask her any questions on how or what happened. Brenda was worried about that.

"Are you okay?" Brenda asked.

"Thanks for coming and letting me know," Kevin said as he turned his back to leave.

"Kev! Please don't do nothing stupid!" Brenda yelled.

Kevin never stopped or broke his stride. He went straight to a heavyset officer and tried to take his head off of his shoulders. Brenda didn't know how many times Kevin hit the man, but the officer's face was bloodied up in ways she never saw before. When more officers came, they were really hesitant. Kevin just lay on the floor with his hands behind his back.

"Visitation is canceled. Visitors exit out this door. Inmates line up against that wall," the duty warden came and said.

Among the chaos and confusion and all the movement, Brenda thought she saw a familiar face in the crowd. She brushed it off to the side and watched four officers take Kevin out. After she couldn't see him anymore, she exited with the other visitors.

*****

Sincere and Lifa were on the road, getting ready to cross the Florida-Georgia line. Sincere was very alert on his trip back to Miami with Bernice. So when it was time to give Lifa more directions, he would be on point. Since Sincere didn't know Georgia and the area so well, he was heading directly to Bernice's place.

Once his money and gun were secure, he would figure out how he was gonna send Lifa back to Miami.

The entire drive north, Lifa didn't ask too many questions. In fact, it wasn't much that she said. It was either "I'm gonna pull over and get some gas" or "I'm gonna stop and grab us something to eat." The only time Sincere got out of the car was to pump gas. Lifa always took care of the rest. On the three separate occasions when Sincere gave her money, he handed her a fifty each time. He knew it was more than enough. All three times she tried to give him his change. He always declined it.

"It's strange how we've been on the road for over ten hours, and we hardly exchanged any words. What makes it weird for me, it actually feels good to just be with someone, listening to the music with no disturbance. Silence to me is better sometimes. It's easier to think," Lifa said in between yawns.

"I couldn't agree with you more. If you're tired, we can pull over at one of those rest stops."

"How much longer do we have to get there?" Lifa asked.

"Two hours, tops. You can make it?"

After the brief conversation, which was the longest one they had, they both stayed silent until they reached their final destination.

Sincere wasted no time taking the bags out of the trunk and placing them inside of the house. He took out some extra cash and met Lifa in the living room.

"I don't know how you plan on getting me back home, but that's gonna have to wait until tomorrow. Where am I sleeping?" Lifa asked.

Sincere didn't like the idea of her sleeping over. Needless to say, she got him here safely. It shouldn't be a big deal for her to spend the night. She did her part in a way Sincere appreciated. She didn't try to get in his business. She drove within the speed limits, and when Lifa called her, she said she was out with a friend.

Sincere led Lifa to Bernice's room, and then he went online, searching for the easiest way to get her back home the following day.

*****

Big Luke, also known as Lukens Jean, had three more years left in his sentence. He was considered the muscle and power of the group Hot Rod created a while back called The Enforcers. After years of reflection, he realized he was placed out front to be the fall guy. It didn't bother him one bit. He had a great run on the streets. Before Hot Rod pulled him in, he didn't have anything. He was living in empty apartments. Working for Hot Rod gave him the opportunity to shine. It put money in his pockets, and money made him relevant.

Big Luke thought of the death of Hot Rod and The Scientist hit the fan all over, but the person that came inquiring about The Scientist, as he described, "The man that loves to throw knives," he couldn't have been on the streets. There was nothing for Big Luke to lose by telling him what he wanted to know. Where was The Scientist? He's dead.

The visit with the strange guy didn't even last that long. A confinement orderly got the entire visitation room canceled. When he beat up an officer, seeing the officer covered up in blood was a great sight to see.

*****

After walking out of the prison, Brenda stayed in her vehicle and cried. She didn't know how long she remained in the parking lot. When she decided to pull off, the sun started to descend.

Brenda paid no attention to the car that was following her for three minutes. She was on a long road, so the car wasn't out of the ordinary. If she was in her right state of mind, her awareness wouldn't have been questioned, but the pain of her biggest loss had her thoughts clouded.

Before making a turn, the back of her window shattered. She felt pain in her shoulders, then she crashed at a crosswalk. Before Brenda could even reach for her gun, the face she saw at the prison came to view. It was indeed a face she was familiar with. It was a face she didn't expect or wanted to see. She knew he was there to kill her. Brenda just didn't understand why. What did she do? Brenda was ready to die. Things hadn't been the same since Keisha left. She welcomed death. The thought of going to wherever Keisha was comforted her.

CHAPTER 26

CHANGES

Snake didn't know anything about The Scientist's or The Source's death. He heard it first from Big Luke after paying him a visit. He didn't fully believe the man, but after doing some research and getting in contact with the ears on the streets, Big Luke was being truthful. Snake didn't care how or who killed them. That's work he longer had to concern himself with. Being in Miami and away from all the activities up north, Snake didn't know what was taking place. He was locked in on his mission. Now that it was over with, He could finally change his focus.

Snake spotted Brenda the moment he entered the visitation park. Running into her wasn't something he expected. Yet seeing her was actually a good thing. She was the only one living that could give someone a description of him. She may just be a standup woman, but why take a chance? He didn't have to take it. Killing her was the best thing to do. So killing her was what he did.

*****

Lifa had trouble sleeping. She never met a guy who didn't even make an attempt to seduce her or show any interest. She knew Sincere wasn't gay. She knew all about him having sex with her little sister and fast-ass friends. Lifa remembered watching the movie *Getting Played*. It was kind of funny how Bill Bellamy tricked Stacey Dash, Carmen Electra, and Vivica Fox. Sincere did something similar. He didn't manipulate any one of them, but just like Bill, he had sex with each of them.

What intrigued Lifa the most about Sincere, he wasn't an open book. Everything about him was mysterious. He was a guy full of secrets. Somehow she knew those secrets had nothing to do with females. He wasn't the type that did any chasing. He was the type that females hunted. The kind of boy all girls wanted for themselves.

Although Sincere was younger than her by at least four years, he was mature than the teenage boys in her school.

Lifa walked into the room she saw Sincere go in. She hoped entering it unannounced wasn't gonna be a big deal. She had on a long T-shirt she had grabbed in the closet after taking a shower. She slipped up by not bringing any extra clothing. She handwashed her panties and stayed pantiless. She didn't know what she was thinking or what prompted her to seek him out, but seeing him staring out the window with a blank stare gave her the confidence she needed to continue.

"Sincere… Sincere… Sincere!" Lifa called out, trying to get Sincere's attention.

"Yeah, what's up? You okay?" Sincere asked without even looking back to face her.

"I'm fine. Having problems going to sleep, but besides that, I'm good. Question is, are you okay? Don't know how long you've been staring out the window. If something bothers you, anything. I have an open ear. I know you don't know me, but for tonight, I could be someone you need. Someone who will be here for you. Someone you can open up to. Allow me to be that. There's no risk or strings attached. Tomorrow I'll be long gone, and we probably won't even see each other anymore. What you say?"

Lifa was nervous and shaking on the inside. She was up front in her invitation. It wasn't much to read into. If Sincere wanted her, he could have her in any way that he wanted. She could be whatever he wanted her to be. As Lisa waited for a response, a reaction, she inched closer to him. To her surprise, Sincere came closer and embraced her. He didn't kiss, caress, or try to undress her. He placed his hand on her shoulders and cried.

When the tears subsided, Lifa didn't wanna push him away by being too aggressive. One wrong question could make him shut any emotions down.

Being forward sexually could also push him away. So she stayed silent and waited for him to make a move. She waited and waited. He finally took her hands and led her to the bed. Her body was on fire and being filled with explosives. If he lit her up, she knew she would explode. In a dream state, she lay on the bed, anticipating his touch, his kisses. All he had to do was pull her shirt up, and she would be all open to him. All he had to do was kiss her. As she waited, it threw her all the way off. When he placed his head on her breast and lay still, *disappointment* wasn't even the word to describe how she felt. She put her foot in her mouth when she told him, she would be someone that's there for him. Now that was proven, she had to figure out a way to make her stay in Georgia a little longer.

*****

Snake was minutes away from Paulette's place. He knew what led him there. As much as he tried to fight off the thought and feelings that already formulated inside of him, he knew it was best to deal with what he felt head on. A person can't run or hide from the truth, no matter how much they try. Paulette was someone he cared about. Someone he found himself thinking about a lot. Snake was tired of hooking up with random women for sex. Each encounter kept his guards up. Some consistency wouldn't be so bad. Snake wasn't justifying for Paulette by any means. He wasn't in denial as well. He liked Paulette and her daughter. They were someone he could see himself protecting. The only family he had was gone; maybe building another one wasn't such a bad idea.

Before Snake made it outside his vehicle, Pamela came shooting out the door in blazing speed, shouting his name.

"Quincy! Quincy!" Pamela almost knocked him down as she hugged him with force. "I knew you would come back."

"What if I didn't?" Snake asked with a smile.

"I would've tracked you down," Pamela said with a serious expression.

"Is that so?"

"Don't be fooled by the baby face. Let's go inside. My mom would be happy that you're back."

Snake was wondering, could this be home? Could this be a life he would want to live? For so many years, his life was based on violence. Violence that he had adapted to. Violence that became a part of him. Could he make the transition and live in peace? At the front door, waiting, stood Paulette. Snake could never remember seeing a woman so beautiful. Her face was pure with no makeup. Her hair was wet from the shower she recently took. The scent she had on was covered in vanilla. The smell was very inviting. Words between them weren't even spoken. The look in her eyes said it all. They hugged each other passionately.

"I'm happy you came back," Paulette whispered.

"I'm happy to be here.

"I know you haven't had a home-cooked meal since you left. We were just getting ready for dinner." Pamela chipped in, grabbing Snake's hand.

Snake didn't know what it was about the little girl, but he liked her. She softened him in ways no one ever had. He also found it funny that she spoke what was on her mind with no shame.

"You can sit by me since you and Mommy have a lot of catching up to do later."

Paulette almost choked on her drink when her daughter made that comment. Snake didn't miss the smile that she was trying to hide. It made him smile too.

Yellow rice, fried cabbage, oxtails, and black beans were on the plate. Snake wasted no time digging into his food. He was never one to just up and eat a woman's cooking. Women couldn't be trusted. Yet he found himself making an exception with Paulette. She fed him while he was recovering from his injuries. If she had any kind of ill intent, he wouldn't be up and about. She could've easily left him for dead and not treated his wounds.

In between his meal, Pamela took Snake and Paulette by surprise with her openness.

"Thanks a lot for taking care of our problems and giving us the money."

"Pam!" Paulette shouted, trying to silence her daughter.

"Calm down. It's okay, right, Quincy?" Pamela asked, daring him to say otherwise.

"What problem? Don't mind her. Pamela, clean this up. We're gonna step outside and take a walk by the lake."

"Sounds romantic. Take your time, Mom, and thanks for being here, Quincy." Pamela hugged Snake and started collecting the plates.

Snake couldn't ignore what Pamela thought she knew. No matter how sweet she was or how good her mother was to him, he wouldn't hesitate to kill them both. He had to find out what Pamela thought she knew.

"Excuse my daughter. Her mouth may get her in trouble one day… To ease your mind and conscience, we appreciate you. I'm not one to ask questions. Blessings come in many ways, in many shapes and forms. So I'm thankful for you."

Snake didn't know how long he and Paulette were talking. Daylight was on the verge of arriving. It seems as if they were talking for minutes. Conversation between them was a lot awkward at first. Paulette was shy and timid. Snake naturally was one who didn't say much. Once the conversation started. It's like they were destined to be together. For the first time, Snake knew what fear felt like.

*****

"Son, being vulnerable to a woman can place you in great danger. I'm not saying to shut all your emotions down, but don't just give anyone your heart. Don't let just anyone in your mind. Circumstances can bring confusion. Difficult situations can weaken you. Too much pressure and overthinking things can make you do irrational things. I don't care how good a girl makes you feel, how sweet the words may sound coming out of her mouth, or how good her look and sex game is. If this girl is not your woman or wife, don't open up. Females are good at what they do,

no matter the age. They have a way of getting what they want. If you're going through it and having problems with your thought process, work it out on your own."

Sincere remembered exactly where he was at when his father said those words to him. Last night, he slipped up. As good as it felt to be comforted by Lifa, sending her the wrong message could be a problem. Females have a way of recanting what they say or forgetting what they said if things were not in their favor. Sincere knew from this day forward, he had to manage his feelings better. Even if he had to suppress it, he would do just that to keep all females at bay. With what he was going through, he shouldn't allow no one to get close. The closer they came, the more of a problem they became.

Lifa was already up when he woke up. Sincere intended to put her on the Greyhound first thing this morning with some extra cash. Most teenage girls would jump on everything Sincere offered in a New York minute.

"Hey! When did you get up? I made us breakfast," Lifa said smiling.

"I don't have time. Gotta make a few runs. The first is getting you on this Greyhound so you can head back home," Sincere said firmly.

"I don't wanna leave just yet."

"That was the agreement. You drive me up here, and I find a way to get you back down."

"I can get back on my own. I'm just not ready to leave," Lifa said.

Sincere didn't know what Lifa was thinking or what she was up to, but she had to go. Whatever game she was playing, he intended to stop instantly.

"Listen, I don't have time for this. I'm gonna give you an extra thousand dollars. Get your ass ready. The bus leaves in thirty minutes," Sincere said with anger in his voice.

"Say less. I'll be ready in five minutes."

Sincere wasn't sure what made Lifa change her mind and attitude so quickly, the extra money she was getting or his aggressiveness.

"You're gonna learn that some females will respect and do what you say once you put your feet down. Sometimes a girl is not gonna take you seriously unless you yell or speak with aggression," his father once said.

Lifa's reaction confirmed what his father told him. In minutes, she was ready to go. Sincere took her to where she needed to be. The extra money was already given to her before they left the house. Sincere didn't make a move to get out of his car once they pulled up at the location.

"Damn, it's like that. You can at least come out of the car and give me a hug," Lifa stated.

Sincere got out of his vehicle and met Lifa halfway. Instead of hugging him, Lifa kissed him. Sincere didn't know what was up with that, but he kissed her back. He'll never see her again, so a kiss wouldn't hurt.

"Here's my number. If you ever need me, call me," Lifa said and walked off.

Sincere balled up the piece of paper and headed back into his car. Everything in Miami would be left in Miami. His next step was to clean up Bernice's place and find somewhere else to stay for the time being. It would be in his car, but his money and guns had to be stashed somewhere.

*****

Pamela was glad that Quincy came back. She connected with him in ways that were unexplainable. She saw the seriousness in his eyes when she mentioned the problem that he took care of. He had nothing to worry about. Coming to the conclusion that he was the one that killed those people wasn't hard. There hasn't been a homicide in that area in probably five years. Thinking that he did it—well, *know* that he did it—wasn't farfetched. Especially when he inquired about them and where they stayed. She wasn't stupid. Once he came in, she would set him straight.

Snake enjoyed his time with Paulette. As they headed back to her place, Pamela was still up, obviously waiting on them.

"We need to talk to Quincy," was all that she said.

"Take that base off of your voice. What's wrong with you?" Paulette said, not knowing what her daughter was up to.

"Can we talk alone?" Pamela asked in a softer tone.

"I'm going to bed. Remember to pick up that order, Pam."

"Yes, Ma."

Snake watched Pamela and could tell that she was frustrated or angry about something. He awaited her to disclose whatever it was.

"You don't trust us."

"I don't trust no one," Snake honestly said.

"Were you always so hard?"

"Always."

"I don't believe you. I see how you look at my mother, and the fact that you came back says you want something different." Pamela pointed out.

"I see you're observant."

"I just want you to know that you can trust us. We don't have to ever speak of certain things, but I trust you enough to tell you. I took someone's life two years ago."

Snake didn't like this admission. When a person takes a life and gets away with it, it's not something they should ever reveal. Pamela had a lot of learning to do.

"First and foremost, don't ever mention that to anyone. I don't care how much you trust a person. I saw parents turn on their kids for money. Best friends turn on each other to avoid prison time. There's always limits to what you can trust someone with. So don't ever make that mistake again," Snake said.

Snake never really had someone who looked up to him. Someone he could teach and love. Someone he could protect and take care of. Pamela needed guidance. She needed a male figure to help her experience. She acted the way she did with him because she needed him. In a sense, Snake knew that he needed her as well. He needed the change.

"Yes. You can trust me."

EPILOGUE

Yolanda was released a month early on her six-month sentence for good behavior. Being incarcerated made her a better individual. It helped her discover things about herself that she didn't know was within. She realized, in darkness, how powerful she was in darkness. There were so many reasons why she shouldn't exist. So many reasons why she should give up, but here she stood, pressing on, defying the odds, and becoming a complete person.

It took only two days to get the information that one needed. A lot has changed since Yolanda was away. A lot would change now that she was back. Yolanda never forgot about those who did her wrong. She would repay all of them with death.

Reading books on mystery and murder sharpened Yolanda's mind. Every act she did, she intended not to be a suspect. She intended to get away with the nine people that were on her list, the first and second being Alexis and Katherine. The two were currently an item now. Their love life or whatever they thought they shared was gonna come to an end today.

Alexis and Katherine were now living together, from Yolanda's point of view. This made things easier for her. The two-birds-with-one-stone concept didn't fit.

Separation would make things easier. Them being together can complicate things. Yolanda was so caught up in her desire for revenge that she didn't notice that she was being followed.

Yolanda knocked on the door the two women were staying at, and Alexis opened the door. Yolanda already had her gun out. Before she could pull the trigger, pain erupted from her sides. Her gun dropped to the floor, and she fell on her knees, looking at the blood.

A man with a badge stood over her. *How did he get here so quick?* she thought. As he pulled out his handcuff, the picture was clearer.

"No. No. No. I can't go back. I won't go back."

"Your crazy ass had no business getting out."

*****

Sincere was enrolled back in school. He had a place to stay, and he was a part-time worker at Foot Locker. Sincere followed and kept an eye on a woman named Jasmine Reed. Jasmine recently got out of a rehabilitation program center and was trying to get back on her feet so she can get her four-year-old son back from The Department of Children's Family. Once Sincere felt as if she was serious about staying clean, he offered her a deal: $500 every other week to have her cousin rent him out an apartment monthly. He also gave her $250 for groceries every month. Sincere convinced her that he wasn't trying to be raised in a foster home. Her having a son that was in the system made her sympathize with him.

Receiving Jasmine's help was temporary. Finding a more reliable source to go through with no ties to the government was a must. Finding a friend with a nice home and family was part of the plan too.

Like his father once said, "Change can be good. In life, you can't be closed off. You'll always need someone for something. You can't do everything on your own. When you're young, make friends. You'll never know who that friend can be or who he or she is."

His father was right. Change can be good. He would live his life to make his parents proud of him. That's why they would want him to do it.

ABOUT THE AUTHOR

Widney Joseph was born and raised in Little Haiti, Florida. Growing up in several neighborhoods like North Miami and North Miami Beach, he lived a lifestyle that drew a lot of attention, which resulted in him being involved with the wrong crowd. These choices ultimately led to him getting incarcerated for twelve years and seven months in federal prison for manufacture and distribution of crack cocaine. Prior to that, he never finished high school or went to college or anything, but the level of his education isn't limited to grade levels or degrees; he ended up obtaining his GED while serving his sentence. During his darkest moments, he found one of his greatest passions, which is him learning about himself. Being in prison, honestly, allowed him to find himself. He gained the desire to write, he learned public speaking, and he got a certification for culinary arts. He also learned craft making handmade purses by reading a lot of DIY (Do-It-Yourself) books. He has gone through a lot in all his years of living, but he was able to overcome everything that was thrown his way. His past doesn't define the person he is today, but the future he's building toward does.

CPSIA information can be obtained
at www.ICGtesting.com
Printed in the USA
BVHW031437011121
620450BV00004B/31